MW01115466

BRAIN

DAMAGE

A NOVEL BY
FREIDA MCFADDEN

Brain Damage

© 2016 by Freida McFadden. All rights reserved.

All rights reserved. No part of this book may be reproduced or transmitted in any form or by any means whatsoever without express written permission from the author

This book is a work of fiction. The names, characters, incidents and places are the products of the authors' imagination, and are not to be construed as real. None of the characters in the book is based on an actual person. Any resemblance to persons living or dead is entirely coincidental and unintentional.

For my patients

NOVELS BY FREIDA McFADDEN

The Inmate

The Housemaid

Do You Remember?

Do Not Disturb

The Locked Door

Want to Know a Secret?

One by One

The Wife Upstairs

The Perfect Son

The Ex

The Surrogate Mother

Brain Damage

Baby City

Suicide Med

The Devil Wears Scrubs

The Devil You Know

PROLOGUE

If someone had asked me before this happened if it would hurt to be shot in the head, I almost certainly would've answered yes. Of course, yes.

It makes sense. A piece of metal rapidly shooting through flesh and bone… how could it not hurt? During my intern year, I spent time in the emergency room and I saw people who had been recently shot. None in the head, but one in the shoulder, one through the knee, and one unfortunate bullet ripped its way right through a man's stomach. I didn't need to ask any of those people if the bullet hurt. I could see it in their faces.

I wasn't someone who had to worry about being shot though. The patients I treated in the emergency room weren't upper-middle-class female doctors living in million dollar apartments overlooking Central Park. They all lived in a poor section of the city, where bullets whizzed through the air as commonly as raindrops.

I, on the other hand, was safe, insulated. I wasn't the sort of person who would be shot in the street while going to buy soda at the local newsstand. When I died, it would be from a stroke or cancer, or if I was lucky, my heart would stop beating one night in my sleep when my hair was as white as my pillow and my face was crisscrossed with deep wrinkles.

Or so I thought.

Back to the initial question of whether it hurt to be shot in the head. Because there is a lot I don't remember, but this part I remember very well.

I remember staring at the gun, not really believing that it would go off, not believing that this could happen to me. And then I remember the explosion, seconds before the bullet discharged, passed through my skull, shattering it to pieces, soaring through gray matter, white matter, neurons, ventricles, then back through my skull again, and finally lodging itself in the well-insulated wall that kept our neighbors from hearing the noise of the gunshot.

And none of that hurt. The truth is, I didn't feel it at all.

What hurt is everything that came after.

CHAPTER 1
Two Years Before

There are times when I truly do hate being a doctor, and one of those times is right now, right this minute, while I'm staring down at the groin of an obese fifty-two-year-old man.

One of our nurses, Jessica, is standing next to me, "assisting me," although in truth, she's actually here to protect me from getting groped by this half-naked man. It's happened before, and I've just gotten sick of it.

Yes, the life of a dermatologist is very glamorous. I still like it though.

"It's a fungal infection," I say, averting my eyes from Mr. Leroy's groin and gratefully redirecting them to his round face.

A fungal infection. Which Mr. Leroy's primary care doctor should have diagnosed himself. What a waste of my time. And dignity.

I try to back away, giving myself a little distance between me and the fungus, but I slam into a wall. Our examining rooms are tiny. Miniscule. Several of my coworkers have complained to Roger, our boss, that we can't work in such tiny spaces, but tiny spaces means more examining rooms to stuff patients into, which means we can see them faster. It's all about the bottom line with Roger.

"That's what Dr. Hanson told me," Mr. Leroy says. His jaws are working together like he's chewing something. Did he start *eating* while I was looking at his groin? Oh God. "And he gave me this tube of spermicide for it."

I purse my lips together, and glance over at Jessica.

"He gave you *what*?" I ask.

"Some spermicide," Mr. Leroy repeats, still chewing vigorously. "And I've been putting the spermicide all over the rash for like a week, but it's not any better. So I figured I should see a skin doctor."

I can tell that Jessica is struggling not to laugh.

"You mean *fungicide*?" she asks.

Mr. Leroy shrugs and rubs his chin. "Oh yeah. Maybe."

I have no idea whether Dr. Hanson gave Mr. Leroy a cream that wasn't strong enough or else he actually did give the poor man spermicide. Either way, I know fungus when I see it. The moist skin folds of Mr. Leroy's groin are ripe with it. If I were a fungus, that's definitely where I would want to live. (Not being a fungus, I live in a very nice apartment by Central Park in New York City. It's my one indulgence.)

I write Mr. Leroy a prescription for a tube of fungicide and explain to him how to use it. He could probably also use some counseling on weight loss and getting his diabetes under control, but I'm not a miracle worker. Considering he doesn't know the difference between spermicide and fungicide, I have a feeling any words of wisdom I have to offer will likely be lost on him. Besides, I've been told by Roger that I've got a ten minute quota for each patient, and I've already used up nine of those minutes.

As I hand over the prescription to Mr. Leroy, I suddenly see the beginning of moisture forming in the corners of his eyes. A second later, they're full on tears. And all I can think is: *What the hell?*

It's not like patients don't cry in here. I've had to hand over more than a few cancer diagnoses in my time, and I've got a box of tissues in the corner of the room that gets replaced on a regular basis. It's something they teach you in medical school: How to comfort a crying patient. Except the first time you actually see it, you panic. You don't know what to do aside from patting their shoulder and saying, "There, there."

But after several years in practice, I've got it down to a science. The compassionate arm rub, the box of tissues, the sympathetic and caring voice. It's not like I'm going to make anything all better, but if I can make them feel even a *little* better, I'll take it. Even if I have to go over my ten minute quota. (Screw you, Roger.)

Still, I have to say, this is the first time I've gotten tears over a diagnosis of jock itch. Did he think I said fungating carcinoma instead of fungus?

Damn, I'm definitely going over my stupid quota.

"Sorry," Mr. Leroy says, dabbing his eyes self-consciously with the back of his hand. "I'm being dumb, sorry."

"What's wrong?" I ask as I reach for our stock of tissues.

Mr. Leroy gratefully swipes a tissue from the box. "It's just that..." He sighs deeply. "My wife left me last year, and I've gained all this weight, and now I have *fungus*. I mean, what woman is going to want me with *fungus* growing on my crotch?"

I clear my throat and force a smile. "Mr. Leroy, I'm sure there are plenty of women who—"

"Would you date a guy with crotch fungus?" he interrupts me.

Would I? I visualize Mr. Leroy's moist, red groin folds and my stomach turns. "Sure," I say.

Mr. Leroy snorts.

"Look," I say, holding up my prescription. "You use this cream and the fungus will be gone in two weeks. Lose some weight and I promise it won't come back."

Mr. Leroy pulls the piece of paper from my hand and looks at it like it could be a winning lottery ticket. "Yeah?"

"I *promise*," I say.

I hold my hand out to Mr. Leroy and he shakes it. His hand is big and warm. In spite of the fungus, Mr. Leroy isn't an entirely unattractive man. He needs to lose some weight, as much for his health as for his appearance, but he has warm, brown eyes and a nice smile.

"You're a nice lady, Doc," Mr. Leroy says to me. "I heard good things about you."

I feel my cheeks color. "Thank you."

He smiles again. I glance up at the clock: fifteen minutes spent with Mr. Leroy. I'm already bracing myself for a lecture from Roger as I work through my twenty-minute lunch break.

Jessica has already put my next patient in a room, and the chart is sitting in the rack outside the door. I grab the chart from the rack and scan the details. Clark Douglas. Thirty-eight years old. Here to have a suspicious mole checked out. I'm just relieved that it's not another teenage acne patient. Not that I mind teenage acne... raging teenage hormones definitely help pay the bills. But when it gets to be August, it seems like that's all you see. I guess the kids figure they want their skin to be clear before school starts up again.

I knock on the door once then enter without waiting for an answer because the doors are inexplicably soundproof.

Let me just say that I may be a doctor, but I'm only human. And sometimes when a patient strips down in front of me for a mole check, even though I am a complete professional in my behavior, I can't help but react to a body that is incredibly wrinkled or covered in skin lesions or thick folds of fat.

Or in this case, the most perfect body I've ever seen. In my life.

Clark Douglas is gorgeous. I'm not sure I've ever used that word before to refer to a man, certainly not in my adult life, but it really does seem appropriate in this case. He is *gorgeous*. And also, he's topless. Topless on my examining table, his pecs and deltoids perfectly toned but not ridiculously so. I can make out the bulge of a six pack on his slim abdomen. This is not a man who's got fungus hidden in the folds of his fat, that's for sure.

And he's just as amazing from the neck up as well. I always thought that chestnut was a nice way of saying brown, but this guy has the most gorgeous thick chestnut locks of hair on his head. He has dimples too, not huge ones, but just enough to be sexy—*perfect* dimples. His eyes lock with mine and they are clear blue, like the untouched waters of the Pacific.

Oh God, I sound like a teenage girl writing terrible poetry.

I've got to get myself under control.

"Mr. Douglas?" I ask, consulting his file. I strip my voice of any sort of emotion.

Clark Douglas smiles at me. God, even his *teeth* are gorgeous. It's almost disgusting. "Guilty as charged."

"I'm Dr. McKenna," I tell him. I hold out my hand to him and he shakes it. His hand is broad and warm, perfectly enveloping my smaller, plumper hand.

"Didn't Jessica give you a gown?" I ask him. I know very well she did. I see it lying unused next to him on the examining table.

Mr. Douglas shrugs. "Isn't it easier if I don't wear it?"

"It's for modesty," I explain.

"I'm not much for modesty," he says with a wink.

I'll bet. He knows how hot he is. That rat bastard.

The mole in question is on Mr. Douglas's back. It's about three millimeters in diameter, light brown, and a perfect regular circle. It's perhaps the least concerning mole I've ever seen in my career. If I were to write a journal article about moles that are completely benign, I might consider including Mr. Douglas's in the article. Not that I would ever write such a frivolous article, although it would actually be an excuse to get in touch with him. Not that I would ever do anything like that.

This guy is really scrambling my brain. Jesus.

"I think you're in the clear," I tell him.

He raises his eyebrows at me. "You don't even want to biopsy it?"

"There's no need," I assure him. "It's completely benign."

"Well, that's a relief," Mr. Douglas says. I notice he doesn't make any movement to put his shirt back on.

"Do you have any other questions or concerns?"

"Yes," he says. "Just one. Are you allowed to date patients?"

Ha ha, very funny.

He's making a joke, obviously. Men who look like him don't actually want to date women who look like me. Not that there's anything wrong with me exactly, but I'm just in a different league than Clark Douglas. He's gorgeous, and I'm just average. Maybe if my blond hair were thick and wavy and luxurious instead of short, practical, fine, and really closer to dirty blond. Maybe if I were six inches taller with long, shapely legs. Maybe if I dropped twenty pounds. Okay, thirty pounds.

Anyway, it doesn't matter. It's just a fact of life. Like that the sky is blue and groin fungus is disgusting.

"No, I don't date patients," I coolly inform Clark Douglas.

"No exceptions?" he asks, turning the full effect of his blue, blue eyes on me. And how does a *man* end up with such beautiful eyelashes? I would have to empty half a bottle of mascara onto my pale lashes to have that effect.

"No," I say, hoping to put an end to this ridiculous line of conversation.

I open up his chart to make a note in it. I happen to notice his occupation: attorney. He's a gorgeous *attorney*. He probably thinks he's God's gift to women, that he's doing me a huge favor by flirting with me. That I'll run home and tell all my girlfriends about it. What a thrill.

He hops off the examining table. He thankfully grabs his shirt and swings it over his head. Unfortunately, he's even more attractive dressed. Well, no. That would be impossible. But he's *equally* attractive dressed.

"What if I stopped being your patient?" he asks. "I can find another dermatologist."

I shake my head. "I'm afraid not."

He raises his eyebrows at me. "So you would never go out with anyone who was *ever* a patient of yours? Even if it was ten years ago?"

I sigh. "Fine. Maybe if it were ten years ago."

"How about five years ago?"

I shake my head again, but I can't help smiling slightly. I know he's still just flirting harmlessly, but he's so freaking charming. It's hard not to fall under his spell, just a little bit. "Maybe."

"Now we're talking..." He nods thoughtfully. "What would you say to... three months ago? What if I ask you out again in three months?"

"Fine," I say, just to put an end to the whole thing. "You can ask me out in three months."

Mr. Douglas pumps his fist. "Alright!" He winks at me again. "I guess I'll see you in three months, Dr. Charlotte McKenna."

I will never see this man ever again. I'm willing to bet the farm on that.

CHAPTER 2
Two Years Before

My apartment is my haven.

No matter how long and exhausting and frustrating my day is, I feel comforted when I walk into my apartment. I live near Central Park, and I have a great view, a spacious living room, a beautifully furnished kitchen, and two bedrooms.

Yes, it's *just me* living there. Thanks for asking.

The one thing I do wish we had is a doorman. We have a buzzer to enter the building, and it always makes me a little nervous. You know, being a single woman living all alone and all. I mean, everyone just lets everyone in behind them even if they don't know them… it's like a free-for-all. Then again, I don't like the idea of having a doorman that I would have to make small talk with every time I leave or enter the building, and buy him an obligatory Christmas gift. Plus we've got Johnny, our burly maintenance guy, who is always somewhere nearby. And I've got a padlock on my door that the locksmith assured me that not even the best spy in the CIA would be able to jimmy open.

So anyway, I feel pretty safe.

When I get home, I toss my keys onto the kitchen counter and let out a long, cleansing sigh. Before I've taken two steps into the apartment, my cat races over to me and meows loudly, then looks up at me with big, longing green-yellow eyes. Two years ago, I adopted a black cat from an animal shelter, which I named Kitty (I'm a doctor—I'm not creative). She's like my best friend now.

I'd wanted a cat forever, but I was afraid to get one. Why? Partially because I work long hours and I wasn't sure if I'd have time to take care of a cat. But also because I was afraid that getting one cat might be a gateway drug to becoming a crazy cat lady—someone who goes to work covered in a layer of cat hair and throws kitties at teenagers playing their rap music too loud.

The crazy cat lady isn't just a terrible stereotype. I honestly believe it's a real thing. At least fifty percent of cats carry an infection known as toxoplasmosis, which is the reason pregnant women shouldn't change litter boxes. I've read that toxoplasmosis can theoretically infect the brain of the owners, effectively causing psychosis. So the crazy cat lady might not just be crazy because she's got twenty cats in her home... it might be because of toxoplasmosis. That's a *real thing*. I didn't want to end up with toxoplasmosis psychosis.

But then I figured, screw it, I'll get a cat.

I open up a can of cat food for Kitty. Kitty refuses to eat any dry food and will only eat gourmet brands of canned cat food. I swear, the stuff looks so good, sometimes I'm tempted to take a taste. (Okay, I admit it, I did try it once. I don't recommend it.) I honestly don't know why my cat is such a spoiled diva, especially considering three months before I adopted her, she was eating out of garbage cans.

For myself, I pull a salmon filet out of the refrigerator and throw it in the frying pan with some olive oil, salt, and pepper. No matter how tired I am at night, I always cook myself a hot meal on the stove. Nothing gourmet, but hey, it's better than a TV dinner.

I hear my phone buzzing inside my purse, and contemplate whether I should answer. It could be my best friend Bridget (well, best friend after Kitty), but more likely, it's my mother. Ever since my father passed on, she's been checking up on me on a daily basis. And our conversations always touch on the exact same topics: the fact that I live alone and the fact that I don't have boyfriend. I'm just not in the mood right now.

Oh hell, I'll talk to her for a minute and that's it.

"Charly!" my mother booms. She must be on her cell phone. She's somehow unable to regulate the volume of her voice when she's on the cell phone. She basically always just shouts into the phone, thinking I won't hear her otherwise. She sounds the way I do when I'm talking to my older, deafer patients.

"Hi, Mom," I say. I glance over at my salmon, which is currently steaming. "I can't really talk. I'm in the middle of cooking dinner."

"What are you making!" she shouts.

"Salmon with a salad," I say as I pull a head of lettuce out of the fridge. Since I read that pre-packaged lettuce is dangerously unhealthy, I've been cutting my own, so I have to balance the phone precariously between my chin and my neck as I slice. I miss the days of ignorance.

"Don't forget to turn off the oven when you're done," she warns me.

"You really think I'm going to forget to turn off the oven if you don't tell me?" I say. I'm trying to keep the irritation out of my voice but it's hard. "I mean, I've cooked *thousands* of meals living on my own, and you think that the *only thing* stopping me from keeping the oven on and burning down the building is you telling me to turn it off? Is that really what you think?"

"It can't hurt to remind you," she sniffs.

I love my mother. I really do. Probably more than anyone else in the world. But somehow it's become impossible to have a conversation with her without my ending up shouting, then feeling guilty about it later. Why does talking to your parents always make you regress to your teenage years?

"Charly," Mom says, "I know you're going to say no to this, but the son of this woman I met playing bridge is interested in—"

"No."

"But if you could just meet him and—"

"*No.*"

"Why are you so stubborn, Charly?" Mom says. "I mean, you're in your mid-thirties. Don't you want to get married and have kids?"

"I told you—if it happens, it happens." I shrug at my salmon. "If it doesn't, it doesn't."

"If you don't make it happen, then it won't happen."

"*Then it won't happen.*"

"But Charly—"

"My dinner is ready," I say as I lift the lid off my pan containing the salmon. The filet has turned that perfect pink color that lets me know that it's cooked to a medium-rare. Perfect. "I'll have to talk to you later."

My mother reluctantly gets off the phone so that I can assemble my plate of dinner. I love being able to eat whatever I want for dinner, then watch whatever I want on television while Kitty settles down on the sofa next to me so that I can stroke her soft, black fur.

The truth is, I haven't met a guy yet whose company I enjoyed better than the peace of my own home. Why wreck something that's already perfect?

But then as the perfectly cooked salmon dissolves on my tongue, I can't help but think about Clark Douglas, that patient from this morning. And how, even though it's practically impossible, I wouldn't entirely mind if he were here, sharing dinner with me right now. And maybe hanging around for a bit afterwards.

CHAPTER 3
One Week After

The light feels like a knife.

Yellow light inches away from my pupil, jabbing at my eyeball like an ice pick through my brain. I want to close my eyes to block it out, but I can't. My eye won't close. Something has wedged it open.

I try to cry out to protest, but my lips don't move. While something holds my eye open, something holds my lips shut. Tape, I think.

"No pupillary response," a voice announces.

With those words, my eyelid is released and I am plunged back into blessed relative darkness, marred only by a large green spot in the center of my vision. I want to live in this darkness.

"No way," a second voice says. "Are you blind? I got a definite contraction of that pupil."

It happens again. My eyelid is yanked open and I see the blurry outline of a face before the light floods my field of vision again. The pain came slower before, but this time it is immediate. I've never been a religious person, but I find myself praying that the light will go away.

Please, God, make it go black again...

"She had pretty eyes," a voice comments.

They are complimenting me in the past tense. That can't be good.

"See?" a triumphant voice announces seconds before the light shuts off. "I told you it contracted."

"Fine," says the first voice. "Keep her breathing on the vent for another month or two instead of giving her organs to somebody who isn't brain-dead."

There's a long pause before I hear: "She's an organ donor?"

"Said so on her driver's license, apparently."

Another long pause. The pain in my head is fading and with it, my consciousness. Blessed darkness. Thank you, God.

"Well, she's not dead yet."

Those words are comforting to me. Something has happened to me, but I'm not dead. I'm alive. I'm still here. Not dead.

Yet.

I hear one last remark before I slip away again:

"Do you think she's really still in there?"

———

I don't know this girl, but she is very pretty and her hair is tied back into a blond ponytail. She is young, maybe in her twenties, with a fresh-faced eager look. There are freckles sprinkled across her nose, which make her look even younger and more fresh-faced and pretty. Her smile fills my vision and makes me feel comforted, optimistic.

"Are you ready to try eating something today, Charlotte?" she asks.

Who is Charlotte?

I have no idea who she is talking to. But her eyes are locked with mine. I think she might be talking to me. Yes, she is definitely talking to me. I am Charlotte. That is my name, I think.

It's a pretty name. Charlotte. I like it.

I look down and see there is a plate in front of me. On the plate, there are three mounds of food. They all sort of look like mashed potatoes, but one is gray, one is white, and one is yellow. Multicolored mashed potatoes. I wonder how they do that.

The girl spoons a bit of the gray material and then lifts the spoon to my lips.

"Open your mouth, Charlotte," the girl says.

I look down and see the badge hanging from the pocket of the girl's bright purple scrub top. Written in big letters is the word Amy. The girl's name must be Amy. That's a pretty name too. Almost as pretty as Charlotte.

"Come on, Charly," she says to me. Amy. Her blue eyes are wide and hopeful. "Open your mouth for me."

She demonstrates by opening her own mouth. She has a little pink tongue.

I really want to make Amy happy, so I do what she did. I open my mouth. Amy's face lights up like a Christmas tree. She's even prettier when she's happy, although I'm not entirely sure why opening my mouth made her so happy. "Great job!" she tells me.

My reward is a mouthful of gray material on a spoon. It's not a very good reward. The spoon tastes metallic and bitter, but the food tastes even worse. It almost tastes like meat, but with an odd aftertaste. I don't like it and I don't want it in my mouth. I want to spit it out, but I don't think Amy will like that.

"Now chew, Charlotte," Amy instructs me as she removes the spoon.

Amy demonstrates this one by letting her lower jaw fall slack, then raising it up again, then lowering it again as if I didn't understand what chewing is. I mimic her movements and Amy looks like she may faint from happiness. Her standards for happiness seem ridiculously low.

"You're doing amazing today, Charlotte," she says.

Amy's standards for "amazing" seem ridiculously low too.

"Now I need you to swallow."

I understand what she wants me to do. I mean, I do and I don't. I know what swallowing is, and I know I've done it before, but I don't entirely know how to do it right now. I'm not entirely sure why.

I see a little crease forming between her brows. Amy isn't happy anymore. I want to make her happy, but I don't know what to do. Whatever it is, I'm obviously not doing it.

"Swallow, Charly," she says. "Come on, *swallow*."

I stop the chewing motion. I feel some of the gray material sliding out of the corner of my mouth. Amy allows the food to trickle down my chin before she dabs at my face with a napkin.

I feel terrible. I want to let Amy know that I am trying my best, I don't mean to disappoint her. I want to do what she'd like me to do.

But when I open my mouth to tell her those things, I lose the rest of the food that she placed in my mouth and it leaks down my chin and splatters on a napkin across my chest.

Amy just sighs and shakes her head.

———

The ball is red and I keep watching it. This is trickier than it sounds. The ball goes up, down, to one side then it's gone. Magically, inexplicably gone. Where did it go? I try turning my head, but I still can't find it.

Where is it?

"Whoa, Charly," a voice says. I feel a hand on my shoulder, pushing me. That's when I realize that I have been falling to the side. The hand is keeping me from falling.

There's the ball again! I found it!

It's red.

The person holding the red ball has short brown hair like a boy, but I don't think it is a boy. Her features are delicate like a girl. And her voice is low pitched, but still definitely sounds like a girl. So I think she is a girl. I'm like ninety-nine percent sure.

Also, I look down and her name tag says Valerie, which is a girl's name. So yes, I am ninety-nine percent sure she's a girl.

"Is this what you were looking for, Charly?" the girl (I think) says.

Who is she talking to? Who is Charly?

Oh wait, I think that's me. I think that's my name.

Valerie rotates the red ball around in her fingers. She holds it in my face. "Do you want to try grabbing it?"

I know she wants me to do something, something to do with the ball, but I don't really understand what. So I just look at the ball. We wait there for a minute, then Valerie's face breaks out into a smile and she shakes her head.

"Wishful thinking," she says with a laugh.

I keep watching the red ball. I watch it goes up, up, up. This time, I swear I'm not going to lose track of it.

"How is she doing today?"

The question was asked by a pretty girl with her blond hair in a ponytail. She looks a little bit familiar. I look at her name tag and read her name. Amy. I'm sure I've seen her before.

Valerie shrugs. "Pretty bad at the beginning of the session, but just now she was tracking this red ball pretty well. I mean, she didn't grab for it or anything, but she followed it almost everywhere."

"Everywhere?"

Valerie smiles. "Well, she loses it when it goes to the left. Her left neglect is still horrendous. She has no awareness at all of her left side. She's practically falling out of her wheelchair to the left."

Who is "she"? Who are they talking about? There's nobody else here besides me. They couldn't be talking about me though. I can't be falling out of my wheelchair because I'm not in a wheelchair. Why would I be in a wheelchair? Those are for old people.

I look down, to my right side. I see an armrest, then a large metal rimmed wheel.

Huh. Maybe I really am in a wheelchair.

"Better than nothing," Amy comments. She sounds a little bit sad, but I'm not sure why. "I don't know… She had one really good day about a week ago when I got her to open her mouth for some food and even chew it a little bit, but then nothing since then. I can barely get her to stay awake through my session."

"We did the coma scale yesterday," Valerie says, brushing some strands of brown hair from her eyes. She has very pretty eyes.

"And?"

"What do you think?" Valerie snorts. "Still vegetative. No purposeful movements."

They are both quiet for a minute.

Oh shit, I don't see the red ball. They were distracting me and I lost track of it. Where did it go?

"It's sad," Amy says. "I just can't get anything out of her most of the time. I hate to give up though. She's so young… and she used to be a doctor."

"Yeah, but her insurance…"

Oh my God, there it is! The red ball! It's in Valerie's hand. I found it!

This time, I am definitely not going to lose track of that ball. Valerie gestures with it and I watch it. It goes up and down. It's easy to follow because it's red.

CHAPTER 4
One month After

"Open your eyes for me."

There is a very pretty girl with blond hair sitting across from me. She is smiling at me. I like her smile. She has very straight teeth. And there are freckles across her pert little nose.

I feel something stroking my hand. I look down and see that the pretty blond girl has my hand in hers. Her hand is so soft, like a baby.

"Very good," the blond girl is saying. "Now I want you to keep your eyes open."

I keep my eyes open, focusing on the blond girl's smile. It's hard. I'm so tired. It would be nice to close my eyes.

"Good," she says. She rubs a cold washcloth over my forehead and my cheek, and I shiver. A droplet of water slides down my cheek and down my neck. "You have such pretty eyes. The color is so unusual. Violet, like Elizabeth Taylor."

Violet is like purple. How could I have purple eyes? Purple is not a normal color for eyes.

"Listen to me," the blond girl says, "I want you to give me a thumbs up if I say your name. Okay?"

I read the name off of the blond girl's name tag: Amy. She looks sort of familiar to me. I think I met her before. Her hand feels very soft, like a baby.

"Is your name Susan?" she asks me.

Is my name Susan? I don't think it is. That doesn't sound familiar.

No, I'm almost certain that my name isn't Susan.

"Is your name Lisa?"

I don't think Lisa is my name either. What is my name again? That seems like something I should definitely know.

But I'm sure if she says my name, I'll recognize it.

I look to my right and see that there is another person in the room besides Amy. It is an older woman, with gray hair that is pulled back into a bun, although dozens of loose scraggly strands have escaped and fallen around her face. She's wearing gray-rimmed glasses that slide down the bridge of her nose. I look for a name tag, but I don't see one.

"How come she always has her head turned to the right?" the older woman asks.

"Injuries to the right side of the brain can sometimes cause a neglect of the left side," Amy explains. "Basically, she has trouble paying attention and noticing stimuli on her left side."

"So she can't see things on her left side?"

"It's not necessarily a question of vision," Amy says. "It's about perception. Like, for example, if I touch her on her left arm, notice how she doesn't really respond, even though her nerves are working fine. She just doesn't *perceive* that I'm touching her. She ignores any stimuli on her left side."

Is Amy touching me right now? I guess she must be. I'm just not *perceiving* it, whatever the hell that means.

"That's so bizarre," the older woman says.

Amy nods. "And weirdly, it doesn't just apply to real life. Patients with hemispatial neglect on the left side can ignore the left side of hallucinations, dreams, or memories too." She turns her attention back to me and smiles. "So tell me. Is your name Charlotte?"

Is that my name? I'm not sure. It sounds familiar.

"Give me a thumbs-up if your name is Charlotte," Amy says.

The older woman is leaning forward eagerly, her blue eyes wide behind the lenses of her glasses. She has dark circles under her eyes. Her blouse is wrinkled, like she slept in it.

"She did it!" the older woman says triumphantly. "I saw her thumb move."

Amy shakes her head. "I… I'm not so sure."

The older woman sniffs. "Well, you weren't paying attention then."

Amy bites her lip.

The older woman stands up. She stands next to me and lays a hand on my shoulder. I try to look up at her, but my head feels funny when I lift it. There's something resting on my head making it hard to move. Something strange and heavy.

"You know your name, don't you, Charly?" the woman says to me.

I'm confused. Is my name Charly then? Or is it Charlotte? Or is it Lisa? Or Susan?

For God's sake, why don't they just tell me my name already?

"She's tracking better," Amy says.

The older woman waves her hand as if this is no consequence to her. She leans forward so I can make out all the wrinkles on her skin. She is so old and smells like flowers. "You know more than you're letting on, don't you, Charly?" she says. She winks at me. "You know who I am, don't you?"

I have absolutely no idea who this woman is.

"Mrs. McKenna," Amy says in a soft but stern voice. Her pretty face looks angry. "We agreed you could sit in on my session if you promised not to disrupt your daughter's therapy."

Amy is angry. Really angry. What have I done to make her so angry? I must've done something terrible to make her so upset.

Oh my God, what have I done?

"Oh, Charlotte," I hear Amy say suddenly. "Don't cry! Why are you crying?"

The older woman starts asking her if it is good that I am crying, and meanwhile, Amy keeps rubbing my hand. How could it be good that I am crying? What is wrong with that stupid old woman?

———

I am dreaming, or at least, I think I am.

A gunshot echoes in my ear, and I try to see where it came from, but I can't. I can see the right side of my apartment so clearly—my bookcase filled with textbooks about skin conditions, a maple wood desk, and my wide-screen television. But I can't see who's making the footsteps coming from my left side.

Even though it's a dream and I know it's a dream, I still can feel hot breath against the left side of my neck. And I hear words hissed in my ear. It feels so real.

Then I wake up.

The room we are in now is real and it's small, with only a bed, a single dresser, and a television. Nobody else is here but the two of us. This is my room. I think so, anyway. That's what everybody says.

The older woman is with me, but she's on the phone. She's speaking in a hushed, urgent voice but I can make out the words she's saying.

"Do you think you could come see her this weekend?" the woman murmurs into the phone.

The older woman is sitting in a chair next to me. I am sitting too. In a wheelchair. I'm always sitting in a wheelchair these days, even though I'm not old or sick. Well, I might be sick. I'm not sure.

The woman's voice raises a notch. "You haven't seen her in over a week. I don't care how busy you are with work—she's your *wife*."

I watch the way the older woman's face is turning red. I wonder whom she's talking to.

"She *does* know who you are!" she cries. "Even if she doesn't greet you by name, she definitely recognizes people. I'm sure of it! I know she'd love it if you came here."

The older woman is nearly yelling now, but I get distracted by the sound of heavy footsteps outside the door. I watch the doorway, waiting to see who will appear.

It's a man. He's wearing a dark suit with a tie. He's tall with a shiny bald head that reflects the lights on the ceiling. He looks important. And scary.

The older woman looks up, then quickly murmurs into her phone: "I have to go now. That detective is here." She pauses as the man waits. "No, I don't know. If you're so interested, why don't you call him yourself!"

She shoves the phone into her purse without another word. She closes her eyes for a moment then opens them again.

"Detective Simpson," she says. "I thought we agreed you weren't going to come here. You *promised* me. I don't want to upset her."

The man shakes his head. "I need to talk to Charlotte. I need to get a statement."

So it turns out my name is Charlotte. Someone *finally* told me. Anyway, since I am Charlotte, I guess that means he wants to talk to me. Which means he is not going to go away until I do what he says or else the time is up.

"A statement?" the older woman snorts. "Does she look like she's in any condition to give you a statement?"

"The trail gets colder every day we wait…"

"It's been over a month," the woman snaps at him. "I think the trail is about as cold as it's going to get."

They keep staring at each other, the man and the older woman. The man takes his arms and folds them across his chest so that his suit creases.

"Mrs. McKenna," he says. "I would think that you of all people would want to see justice brought to the person who shot your daughter."

"I told her it was dangerous to live so close to the park," the woman murmurs. "I told her a hundred times. She never listened to me and now..."

Her eyes fill up with tears and she looks away.

"If we could track the jewelry that's missing..." the man says.

The woman snorts. "What a waste of time. Is this what our taxpayer dollars are being used for? You should have spent more manpower when she first got shot, when there was actually a chance of catching him."

"There were no matchable fingerprints," the man says. "No eyewitnesses. And the weapon was your daughter's own gun, so it wouldn't have helped to trace it to a dealer."

"God only knows what Charly was doing with a *gun*," the old woman mutters. "She really must have lost her mind."

"Also," the man adds, "there's the matter of the rather large life insurance policy that Charlotte had. You know, her husband stood to gain two millions dollars."

"No," the old woman says firmly. "Clark never would have…"

"We just have to explore all avenues…"

"Fine," she says abruptly. She turns away from both of us. "Go ahead, ask her your questions. Explore your avenues. Do what you need to do. I just… I don't want to be here…"

The older woman races out of the room, leaving me alone with the man. His shoulders sag slightly, and he lets out a long sigh. Suddenly, he does not seem quite so scary anymore, so it's okay that I am alone with him. He pulls a notebook and a pen from his pants pocket.

The pen has a red cap.

"Now Charlotte," the man says to me. "What can you tell me about the night of December ninth?"

I stare at the red cap of that pen. Watch the red. Follow it when it moves. Don't lose it, Charly. Don't lose it.

CHAPTER 5
Two Months After

I wake up to the sound of voices. Angry voices. I try to go back to sleep, squeezing my eyes shut as tight as I can, but the voices won't let me escape. They are like metal pans clanging together in my brain.

"Two weeks is the most you're going to get," a male voice says.

I roll my head in the direction of the voice. It belongs to a tall man with thinning dark hair that is graying heavily at the temples. He wears a long white coat that comes down nearly to his knees. He has his arms folded across his chest, and his eyes are sharp behind a pair of rimless spectacles.

"So you're just giving up on her?"

This voice comes from the older woman, who has been around more and more. She is always sitting by my bed, talking to me in a soft, kind voice. But right now her face is contorted, making her look older and uglier.

"We're not giving up, Mrs. McKenna," the man says. "But she's been here over a month and we haven't seen *anything* in the way of progress. She's exactly where she was on the first day."

I think that they're talking about me, even though they never say my name. Everyone comes in here to talk about me. These conversations never seem happy.

"You just said you're not giving up," the older woman retorts, "then you tell me that you're giving up."

The man sighs. I'm not sure anymore if he's angry. He looks kind of sad actually. He shoves his hands into the deep pockets of the long white coat. I notice that his tie has cartoons of little yellow ducks on it. It makes me smile.

"We've given her a lot of time, Mrs. McKenna. If it were up to me, I would let her have longer. You know I would. But the insurance is cutting her off."

"So if she gets better," the older woman says, "you would take her back?"

The man is quiet for a long time. So long that I almost go back to sleep. My eyelids are heavy and they start to droop. Finally, he says to her, "Mrs. McKenna, you have to face the reality that she probably isn't going to get any better than this."

The older woman's head droops down. "You're wrong."

"I hope I'm wrong. Believe me."

The older woman just shakes her head. "So what do we do now?"

"It's up to you," he says. "You know how much is involved in her care. She can't dress herself, bathe herself, eat... do you feel like you can take that on?"

I understand what he is asking. He wants to know if the older woman will take care of me. I know she will. She loves me. I can't remember much, but I know this much.

"You have to understand, Dr. Greenberg," the older woman says. "I have arthritis and my husband died a few years ago. I'm in my seventies. I just can't…"

The man holds up his hand. "I understand. I'll talk to the case manager about arranging for a nursing home."

The older woman's wrinkled skin turns a shade paler. "A nursing home?"

"It's the best thing for her."

"She's only thirty-seven…"

A crease appears between the man's eyebrows. "I understand how you feel. But you can't feel guilty about this. Charlotte needs twenty-four-hour-a-day care and you just can't provide that."

The older woman looks over at me, and seems surprised to see that my eyes are open. She gasps slightly and clasps her hand over her mouth. "Oh my gosh, she heard all this. We shouldn't have had this conversation in front of her."

"Mrs. McKenna," the man says patiently, "you have to realize that she can't understand—"

"You have *no idea* what she can understand," the older woman snaps at him.

The man looks over at me and for a moment, our eyes meet. His are brown but the whites are lined with red. He looks tired. He squints at me a minute, then he shakes his head.

"We'll get you that list of nursing homes tomorrow," he promises.

CHAPTER 6
Two Months After

The pain is like white hot coals sliding across my belly. It wakes me up from sleep, and when I realize that it has no intention of stopping, I crack open my eyes and whimper. Well, at first I whimper, but then it turns into a moan. Then a scream. Or my best attempt at a scream.

There's a woman standing over me wearing flower-patterned scrubs with dark hair pulled back into a painful-looking bun, and she's doing something to the tube that comes out of my belly. I hate that tube. I have tried to remove it on multiple occasions, but they won't let me. Once they even covered my hand in a big white mitten covered in mesh to thwart my efforts.

That tube hurts so much. The skin around it on my belly is red and angry and goopy. They keep putting bandages and creams on it, telling me it will help with the pain, but it never does. Anytime anyone touches that tube, I want to scream.

I reach for the tube with my right hand, trying to push away the woman. She has bags under her brown eyes, which narrow at me angrily.

"Will you just let me do this, Charlotte?" she snaps at me. "I'm not in the mood."

Well, I'm not in the mood to have excruciating pain in my belly. I swipe at her hand, in my best attempt to keep her away.

"If you keep this up," the woman says to me, "I'm going to get out the restraint."

Then she takes one hand and physically pins down my right arm hard enough that I can feel her fingernails biting into my skin. I'm sure I have another arm somewhere that I can use against her. For right now, I'm not sure where it is. And with my right arm restrained, I'm helpless. The pain commences. It's just as white-hot as before. Burning. That's the only word that runs through my head as tears well up in my eyes. Burning.

"Stop!" I croak. "No! Stop!"

It's a miracle. The woman stops, her brown eyes now wide, staring at me. She doesn't look angry anymore.

"Did you say something?" she asks me in a soft, bewildered voice.

I just stare at her. Now that the pain is fading, I feel like I could go back to sleep. I'm so tired.

The woman leaves the room. The pain in my belly has subsided to a dull ache. My eyes start to drift closed. So tired...

I am nearly asleep when the woman returns. By her side is the blond pretty woman with the ponytail and freckles. I know her name. What is her name?

Amy! That's her name.

"Charly," Amy says. She picks up my hand from the bed and holds it in her own. Her fingers are so soft, like a baby. "Megan says that you talked. Is that true?"

Amy's hands are so soft. I'm so tired. I think I will go back to sleep.

"What was happening when she spoke to you?" Amy says. She is talking to the other woman now. Maybe she will leave me alone so that I can sleep

"I was cleaning her feeding tube."

"Let's do it again then."

My eyes have nearly drifted shut when the pain begins again. I gasp. Why does it hurt so much? My belly didn't hurt this much before. Although I don't really remember that much about before.

"Stop!" I plead, because it worked before. "Stop!"

Again, like magic, the pain halts. It worked. Thank God.

When my vision focuses in again on Amy's face, she has the biggest smile I've ever seen.

"Charly," she says. "You just made my day."

CHAPTER 7
Two and a Half Months After

Honest to God, my head is so itchy. I don't know what is making it so itchy. Maybe somebody is coming in during the night and putting itching powder on my scalp. Or maybe there are tiny little bugs crawling all over my skin. That's how it feels anyway. And all I can think of is scratching my scalp over and over until the itch goes away. Right now, that's my idea of heaven.

But they won't let me do it.

Every time I tried to scratch the itchy spot on my scalp, somebody grabs my hand and says, "No, Charly! You don't have any skull under there!" Which I guess explains why my scalp is so soft and squishy.

Also, I've got a huge helmet on my head, so just getting my hand in there is a challenge. I've tried to take off the helmet, but nobody is very excited about letting me do that either. I guess because of the no skull thing.

I keep trying to explain about my scalp being itchy. I really don't think they get it. It gets me upset because what if there really are bugs all over my scalp? You would think they would want to check and maybe try to get rid of them. But nobody seems to care.

Dr. Greenberg is my doctor here, and every day I try to explain to him about the itch in my scalp. I figure, if anyone should be able to help me, it's a doctor. People tell me that I was a doctor before, and I know I could help myself, but that would involve taking off the helmet and scratching my head, which nobody will let me do. Since I'm a doctor, you'd think they'd let me treat myself.

"How are you doing today?" Dr. Greenberg asks me during his daily visit to see me in my room. I like it when he comes to see me. I like how he always has funny ties, like today he has balloons on his tie. He seems like a really nice man. Maybe he can help me stop being itchy.

"My head itches a lot," I explain. I raise my right hand and try to snake it under my helmet, but earlier today, a nurse attached a thick white mitten to my hand, so I can't really do much with it.

"I know it's uncomfortable," Dr. Greenberg tells me, "but you really can't scratch there. You don't have any skull covering your brain, so you could hurt your brain."

"I wouldn't hurt my brain," I say.

"You might."

"I already hurt it pretty bad," I say. "How much worse could it be?"

Dr. Greenberg chuckles. I don't know why that was funny. It's true.

"Are you ready to do our questions?" he asks me.

I shrug.

"Tell me your name," he says.

"Charly."

"Charly what?"

I know this one. I stare at him for a minute, then I finally come up with, "Itch?"

Dr. Greenberg shakes his head. "No. Your last name is McKenna."

I knew that one. If my head wasn't so itchy, I would've gotten it.

"And where are we, Charly?"

I hate these questions. It's so hard to concentrate when I'm so itchy. "We're here."

"But where is here?"

"My room."

"Right, but what kind of place is this?"

"It is…" I try to focus. I know he expects me to give him an answer. But all I can think about is how itchy my scalp is. I try to scratch it again, but the damn glove stops me again. "An itch?"

Dr. Greenberg smiles at me. "It's a rehab hospital, Charly."

"Oh."

"And how old are you?"

I think hard. I feel like I remember somebody saying I had a birthday coming up. So I'm going to be older than I was before. But how old am I now? "I'm going to be twenty."

Dr. Greenberg laughs again. "Don't we wish? Try again, Charly."

"Twenty-two?"

"You're thirty-seven," he says.

Oh my God, could that be true? I try to look down at the wristband on my arm, which has all my information, but I can't see it because of the mitten. How could I be thirty-seven though?

"That's so old!"

Dr. Greenberg smiles down at me. "You're younger than I am."

If I'm thirty-seven, does that mean I have wrinkles on my face? Is my hair turning gray? Thirty-seven is pretty old, right? I don't want to be thirty-seven! That's *so old*! I would rather be twenty. But I guess if he says I am thirty-seven, I must be.

Dr. Greenberg takes out his stethoscope and starts listening to my chest. I take a deep breath so that he can hear me breathing. He always tells me when he's done that my breathing sounds very good. Then he touches my belly, which I really don't like because the feeding tube is still there and it hurts a lot. The good news is that if I eat enough, Amy said we could take it out.

"Sounds great, Charly," he says.

I smile.

"Just one more question before I leave," he says.

I nod, determined to answer this one correctly.

"How old are you?"

I stare him straight in the eyes. "Twenty-itch."

By the look on his face, I don't think I got it right.

———

Amy, who is my speech therapist, says that the only way I will get that stupid tube out of my belly is if I eat. She's allowed me to start eating food, but it's not real food. Not in any sense of the word.

I am sitting in my wheelchair in my room, and my mother is sitting beside me. She is almost always around during meals, and I hate it. She keeps saying things like, "you have to eat, Charly," or "just one more bite." Of course, after she tells me one more bite, then she says again that I have to take another bite. So it's all just a big fat lie.

Today I am having steak, potatoes, and green beans for lunch. My mother circled it for me on the menu I got this morning, and it sounded good at the time. There's nothing wrong with steak, potatoes, and green beans. But now I look down at my plate, and it doesn't look so good. The steak is a big pile of gray mush. The potatoes are big pile of white mush, and the green beans are… you guessed it, green mush.

If I had to pick one to eat, I guess it would be the potatoes, because potatoes are usually served kind of mushy anyway. I definitely don't want to eat the meat, and I've never liked green beans. In any case, they don't benefit from being mushed up. I don't think green bean purée is going to turn into a hot new food trend.

"Come on, eat something," Mom says to me.

I pick up the fork with my right hand. I take a little bit of potatoes and bring it to my mouth. They taste terrible.

"Oh, Charly," Mom sighs. "Please don't spit it out."

I wasn't intentionally trying to spit out the potatoes. Sometimes it's hard to keep food from dribbling out the side of my mouth unless I swallow it right away. Which is hard to do if the food tastes awful.

"Why didn't they bring me a drink?" I ask.

"They *did* bring you a drink," my mother says. "It's right here."

I look down at my tray. I see my plate of three piles of mush, my knife and fork, and that's it.

"It's over to the left, Charly," she says.

This keeps happening to me. I keep looking for something that supposed to be in front of me but I can't find it, and then somebody tells me that it's over on the left. That doesn't make a lot of sense to me. But when somebody asks me where something is, something that I can't find, I've figured out the correct answer is: "It's on my left."

My mother does something to my tray, and all of a sudden, a cup with orange liquid comes into view. It's not really liquid though. It's sort of the texture of those ice slushies I used to drink when I was a kid, except it's not ice cold, so it tastes sort of weird. I mean, who wants to drink a lukewarm orange slushy? But something has to wash down the mashed potatoes.

"Good, Charly," mom says. "Now take another bite."

All my solids have been turned into almost liquid, and my liquids have been turned into almost solid. I don't know how they expect me to really eat this stuff. But I have to try. If I can get the feeding tube out, it will be worth it.

CHAPTER 8
One Year, Nine Months Before

I had planned to run a marathon next month. That's not going to happen. My training is completely screwed.

I can run five miles. That's the upper limit before the pain starts up in my right knee. It hurts on the lateral side of my knee, a sharp unrelenting pain that won't stop until I do. At first, I hoped I could run through it. But it's obvious I can't.

I saw a doctor and he said it was my iliotibial band. His brilliant suggestion was to try stretching it out, maybe do some physical therapy. If that's the best he's got, this race is definitely not going to happen.

I'm on my first mile now, running around the small park by the office where I practice, while listening to a Fleetwood Mac album on my iPhone. I already feel a tiny twinge in my knee. This is so freaking depressing. I keep hoping that maybe the problem will go away on its own. Like maybe I would start running today and it would just be magically gone.

Guess not.

"You're pretty fast," a male voice says from behind me. "What's your time for a mile?"

I slow down to a stop, channeling my frustration into anger. I don't like it when people talk to me when I'm running. The last thing I want when I'm trying to train for a marathon is comments from the peanut gallery.

But when I turn around, I get a surprise. Jogging behind me is none other than Clark Douglas.

You know, the hottie? The one I thought I'd never see again in a million years? The one with the blue eyes like the Pacific Ocean, or maybe like my laundry detergent. They're both pretty blue.

"Hello there, Dr. Charlotte McKenna," he says, smiling that perfect smile as he too slows to a stop.

This is a coincidence, I'm sure. But still, I can't help but feel the tiniest bit excited. He couldn't possibly be here just to see little old me. Could he?

Figures that today I'd be wearing an old baggy pair of running shorts and a T-shirt two sizes too big.

"What are you doing here?" I ask, pulling out my earbuds. Stevie Nicks's voice fades into the background.

"It's been three months," he reminds me.

Oh my God, he really is here to see me.

I need to put a stop to this. Right now. Damn, why does he have to look so good in his shorts and T-shirt?

"Mr. Douglas," I begin.

"Clark," he corrects me.

"*Mr. Douglas*," I say again, more firmly this time. "This isn't appropriate."

"You said that after three months," he says, "you'd consider going out with me."

I shake my head in disbelief. The most handsome man I've ever met in my life is standing in front of me, *begging* me for a date. There's something very wrong with this picture.

"I'm sorry," I say. "I just don't think it's a good idea."

Clark nods. For a minute, I think he might actually accept my refusal and put an end to this ridiculousness. But then he says, "How about a race?"

At first, I think I've heard him wrong. "*What*?"

"I'll race you one lap around the park," he challenges me. "If I win, I get to take you out on a date. If you win, I'll leave you alone." He grins at me. "Seems like a pretty good deal for a runner like you."

I look down at Clark's muscular legs. He's got more power than I do and more length. In a race around the park, he could beat me easily.

"Make it twenty laps," I say. Clark might be able to beat me during a single lap, but I'm willing to bet I have much better endurance.

Clark's smiles. "You're on."

He starts to run then, giving himself a few second head start, but I'm right behind him. Too late, I remember the issue with my knee. Twenty laps will put me over the five-mile mark. If I'm in agony from my knee, it might slow me down.

I square my jaw and pick up my pace. I'm going to win this race. Now it's a matter of pride. I can be pretty competitive when I want to be.

Just as I suspected, Clark is ahead of me after the first lap. After the second lap, he's still in the lead. But by lap number eight, he's slowing down considerably. I can tell he's starting to breathe heavier, and I wonder if he's even going to make it the entire distance. I'm going to *clobber* him.

"You're going to lose," I inform him, as I pull up beside him, running with easy strides. I'm trying not to sound too braggy, but it's hard.

"We'll see," Clark huffs.

Except I can tell that even talking is becoming an effort for him. He is so going to lose.

For the next few laps, I'm ahead of him. But not by as much as I could be. My knee feels wonderful for a change, and I could probably be two laps ahead by now. But here's the weird part:

I feel myself hanging back.

I keep glancing over my shoulder, seeing Clark about half a block behind. I could zip ahead, and finish the race with an embarrassingly big lead, but I don't do it. I always keep Clark in my sight.

Finally, at around lap number nineteen, Clark stops running altogether. He had been steadily losing his steam for the entire last lap, so I'm not surprised. When his footsteps go silent, I turn around and I see him resting his hands on his knees and leaning forward, gasping for air.

He's done. There's no way he's finishing the race before me.

I could walk away right now. I could inform Clark that he's lost and that he is now *required* to leave me alone. But naturally, I'm far too stupid to do that. Instead, I walk back to where Clark is busy catching his breath.

Clark's face is red from exertion. When he lifts his face to look at me, his blue, blue eyes meet mine and he gives me an apologetic half-smile.

"You're too fast for me," he manages. I can see a droplet of sweat roll down his temple. "I guess you win, Dr. McKenna. I'll leave you alone."

God, I'm such a loser for having a crush on this guy.

"Come on," I say. "Only one more lap."

Clark's eyes widen. His half-smile widens into a grin, and he straightens out with a newfound burst of energy. We jog together side-by-side for the last lap, and I hang back at the end to let him win.

CHAPTER 9
One Year, Nine Months Before

"Oh my God, this would look so cute on you!"

As I huddle between two large racks of dresses at Macy's, trying not to feel stifled by the crowds of Saturday shoppers, I wish I could be anywhere else. Somehow I've allowed my friend Bridget to talk me into a shopping trip in honor of my upcoming date tonight with Clark. I didn't even want her to know I had a date, but somehow I let it slip, and I swear, I think she's more excited than I am.

It's been a while.

"You need to try this on," Bridget insists. She's holding up a green dress that's covered in shiny beads and sequins. What sort of person wants to be seen in a dress that looks like that? Do adult women actually wear dresses with *sequins*? The sight of it makes my eyes hurt.

"I don't think it's me," I say. I gently attempt to pry the dress out of her fingers and return it to the rack.

"And what's so wrong with that?" Bridget says.

"Because if I show up to a date wearing a dress that's not me," I explain, "then the guy won't actually like *me*. He'll just be liking some weird bead, sequin girl. I need to be myself."

"Yeah, and where has that gotten you?"

Ouch.

Okay, to be fair, I haven't been out with a man in close to a year. Honestly, I'm not entirely sure how that happened. I used to go out on dates, I swear. Things have just gotten so busy at work, and more and more, my dates were beginning to feel like a huge waste of time. They felt more like a chore... the obligation of trying to find another person to spend the rest of my life with. There was certainly nothing enjoyable about the forced, awkward conversations with variably attractive men.

So I took a break.

A year isn't that long though. Obama was president during my last date. It isn't like it's been *decades* or something. It's just a short dry spell. Bridget is really overreacting.

Bridget reluctantly drops the green dress and makes her way to a rack of little black dresses courtesy of Ralph Lauren, while I nearly get elbowed in the boob by two eager shoppers. Why is it so crowded here? Don't people have better things to do on a Saturday than go shopping for dresses? I want to shake them and tell them to enjoy the sunlight.

"Okay, how about one of these?" Bridget asks.

The Ralph Laurens are classy, at least—something I could conceivably wear. I pick up the price tag on one of the dresses and gasp.

"Bridget!" I cry. "Look how expensive these are!"

Bridget rolls her eyes. "Charly, you're a *doctor*. You can afford a stupid dress."

She's right. I spent so much of my early life being poor that it's hard to transition to thinking of myself as moderately wealthy thanks to my income and my lack of a social life. It also doesn't hurt that I've had some really good investment tips from Bridget, who works for a pharmaceutical company. *Really* good tips.

Bridget had money growing up, and you can tell by the way she shops. Watching Bridget shop is more mesmerizing than watching a lava lamp. She can pluck a thousand dollar vase off a shelf and buy it without a second thought. She doesn't seem to experience the soul-crushing guilt that I feel whenever I spend a lot of money. Right now, she's in her second trimester of pregnancy, but instead of food, she craves clothing. It's the weirdest thing ever.

"This," Bridget says, pulling a short, clingy black number off the rack and shoving it in my direction. "Try this one on."

The price tag is swinging in my face, and it makes me feel almost nauseated. But I don't say no. The truth is, I haven't been this attracted to a guy in a long time. I want to look hot for this date. No, not just hot, I want to look *hawt*. I want Clark to see me and do a wolf howl.

"Okay," I say.

Bridget smiles triumphantly. "And then," she says, "we're going to look at shoes."

———

I don't want to admit how much money I've spent in preparation for this date. Let's just say it's a lot. I could feed a family in Ethiopia for a month with that money. I could cure over a hundred children in a developing nation of parasitic infections all for what I paid for an outfit I very well may never wear again.

I can't remember what happened to the Charly who showed up to dates in jeans and a blouse, and said take it or leave it.

The little black dress is sexy though. It's *perfect*. It somehow makes me look like I have this gorgeous hourglass figure and it even makes my muscular calves look dainty. It's a *magical* dress. (It ought to be for what it cost.)

I wish I had a little black dress for my face. I blow a layer of dust off my bag of make-up, and examine the contents critically. I only left myself half an hour to work on my make-up, which isn't nearly enough time. Really, I could use hours, and possibly a plastic surgeon. I do my best to use the tricks I know to make my lips look fuller, and I even dig out my eyelash curler. But then again, it's an eyelash curler, not a magic wand. Kitty watches me the whole time I'm painting myself, with an expression on her face that seems to say, "What are you *doing* to yourself?"

Good question, dear cat.

When Clark rings for me downstairs, I am in full on panic mode. I start looking around my apartment, wishing I had time to clean it better. Not that I've got dirty socks lying around or anything like that, but I'm really paranoid that the apartment has a cat odor that I've become immune to. While I'm waiting for Clark to make his way upstairs, I desperately start spritzing cucumber-scented body mist everywhere. By the time the doorbell rings, my armpits are sweaty.

Clark is standing at my front door, holding a single red rose. He's wearing a dark dress shirt and tie. Jesus, he looks *good*. And that rose is admittedly a nice touch.

"For you, mademoiselle," Clark says, grinning as he holds the rose out to me.

I take the rose and make a big show out of smelling it, although I'm not sure what to do with a single rose. I'm not really into flowers—the only life I can sustain these days is Kitty's and possibly my own. I toss the rose on my dining table, where it will probably die within a day. Or else Kitty will eat it.

Clark is smiling at me, and my knees start to wobble. Honestly, I've never dated a man who looks like him before. They may not have been ugly, many were even passably cute, but Clark is in a whole other category of handsome. If somebody were making a movie about my life, Clark *could play himself*. That's how handsome he is.

"I'm ready to go," I tell him, clutching my purse. I'm desperate to leave before he stumbles on some pantyhose I forgot to throw in the laundry, or a box of tampons I left lying on the bathroom sink.

Clark sniffs. "Are you making something with cucumbers?"

I swallow. "No."

Clark glances over my shoulder. "How about a grand tour?"

Damn it. "Sure, I guess. I mean, if you want."

Clark follows me around as I lead him into my small kitchen, followed by the living room, the bedroom, and the second bedroom that I have converted into a study. I had to field the second degree from my real estate agent, who couldn't seem to get it through her head that the two bedrooms were just for me.

I watch Clark run his finger along the side of my armoire, which I purchased on sale from Ikea. Nervous and excited as I am about this date, somehow I'm certain that he will not be the bearer of any children for my empty bedroom.

"You own this place?" he asks.

I nod. "I bought it two years ago. I wanted to wait, but I figured…"

I stop myself before I inform him that I figured I might as well buy a place myself since I obviously wasn't getting married anytime in the near future. That's not a first date conversation topic. When you're a single woman in her mid-thirties, the goal during the first date is to pretend like you've never heard of the word marriage.

Marriage? Gee, what's that? Is that a drink? A new Internet start-up company?

"What's the square footage?" he asks.

I look at Clark sideways. I swear, if I didn't know he was a lawyer, I'd guess he was a real estate agent who was only going out with me to convince me to sell my apartment.

Oh God, is he a real estate agent who's only going out with me to get me to sell my apartment?

"I can't remember," I say as I squeeze my fists together. I'm not used to feeling this nervous on a date. I hate the way that Clark is making me feel. Hate it and love it.

Clark walks over to the window, and gets so close to the glass, I'm worried he might leave smudges. "You have an incredible view of the park."

I try to smile as I join Clark at the window. The view was what sold me on this apartment—I love looking at the expanse of green right outside my window. No matter what kind of lousy day I'm having, it always cheers me up. "Yeah, I love it."

He's close enough to nudge my shoulder with his. "Sort of romantic."

I feel a flush rise in my pale cheeks. I know I must be blushing, and I'm sure he can tell. "Yeah, sort of."

A loud meow from behind us interrupts the moment and whatever was about to happen. We turn around and see Kitty, perched on the floor behind us, as if waiting to be introduced. Clark cocks his head at her.

"This is your cat?" he asks.

No, she's a stray that wandered in through the back door.

I nod. "Her name is Kitty."

Clark grins. "Black cats are bad luck, you know."

"So they say…"

I actually hate that superstition. Down at the shelter, they told me that black cats have the hardest time getting adopted because nobody wants the bad luck.

"She's cute," Clark says. He bends down and attempts to pet her, but she backs away and hisses at him. So much for wanting to be introduced. "What breed is she?"

I shrug. "She's a cat."

"The breeder didn't tell you?" he asks, raising his eyebrows.

"I didn't get her from a breeder," I explain. "I rescued her from a shelter."

Clark stares at me, aghast. "Are you serious, Charlotte? You got her *off the street?* She could have fleas! Or be pregnant!"

"She doesn't have fleas," I say defensively, as Kitty nuzzles against my bare calf. "They checked her out at the shelter. And she's been fixed."

"Yeah, that's what they *say*," Clark snorts.

"Are you suggesting they *lied* to me?"

He shrugs. "You get what you pay for."

"Well, I'm not returning her," I say. Clark is seeming less and less attractive by the minute. As if some snooty cat from a breeder would be better than my Kitty. What an ass. No wonder he's still single. "I've had her two years and she's been checked out by the vet. She's fine."

"I suppose you're right," Clark concedes. He crouches down again to make another attempt to pet

Kitty. This time he nearly gets his hand on her black fur before she hisses again and scratches at his hand.

Clark lets loose with a string of profanity. He jumps up, clutching his hand. I am totally shocked. In the two years I've had Kitty, she's never once scratched anyone. Even when one of my coworkers brought her two-year-old son over, who tried to ride Kitty like a horse.

"You didn't have her declawed?" Clark asks accusingly.

"It's inhumane to declaw a cat," I say.

Clark shoves his hand in my face, which is actually bleeding not insignificantly. "Look what she did! You think that's humane?"

Well, this date isn't exactly getting off on the right foot.

I offer to disinfect and bandage Clark's hand, but he waves me away angrily, cleaning it off in my bathroom with soap and water. I would just as soon call off the date entirely, but when Clark emerges from the bathroom and says, "Let's go," I follow him out the door.

CHAPTER 10
One Year, Nine Months Before

I stare at the name on the first chart of the day, trying to remember why the name sounds familiar. *Leroy... Leroy...*

I flip it open and it suddenly all rushes back to me. Of course—Stanley Leroy. Groin Fungus Guy. I look at the reason for the visit and it simply says "follow-up." I guess groin fungus has reared its ugly head once again, as it is apt to do.

I knock once then open the door to the small examining room. The dark-haired man sitting on the examining table in the blue gown we provided looks vaguely familiar, but I honestly don't recall Groin Fungus Guy being quite so attractive. He's thinner than I remember, but he still has the same sorrowful brown eyes. I can't help but notice the way his face lights up when he sees me. I guess it's not surprising though, considering I am the keeper of groin fungus medication.

"Hello," I say with a smile. "What can I do for you today, Mr. Leroy?"

I'm assuming the answer involves looking at groin fungus.

"Please call me Stan," he says. "And I'm just here for a follow-up."

I raise my eyebrows. "Are you still having symptoms?"

He shakes his head. "Nope. It's all cleared up. Thanks to you, Doc."

"All in a day's work." I shrug modestly. "You didn't have to come back to tell me it was better though."

Stan Leroy hesitates. "I know. I just…"

I frown, my fingers getting ready for another Stan Leroy revelation. The tissue box is in the back of the room.

"I actually wanted to thank you, Dr. McKenna," he says, looking straight into my eyes. "You inspired me. Because of you, I lost twenty pounds, I got in shape, and… I feel a lot better about myself."

"Wow," I say. I get that nice, warm feeling in my chest that I always get when I feel like I've genuinely helped someone in the course of my job. Sometimes I love being a doctor. "That's great. Really. You look great."

Mr. Leroy takes a deep breath. "And I was just wondering…"

Uh oh.

"Do you think I might be able to take you to dinner sometime?" he asks. His brown eyes are hopeful, like a little puppy dog.

Dating patients is a big no-no. It's the kind of thing that can lose you your license. I already made an exception for Clark Douglas, and all that got me was a miserable evening that I wished desperately could be over for the entire hour that it lasted. So there's only one answer to Stan Leroy's question.

"I'm sorry," I say. "I'm not allowed to date patients. I could get in a lot of trouble."

"Oh." Mr. Leroy's face falls. But unlike Clark, I know he's not going to pressure me further. He's not that kind of guy. "I understand."

I wish Mr. Leroy the best of luck and send him on his way. I don't put in a bill for his visit. I figure I very well can't charge the insurance for a failed date request, no matter how much it will irritate Roger.

It isn't until I'm pulling a second chart out of a patient's door that I feel a twinge of regret. I wonder if I made a mistake turning down his request. I'm still smarting from my date with Clark last week—I was so excited for my first date in over a year with this incredibly attractive man, and all we did was stare at each other across the candlelit table in an Italian bistro, saying practically nothing. It was bona fide disaster.

But it wouldn't necessarily be that way with Stan Leroy. I could see in his eyes that he's a genuinely nice man. He wouldn't spend the night pissed off because my bad luck cat scratched him. Kitty wouldn't scratch him in the first place, most likely. And having seen him for a skin infection months ago doesn't really make him my patient, per se. I mean, it's a grey area.

Maybe it's not too late to change my mind.

Before I can second guess myself, I drop the chart I'd been holding back in the rack and rush out into the waiting room. I push past the heavy door that leads into our waiting area, a small, brightly lit room with about a dozen wooden chairs, littered with every magazine known to man. But before I have a chance to scan the room for Mr. Leroy, another unfamiliar man quickly steps in front of me.

"Dr. McKenna!" the man booms.

I've never seen this man in my life. I've seen more patients in my day than you can imagine, but I know I'd remember this one. He's at least a head taller than me, even in my heels, with a shiny bald palate and the burly frame of a football player. I instinctively take a step back.

"Yes…" I say. I glance over at our front receptionist Margo, who is shaking her head.

"Mr. Barry," Margo says. She's really good at dealing with troublemakers, probably because she has three sons at home. "I told you that Dr. McKenna has a very busy schedule this morning…"

Barry. Oh great. I know exactly who this is.

"Dr. McKenna," Mr. Barry growls under his breath. "I want to talk to you about my wife Gina."

Regina Barry visited my clinic over a year ago. She was suffering from severe psoriasis, a skin condition that caused her to have shiny scales over large portions of her skin. Most people don't know it, but psoriasis causes more depression than most other medical conditions, including cancer. Having scales on your skin, especially for a young woman like Regina Barry, results in a tremendous loss of self-esteem.

On one visit, Mrs. Barry sobbed to me how horrible her husband was to her, how he was an asshole who tried to control her, but she didn't have the self-esteem to leave him. My box of tissues was working overtime that day.

"Your wife is much better," I say defensively. Mrs. Barry responded well to a combination of medication and light therapy. At her last visit, she was actually doing great.

"She sure is," he growls again. "She's so much better that she told me she doesn't want me anymore. She thinks she's too good for me now."

Well, good for her.

"I'm sorry to hear that," I say stiffly.

"I'll bet," Mr. Barry snaps. "Whatever witch medicines you gave her messed with her brain."

Despite everything, I almost laugh at how ridiculous he's being. "That's impossible."

"I know it's all your fault, Dr. McKenna," Mr. Barry says, sticking his face in mine. "And believe me, I'm going to make you pay."

I'm going to make you pay.

The words make my mouth go dry. Believe it or not, I've never been threatened before by a patient. I've had patients who were psychopaths, jailbirds, or just plain jerks. But this is my first threat. And when he says it, standing over my with his biceps as thick as tree trunks, a thrill of fear runs down my spine.

"Excuse me," a voice speaks up, "but you can't talk to Dr. McKenna that way."

The trance is broken. I look over to identify my savior, and see none other than Clark Douglas, standing behind Mr. Barry. Looking, by the way, *achingly* handsome in a crisp white dress shirt and tie. I've never been so grateful to see a person in my life.

Mr. Barry snaps his bald head around. "Mind your own business, asshole."

Clark swiftly steps between Mr. Barry and me. Despite the fact that he isn't as tall or burly as Mr. Barry, he's easily as physically fit. "Dr. McKenna healed your wife," he says. "So you have absolutely no grounds for a lawsuit against her. Making these public accusations against her is outright slander, for which *she* could sue *you*."

Mr. Barry's eyes widen, and then Clark lowers his voice a notch, "Of course, if what you're threatening is not a lawsuit and rather some other sort of *payment*, then we'd have to get the police involved in the matter." He raises his eyebrows. "Should we call the police?"

I have to hand it to Clark. Mr. Barry looks pretty freaked out.

"No," he mumbles. "Don't call the police."

Mr. Barry allows Margo to quietly escort him out of the waiting room without leveling any further threats at me. And now I'm alone with Clark (and the handful of patients who got to witness the show).

"Are you okay?" Clark asks me. An adorable crease forms between his eyebrows.

"Fine," I lie.

Clark takes me by the arm, and somehow he locates the one examining room that doesn't already have a patient stuffed into it. He instructs me to sit down, and so we sit together until I stop shaking. Clark doesn't say anything, just sits there, holding my hand. We're as silent as we were on our date, but it's a different kind of silence. The nice kind.

"What are you doing here?" I finally ask him.

Clark smiles crookedly. "I came to apologize, actually. I was a jerk last week and I wanted to say sorry."

"Oh," I mumble. "Um, well, that's okay."

I reach for his hand and I notice that he winces. That's when I look down and see that the scratch marks from Kitty have turned an angry red color that's spread all over the back of his hand.

"Clark!" I gasp. "Have you been to a doctor about this?"

He shrugs. "Nah. It's just a scratch."

"It's not just a scratch!" I say. "It's clearly infected. You need antibiotics." Clark shrugs again and I shake my head. "If I write you a prescription, will you take it?"

Clark thinks for a minute. "If you write me a prescription, does that mean you're my doctor again?" He gazes at me with those blue, blue eyes. "Because I'd really like another chance at a date with you."

I hesitate for only a second. "I'd like that too."

CHAPTER 11
Two and a Half Months After

Every day, I go to a group where we play games to help us remember things. Sometimes, for example, we play Jeopardy. Except that instead of questions about famous novels or figures in history, the questions are about where we live or when our birthday is.

Unfortunately, it's still very challenging.

There are four of us in the group. It's me, a girl who is about twenty, and then two older people, a man and a woman. We get pushed into a small room in our wheelchairs, and then sit in the circle around a small wooden square table.

The two other women in the group don't talk much. Amy, who runs the group, usually has to ask them questions several times before they answer. The younger woman often falls asleep during the group. The man, on the other hand, talks way too much. Amy has to tell him to be quiet a lot.

I secretly think of myself as the only normal person in the group. But I'm concerned that Amy doesn't see things that way. She's always telling me I need to talk more.

Today we are playing a game that I really hate. It involves a beach ball on which Amy had written about a dozen questions. We toss the beach ball around between us, and when it's our turn, we have to answer one of the questions on the ball.

I don't like this game for many reasons. First of all, I'm not very good at catching the ball. I can't seem to use my left hand very well, so I have to catch it one-handed. It is not easy to catch a beach ball with one hand. The other reason I don't like the game is that I can't read very well right now. I'm not sure exactly why, but when I look at a page of words and read them out loud, they don't make sense to me. Amy says it's because I'm not reading all the words. When she asked me if I know why I'm not reading all the words, I quickly tell her it's because I'm not looking to the left. I'm totally on top of my issues with the left side. If only I could fix them.

When it's my turn to catch the beach ball, Amy helps me. Otherwise, it would almost definitely end up on the floor. She helps me steady the ball in my right hand, and points to one of the questions she's written.

"Read the question, Charly," she says.

I look at the question she's pointing to. I read, "What does the president ate?"

What? What the hell is that supposed to mean?

"How are we supposed to know what the president eats?" the old man speaks up. "Probably lobster. Or steak."

Amy smiles patiently. "Charly, you didn't read the entire question."

I suppose that's possible. I look back down at the ball. I see the words "What", "president", and "ates". Amy reaches into her pocket and pulls out the red pen. She's done this before, so I know before she does it that she's going to put the pen just to the left of the question. That way, I can look for the pen to know where to start reading.

"What is the name of the President of the United States?" I read carefully.

Before I can answer, the old man quickly pipes in with, "His name is Dave."

I frown at him. I don't think the president's name is Dave. I can't remember his name though. I think it might be Alabama.

"Well," the old man says, "that's not the *real* president's name. That's just the guy who is pretending to be the president because the president had a stroke and is sick. So Dave steps in and everybody thinks he's the president. Except his wife, who is that woman who sort of looks like a man. She knows the truth because Dave looked at her leg and her husband *never* looked at her leg anymore."

"Um," Amy says, "I think that was all from a movie called *Dave*."

"Of course it was a movie," the old man snorts. "Dave was just pretending to be the president, but then the president had a stroke and he had to step in and be the real president. And his wife was played by that actress, the one who looks like a man. You know who I mean. Anyway, he looked at her leg. When they were in the car.

And that was how she knew that he was Dave and not really her husband. And…"

Oh God, the old man is still talking. How does he talk so much?

I try to listen, but I get distracted by a face peering into the small window on the door to the room. It's a man who looks incredibly familiar to me. He's very handsome. Like, just so incredibly handsome. He looks like a movie star or something. He has perfect hair, the color of chestnuts, and a powerful jaw. My heart leaps when he raps on the window.

Amy holds up a finger so that the old man will stop talking, but it doesn't work. Surprise, surprise. He's still babbling about *Dave* when she goes to open the door.

"I'm sorry," she says to the man. "We're in the middle of doing the orientation group."

The man smiles and dimples pop up on his cheeks. Jesus, he's handsome. My heart flutters in my chest.

"I'm here to see Charlotte," he says.

Me?

"I understand," Amy says, "but we're right in the middle of group. Do you think you could wait fifteen minutes?"

"I cancelled an important meeting to see my wife," the man says. "Are you really going to make me sit out here and wait?"

My wife.

He called me his wife.

Oh, so that's why he looks familiar.

I look up at the handsome man again. Could he really be my husband? He's certainly really attractive, but he seems much too old for me. He is probably at least forty. Except I keep forgetting that I'm not twenty years old. How old did Dr. Greenberg tell me I was? Fifty-seven, I think. So that means this man is much too young for me.

"I'd really prefer if you'd wait outside," Amy says. "We'll only be another fifteen minutes. I prefer not to distract the members of the group."

"I wouldn't distract anyone," the man insists. Then, without being invited, he moves towards an empty chair in the corner of the room. "I'll just sit right here."

Amy doesn't look happy, but she doesn't say anything else to the man. But after that, it's very hard for me to concentrate on the group. The man is mostly looking at his phone, but I can't stop staring at him. As a result, I can't answer most of the rest of the questions on the ball, and at one point, the ball hits me right in the nose. If it wasn't made of plastic and filled with air, it could've seriously injured me.

When the group ends, usually Amy takes us back to our rooms one by one. But since the man (who is apparently my husband) is here, she says to him, "Would you mind taking Charly back to her room?"

The man blinks his eyes a few times. He has really nice eyes. They are blue like the hand soap. "Oh. I didn't realize she could walk."

"She can't," Amy says with a frown. "You'll have to wheel her. She's in Room 201, right by the nurses' station."

The man nods and steps behind me, seizing the handles of my wheelchair. He tries to push me around the table, then through the door to the room, but he misjudges the width of the doorway, and the footplate of the wheelchair bashes into the doorframe. "Sorry," he says.

Okay, that really hurt. But I guess since he's my husband, I'll forgive him for being clumsy.

He pushes me down the hallway for a while in silence. When we get to the nurses' station, he stops and comes around the side of my chair to face me. He smiles at me, which makes his dimples widen. Why am I married to such a handsome man? And why is this the first time I'm seeing him here?

"You know who I am, don't you, Charlotte?" he asks.

I nod. "You're my husband."

I'm rewarded with an even wider smile. "Right. And what's my name?"

His name? Doesn't he realize that I was in that group because I barely know my own name?

Except then, all of a sudden, it comes to me. "Clark."

He nods, still smiling, but somehow he doesn't seem quite as happy anymore. Amy sometimes shows me drawings or photographs of faces with different emotions and tells me to identify them. If I had to identify this man's emotions, I would say that he's nervous.

"Listen, Charlotte," he says. He rubs his palms together. "I'm sorry I haven't visited more. I've just been really busy. With work and all."

"It's okay," I say.

Except I'm not sure if it *is* okay. If he's my husband, shouldn't he be here all the time? I always see husbands and wives visiting other patients.

I just stare at him. I'm not really sure what to say. I know he's supposed to be my husband, but he's really handsome. It's throwing me off. Actually, the whole thing is making me super nervous.

"Anyway," he says. "You look great, Charlotte. Honestly."

I smile at the compliment. Except when I smile, his eyes widen.

"What's wrong?" I ask him.

"Your face..." he says.

My face? What's wrong with my face?

He continues, "It's just... well, just a little bit lopsided. It's not a big deal. Hardly even noticeable."

My face is lopsided? What does that mean? I'll have to try to remember to ask Dr. Greenberg in case it's something important. Maybe it's something we can fix.

My husband, Clark, glances down at his watch. "God," he says, "I didn't realize how late it was. I actually have to get going."

Get going? Didn't he just get here? I thought he canceled a whole meeting to come here. Maybe I'm confused though. Maybe he's been here a long time and I didn't realize. That happened to me before. Although usually it's the opposite. I feel like I've been in therapy for hours and they tell me that I've only been there for like two minutes.

For a moment, Clark leans in like he's going to kiss me, but then he hesitates. Instead, he reaches out and pats me on the head. Except I'm wearing my helmet, so it just make this loud rapping noise that reverberates in my ears even after Clark has waved goodbye and walked down the hall and gotten into the elevator.

He didn't even bother to take me all the way to my room.

"He's gone already?"

I look to my right side and see the old man from my group has been placed beside me in his wheelchair. He's frowning so that his thick, bushy white eyebrows are bunched together.

"He didn't realize how late it was getting," I explain.

"But he just got here!"

I don't know what to say to that one.

"I don't like him," the old man says. "He reminds me of that guy who was president before Dave took over. That guy was a really bad president. He did a lot of things that hurt poor children and he wasn't good to his wife. His wife was played by that woman who looks like a man. You know who I mean?"

"Sigourney Weaver," I say, and a nurse at the station who had apparently been listening to our conversation looks like she's about to fall over in surprise. Sometimes I

surprise myself. Maybe my brain isn't completely broken.
Although it's definitely pretty damaged.

CHAPTER 12
Two and a Half Months After

I have the dream again.

It's clearer this time, less foggy. I am walking down a long hallway then come across a door. The door to my apartment. I fit my key into the lock, and open the door. And someone is waiting for me.

Then: a gunshot.

I'm lying on the floor, bleeding, dying. I feel myself choking on blood. I cry out for help. *Please help me.*

Then I hear the footsteps coming from the void that's on my left. Everything on the right is so clear: my bookcase, the television… but the left is a blank space.

And even though it's a dream, I feel the hot breath on my neck, and the whispered words. Only this time I can hear the words clearly:

"You deserve this."

I wake up in my bed, my hospital bed, and I'm shaking. I'm drenched with sweat. It takes me a few moments to reassure myself that I'm safe now. I'm not lying on the floor of my apartment, dying. I'm alive and safe in a hospital.

And then I see that a strange man is standing in my room.

Unfamiliar visitors are not completely unusual around here. Actually, it's entirely possible that I have met him before, maybe many times before, and I just don't remember him. I know, at least, that he's not my husband. I assume he works here, based on his blue scrubs and ID badge hanging off his chest pocket. But there's something ominous about him.

I squint at the ID badge and read off his name: "Chris."

Then underneath his name, I read off his title: "rapist."

Oh my God.

This man is a rapist. A rapist is in my room.

I look up at Chris's face, at the stubble of a beard on his chin, and his dark, foreboding eyes. To say that I am terrified would be an understatement.

I suck in a breath, hoping that the rapist will lose interest in me. Maybe Amy will come here and he will like her better. Any man in his right mind would prefer Amy to me. She's very pretty, after all, and she doesn't have to wear a helmet on her head. The rapist would certainly want her over me.

Not that I want Amy to be raped either. I don't. But Amy could make a run for it and probably escape. I can't.

"Hello, Charly," Chris, the rapist, says to me. "You feel like getting dressed?"

That's when I realize, to my horror, that the rapist has actually *been sent to see me*. They have sent him here to rape me.

I guess this is part of my therapy. It's been a long time since I've had sex. Months. So I guess maybe they feel like part of getting better is getting back in the swing of things. Sexually.

The rapist approaches my bed and I feel my heart starting to race in my chest. I don't care if this is part of my therapy—I don't want to be raped. First someone tries to murder me and now this? But I don't think I can fight this man off. So what can I do? I can't just lie here and let him rape me, can I?

There's only one thing I can do:

Scream.

Chris looks incredibly startled. I guess other patients are more accepting of their therapies. He takes a few steps back, and looks around nervously. I think I have deterred the rapist for now. Hopefully, somebody will come rescue me soon.

A minute later, a nurse that I know named Nicole comes running into the room. Nicole looks as panicked as I feel. I didn't even realize I was still screaming, until Nicole puts her hand on my shoulder, and says, "Charly, what's wrong? Why are you screaming?"

I snap my mouth shut, and take a deep breath to calm myself. I am shaking.

"He was going to rape me," I tell Nicole. It's all I can do to keep from bursting into tears.

Hopefully the rapist won't want to rape Nicole. I don't think I can protect her.

Nicole whips her head around and stares at Chris accusingly. His evil black eyes widen and he holds up his hands.

"I didn't do anything," he says. "I'm supposed to be doing her occupational therapy, and I asked her if she wanted to get dressed. Then she just started screaming her head off for no reason."

Occupational therapy. Yeah, right.

"Is that so?" Nicole asks, folding her arms across her chest. She looks back at me, and says in a gentle voice, "What did he do, sweetie? Why did you think he was going to rape you? Did he touch you in a way you didn't like?"

"I didn't touch her at all!" Chris interrupts. "I didn't even lay one finger on her!"

Nicole shoots Chris a dirty look, and she takes my right hand in hers. She gives me a comforting squeeze. "Tell me what he did, Charly. Tell me why you thought he wanted to rape you."

"It says on his chest that he's a rapist," I explain.

Nicole just looks confused for a minute. Finally she squints at Chris's badge. "Charly," she says, "the badge says 'occupational therapist.'"

"No it doesn't," I cry. "It says rapist!"

Nicole furrows her brow then, all of a sudden, she starts to giggle. "Oh my gosh, the right side of 'occupational therapist' is 'rapist'! She can't see stuff on the left. That's why she thought you were rapist!"

Nicole and Chris both start to laugh, but I don't really see what's so funny. They explain it to me about how I didn't see the left side of the word, so I misunderstood what it meant. But honestly, I don't see why it's funny that I thought that he was going to rape me. I was really scared.

Anyway, I still don't like him. I definitely don't want him to get me dressed anymore.

―――――

I have to go to the bathroom.

The urge came on suddenly, the way it always seems to these days. I was sitting in my room, in my wheelchair, watching television. I like watching game shows. It's sort of hard to follow sometimes, but I like how happy everyone gets when they win a prize. They should give prizes during therapy. That would make it more fun.

Before the nurse brought me to my room, she asked me if I had to use the bathroom. At the time, I said no because I didn't. But now I do. I do so badly that I know if I don't get there fast, it will be too late.

It's too late a lot.

Since I've been here, the nurses keep putting me in briefs. If you didn't know, "briefs" are another word for diapers for adults. I can stop wearing them as soon as I can make it to the bathroom on time. But the problem is that I often don't have any idea that I have to go until I really, really need to go. Like now.

And the bigger problem is that I can't find my call button for the nurse.

I look on my lap and it isn't there. That's where they usually put it. I look on the table to my right, and it isn't there either. I know where it must be. It's probably on my left. But it may as well be in another country for all the good it does me.

I really have to go to the bathroom. So bad.

The bathroom in my room is only about five feet away from me. I think I could probably make it over there on my own. It's only five feet. I'm taller than five feet, so I would only have to go the length of my body.

I put my right arm on the push rim of the wheelchair. I'd like to go straight, but the chair just turns in the circle. If I could use my other arm, I think I could probably go straight. But much like the call button, my arm may as well be in another country for all the good it does me.

Okay, this isn't working.

My only other option is to walk.

There's a belt across my lap, strapping me into the wheelchair, but it's actually very easy to undo with my right hand. In spite of the fact that I can't figure out where my left hand is, my right hand still works very well. I've got the belt open in about two seconds.

Of course, then that stupid alarm starts going off. I try to ignore it.

I grab the armrest of my chair with my right hand and push myself into a standing position. It probably would have been smart for me to take my feet out of the footrest before I did that. It probably would've been even smarter for me to wait for the nurse to come help me to the bathroom.

In any case, in about five seconds, I find myself face-to-face with the floor of my room.

I have caused a great deal of excitement. Almost instantly, practically every nurse on the floor comes running into my room. They surround me on the floor, asking me if I'm okay, and trying to figure out the best way to pick me up again.

"Why did you do that?" I hear someone asks me.

"I had to use the bathroom," I try to explain.

"Oh God," a nurse says, "she's all wet."

I guess it's too late to make it to the bathroom.

The whole thing ends up being a huge mess. Literally. They drape a bunch of towels over the seat of my wheelchair, and help me get back into it. Then I have to get back in bed and get cleaned up. The entire process takes at least twenty minutes.

After I'm clean and dry again, Dr. Greenberg comes into the room to see me. His arms are folded like I am definitely in trouble, and even the monkeys on his tie look angry. I drop my eyes. I feel bad about what I did. And the worst part is that I didn't even get to the bathroom in time. I'm sure Dr. Greenberg will find out about that too.

"Charly," he says to me. "Are you okay? Does anything hurt?"

"Only my pride," I say.

Dr. Greenberg raises his eyebrows and laughs like I just said something really hilarious. He turned to the nurse sitting with me. "Doesn't she have an alarm on her wheelchair cushion and on her belt?"

The nurse nods. "Yes, but she was too fast. By the time we got here, she was already on the floor."

"Too fast, huh?" Dr. Greenberg strokes his chin. "I think we're going to have to park you in the hallway from now on, Charly."

I don't want to be in the hallway. I'd rather be in my room. But I guess I don't have a choice in the matter. And anyway, this way if I need to go to the bathroom, it will be easier to tell someone about it. So maybe that's a good thing.

CHAPTER 13
Two and a Half Months After

Well, I am now a Hallway Parker.

That's what everybody says about me. Like, constantly. When I got up in the morning, my nurse told the aide working with her that I was a Hallway Parker. When my therapist Valerie got done working with me today, she told the next therapist that I was a Hallway Parker. They should just write it on my helmet.

Basically, what it means is that when I'm in my wheelchair, I have to be in the hallway. That's so everybody can watch me and make sure I don't get up and fall on my face again.

Right now, it's lunchtime, and because my mother isn't here to watch me, I get to sit out in the hallway with my food with the other handful of Hallway Parkers. Technically, it's not really the hallway though—it's actually the intersection of two endlessly long hallways, both coated in sterile white paint that's so bright, it hurts my eyes.

The "hallway" is more interesting than my room, at least. I'm just next to the nurses' station, so I get to watch the nurses going about their work, and sometimes gossiping about patients because they think we can't hear them even though we're only about five feet away. I get to watch visitors coming and going with their big families and toddling children. And when it's quiet, they roll out a television for us and use the finicky VCR to put on a movie. The movies are all really old movies that I haven't seen in many years, like *National Lampoon's Christmas Vacation* or *Grease*.

Recently, Amy started letting me have food that wasn't completely mush. It's very exciting. I can have sandwiches, for example, but they can only have cheese or tuna salad in them—nothing really hard or difficult to chew or swallow like chicken or beef. If I do want meat, it has to be mushy, unfortunately. Maybe I'll become a vegetarian.

The really, *really* exciting thing though is that I get to have water. I really missed being able to drink water. I felt like my mouth was always dry and yucky before.

I feel like I could just drink water all day. I could drink the ocean. And not just a small ocean, like the Arctic Ocean. I could drink the Pacific.

A lot of the people in the hallway right now are old. Most of them have thinning hair, and what little hair they have is white or gray. They are all wrinkly, and have bleary, watery eyes. Plus they are all really deaf, so when they try to talk to me, they usually don't hear what I say back. It's sort of depressing.

Maybe I should tell them to readjust my position so that all the old people are on my left, so I don't have to see them.

Directly to my right is one guy who seems a little younger. He is maybe in his thirties. His brown hair is shaved short like mine, which I guess has something to do with the staples punched into the left side of his skull. But unlike me, he still has his skull. Otherwise, he'd be wearing a helmet like I am.

The guy is eating some cut-up pieces of meat, and I can't help but watch. He's really not doing very well at feeding himself. He's actually horrible at it. He's able to spear the meat with his fork, but after that, his hand seems to go all over the place, when it's obvious that he'd like it to go to his mouth. He does eventually get the food in there, but it takes a while. I feel bad for him because it looks really frustrating.

As he's chewing, the guy realizes that I'm watching him. He turns to me, blinking his brown eyes. He isn't super handsome in the same way that my husband is, but he's cute and I like the way he looks. He looks like he'd be a nice person, like he'd have a friendly smile.

"What are you looking at, Helmet Girl?" the guy snaps at me.

Okay, maybe he's not so nice.

I look away, back down at my own sandwich. I know that I'm not supposed to be staring at someone else. But I don't want to look at the depressing old people, and there really isn't all that much else to look at in the hallway, so almost right away, my eyes get drawn back to the guy with shaky hands. Now he's trying to get open what looks like a container of cream cheese. It takes him a minute, but then he's got the cover off. I watch as he digs his fingers into the soft, white cheese.

I thought for sure he was going to eat the cream cheese, especially considering it's obvious he hasn't eaten much yet for lunch. But instead, he starts smearing it on his cheeks like warpaint. He's actually much better at doing this than he is at feeding himself.

He's emptied almost the entire container of cream cheese onto his face before a nurse whose ID badge reads Betty notices what he's been up to.

"Jamie!" Betty exclaims. "What did you do to yourself?"

His name must be Jamie. He blinks innocently. There's cream cheese in his eyelashes. "What do you mean?"

"There's cream cheese all over your face," Betty says accusingly.

Jamie glances in my direction. "Helmet Girl did it."

Before I can have a chance to protest my innocence, Betty studies me and shakes her head. "Nice try, Jamie," she says. She holds out her open palm to him. "Give me the cream cheese container."

Jamie grins at her. I was right—he does have a nice smile. "I don't have it."

Betty's voice becomes more stern: "Where is it then?"

"It's in my butt," he reports very seriously.

I start to laugh. Hard enough that I almost start choking on the water I worked so hard to be allowed to have.

"That's not funny," Betty says.

"Helmet Girl thinks it's funny," Jamie says. He winks at me.

Betty folds her arms across her chest and taps her foot angrily. After a few seconds, Jamie pulls out the package of cream cheese from the seat of his wheelchair, and throws it in her general direction. It misses her by about two feet and lands on the floor.

Betty sighs and scoops up the package of cream cheese from the floor. "Come on," she says to him. "Let's get you cleaned up."

I watch as Betty wheels him away. Lunch in the hallway really isn't so bad.

CHAPTER 14
Two and a Half Months After

Today is my first day of Walking Group.

I'm very excited to be in Walking Group. So far, I haven't gotten to do much walking. Mostly, I've been stuck in my wheelchair. We've done a little bit of standing, and taking a few very careful steps in my room. But that's about it.

I'm assuming we're going to do a lot of walking in Walking Group. After all, it's called "*Walking* Group."

Walking Group is held in a small gymnasium, which has large windows on either side that pour light into the room. There are four other people in Walking Group, and we gather together at ten in the morning, forming a semi-circle with our wheelchairs. The first thing I saw when an aide pushed me into the room was a set of parallel bars, like the kind I used to use when I took ballet class when I was a kid.

"Are we going to do ballet here?" I asked in surprise.

It's not that I didn't want to do ballet, but I just didn't really see the point. If I can't even walk yet, what good would it do for me to be able to plié?

A small woman in green scrubs with straight brown hair pulled into a ponytail smiled down at me. "We're not going to do ballet," she said. "Those bars are to help balance during walking."

That made a lot more sense, I guess.

The woman with straight brown hair turns out to be named Natalie, and she is joined by a young black man named Steve, who is also wearing green scrubs. They start together on the far right, helping us to walk one by one.

I recognize only two other people in the group. One is an older woman, part of the deaf old person crew that populates the hallway. The other is that guy Jamie, the one who smeared cream cheese all over his face. I wasn't sure if he would recognize me, but then after a minute of my sitting next to him, he says, "Hey, it's Helmet Girl."

So one thing I soon realized about Walking Group is that nobody in Walking Group walks very well. It's sort of ironic. The first person, an elderly man, needs to use a walker, and even then, Natalie is mostly holding him up. The man keeps leaning more and more forward, until his top half and his bottom half have nearly formed a right angle. When that happens, Natalie yells for Steve to bring her his wheelchair, and they get him to sit back down again. His turn is over.

Jamie goes next. Natalie wheels him over to the parallel bars, and says to Steve, "I'm going to need your help with this one. He's a lot of work."

Unlike me, Jamie seems able to move his arms and legs pretty well. But that doesn't help much when he tries to walk. He's able to stand without a problem, but then when he tries to take a step, he's all over the place. He lurches forward drunkenly then nearly falls to the side. He looks like he's intoxicated, although he clearly isn't. Natalie and Steve are both straining to keep him upright, even as he grabs onto the parallel bars with his right hand. He takes a few steps then they carefully lower him back into his wheelchair.

"Wow, that was terrible," I comment.

Too late, I realize how mean of a thing to say that was. Sometimes I honestly don't know what I'm about to say until the words are already out of my mouth.

Jamie whips his head around to glare at me. His ears are bright red. "Let's see you do better."

Natalie wheels me over to the parallel bars for my turn. I feel a twinge of excitement in my stomach.

"Do you need my help?" Steve asks Natalie.

Natalie looks at me thoughtfully. "She's small," she says. "I think we'll probably be okay."

Natalie guides my right hand to the parallel bars. I close my fist around the cold metal. She instructs me to stand up, so I try, but I immediately start pitching forward. Natalie catches me then helps me onto my feet.

"Steve!" Natalie gasps. "You have to help me!"

Steve rushes over, and between the two of them, they keep me upright. I don't know exactly what I'm doing wrong. Natalie keeps telling me that I have to try to stand up straight, that I am leaning too much to the left, but I'm trying to stand up straight the best I can. When they tell me I'm completely straight, that's when I feel like I'm going to fall over to the side.

It takes several minutes and all we manage to do is just stand up. I don't even get to take a step. By the time Natalie and Steve lower me back down into my seat, I can see a line of sweat along Natalie's forehead. It's definitely a disappointing start to Walking Group.

"Oh my God," Natalie says, shaking her head. "That was really hard. I don't know if she's ready to be in this group."

Oh no, no, no! I don't want to leave Walking Group! I don't want to be stuck in my stupid wheelchair all the time! Please let me stay!

I want to beg Natalie to give me another chance, but I don't. I just sit there silently, biting my lip as Natalie and Steve talk about me, deciding if I should be allowed to stay. Finally, they agree to let me have a few days to see if I improve.

When Natalie wheels me back to my spot in the semicircle, Jamie's brown eyes meet mine. I expect him to make a comment on how badly I did. I would deserve it. For a lot of reasons.

But he doesn't say a word.

CHAPTER 15
Three Months After

My favorite of all my therapies is speech therapy. It's the only one I really look forward to.

My speech therapy sessions with Amy are usually held in my room. We sit by the window, me in my wheelchair, Amy in a regular chair, with a rolling table between us. Every day, we start our session with the same set of questions.

"Where are we, Charly?" Amy asks me.

"We're in a rehab hospital," I reply.

Amy smiles. "Very good. And what's the date?"

"March sixth," I say.

Except the only reason I know is that it's written on the whiteboard hanging from the wall in my room. And pretty much everywhere I go, somebody has written down the date. And people are constantly asking me what the date is. So it would be almost impossible not to know at this point.

I pointed out to Amy once that I just look up at the wall to tell her the date, and she said it was okay, that I wasn't cheating. She said just knowing where to look for the date was pretty good.

"Great!" Amy exclaims. She makes a note on her clipboard. "And why are you here in the hospital?"

This is the part I always have trouble with. I'm not entirely sure why.

"I got hurt," I say.

"What part of your body did you hurt?"

"My head."

"And how did you hurt it?"

I lower my eyes because I know I'm about to give the wrong answer. "I fell."

"No, Charly," she says. "You got shot. In the head."

I guess the reason I have trouble with this part is that I don't believe it. How could I have been shot? I'm just a normal person. Normal people don't get shot. Only police officers or criminals or people in the movies get shot.

"Who shot me?" I ask her.

Amy gets very busy all of a sudden making notes on her clipboard. "I'm not really sure."

As I watch her scribble on the clipboard, I suddenly remember a conversation I had with my mother yesterday.

"Was it a burglar?" I ask.

Amy puts down her clipboard. Her blue eyes are wide. "Why do you say that? Do you remember something?"

I shake my head. "No, that's just what my mom told me."

Amy sighs and shakes her head sadly.

The next thing Amy does is whip out a piece of paper from her clipboard. She places the paper on the table between us so that I can see it's a drawing. I know we've done this task before.

"Can you tell me what you see, Charly?" Amy says.

I look down at the black-and-white sketch in front of me. "It's a mom washing the dishes."

"Right. Anything else?"

I study the drawing. "The mom is distracted and the sink is overflowing."

"Anything else?"

I shake my head no.

I already know what Amy is going to do next because the same thing happens every single time. She whips out a bright red ruler and places it on the left side of the drawing. I turn my head to the left, looking for it. Finally, I spot the red. And now that I have it as a guide, I can see the rest of the drawing.

"There are two kids trying to steal the cookie from the cookie jar," I say. "And the little boy is on a stool that is going to fall over."

"Good," Amy says. She leans back in her chair and gets this thoughtful expression on her face. "Charly, why did you say that the woman was a mom?"

"I guess because there are two kids in the picture," I say with a shrug.

"Yes," Amy says, "but you couldn't see the two children until I put the red ruler on the paper."

"I don't know then," I say. "Maybe she just looks like a mother."

"Or maybe," Amy says, "your brain was able to see the two children, but you just couldn't put the whole thing together. Maybe you're absorbing everything that's on the left, but you just can't process it."

Maybe. I guess it's possible. But the woman in the drawing really does look like a mom. She has an apron and everything.

———

There are two parts to every dinner I eat:

First, the aide sets me up in the hallway, so everyone can keep an eye on me, then she puts my tray down in front of me. I eat everything on my tray and let them know that I finished.

Then comes the second part of the meal. When a nurse or nurse's aide turns my tray around, and all of a sudden, it's filled with food again.

Right now, I'm on part two of dinner. That guy from my Walking Group, Jamie, is sitting on my right. He's only out here in the hallway sometimes, but now I wonder if maybe he's here every time I'm here, but sometimes he's on my left so I don't know he's there.

He's got a plateful of chicken, cut into pieces, as well as peas on the side of his plate in a big green pile. He's not much steadier than he was last time I saw him feed himself. Anyway, I'm not sure who thought it was a good idea to give him peas to eat, but it really isn't. He takes a spoonful of peas and carefully brings it in the direction of his mouth. He actually gets almost all the way there, before his hand jerks in the wrong direction and the peas spill everywhere. Like, all over his plate, his tray, his pants and the floor.

And on top of that, he pokes himself in the eye with the spoon.

That's when I burst out laughing.

Jamie rubs his eye and glares at me. "You think that's funny, Helmet Girl?"

"Yes," I say. Obviously I think it's funny. I'm laughing.

Jamie puts down his spoon. He reaches over towards his tray with his hand and scoops up a handful of peas. I watch him carefully, wondering if he's going to start smearing them on his face. But instead, he hurls the handful of peas in my direction.

His aim is actually very good this time.

The peas wind up going everywhere, just like they did to him. A few hit me in the face but most hit me in the chest. My shirt has a pretty wide neck, just in case I need to get it on over the helmet, so several peas go down my shirt and pool in my bra.

"Mr. Knox!" There's a nurse rushing over to us who apparently saw the whole thing. Maggie, I'm pretty sure her name is. "Did you throw peas at Charlotte?"

"No," Jamie lies.

I don't say anything, but then Maggie looks down at his plate and at all of the peas on my shirt. I don't have any peas in my lunch. She can figure out the truth.

"Tell Charlotte that you're sorry," Maggie instructs him.

"I didn't do anything wrong," Jamie insists.

At that moment, an elderly man suddenly appears out of nowhere. Like he just materialized out of thin air. That means he probably came from the left. Also, he's wearing a checkered shirt and khaki slacks, which means that he's not a patient because we mostly all wear sweatpants and t-shirts or sometimes jeans. Sometimes it can be hard to tell the visitors from the patients, especially when they're old.

"What's going on here?" the elderly man asks.

Maggie shakes her head. "Your son just threw peas at this woman over here."

"James!" the old man says in a stern voice. "Why did you do that?"

Jamie is quiet for a minute. Maybe deciding if he has any chance of getting away with it. Even *I* know that he doesn't though.

Finally, he says, "She started it."

Maggie shakes her head again. "Trust me," she says to the old man. "This patient did not start anything with him. She hardly ever even talks."

"She did!" Jamie insists.

Then he picks up another handful of peas from his plate and throws those at me too. God, they gave him *way* too many peas.

"James!" his father yells. "You stop that right now!"

Jamie picks up what remains of the peas on his plate. At this point, it's painfully obvious to everyone what he's going to do. Maggie grabs his arm and attempts to wrestle the peas away from him. She at least manages to get his fist open, and the peas scatter all over the floor.

Better on the floor than on me.

"God, I'm so sorry," the old man says to Maggie. "You have to understand, he's not like this… usually. I mean, *before*."

"It's understandable," Maggie says as she bends down on the floor to scoop up stray peas. The old man bends down to help her, although it looks like it's hard for him to get on the floor. "He has a head injury. This behavior is part of the recovery."

"I know, but…" The old man bites his lip. "Jamie's the last person you'd expect to act this way. Honestly. He's just the nicest guy you'd ever meet. And he's always been so responsible. When he was growing up, he never gave me the slightest bit of trouble."

Maggie glances at Jamie, like she doesn't quite believe it. "Is that so?"

The old man nods. "I'm not sure if you know this, but he's been raising his son all by himself for the last six years. The kid's mother… she just took off." His eyes cloud up for a second, then he shakes his head. "Anyway, you have to believe me that if Jamie had any idea how he was acting, he'd be completely mortified."

"Don't worry about it," Maggie says as she scoops the remainder of the peas into her hand. She gets back on her feet. "However, we *would* like Jamie to apologize."

"Of course," the old man says. He looks down at his son. "Jamie, tell this woman that you're sorry for throwing food at her."

Jamie's eyes widen. "She started it," he insists. "She should apologize to me first."

"Say you're sorry, Jamie," his father says in a stern voice.

Jamie screws up his face for a second, like he's going to throw a fit. But then I guess he thinks better of it. He sighs and faces me. "I'm sorry, Helmet Girl."

"And I apologize for him too," the old man says to Maggie.

Maggie smiles. "Really, it's okay. He's probably just bothering her because he thinks she's pretty and he likes her."

"I don't!" Jamie yells.

And to emphasize his point, he picks his roll up off his tray and throws it at me. It bounces off my helmet.

CHAPTER 16
Three Months After

I always see family members coming to visit other patients. I only get one visitor: my mother.

I asked her once where my father was, and why he never comes to visit. About a minute after I said it, I suddenly remembered a phone call from my mother many years ago, telling me that Daddy died from a heart attack. If he were alive, I'm sure he would visit me. If I had a sister or a brother, they might come. But my mom told me that I don't have a sister or brother.

I do have a husband, of course. Clark. He came that one time but never again. I'm sort of hoping he'll come again, but part of me sort of hopes he doesn't. I'm not sure why but he makes me nervous.

My mother can be sort of annoying when she visits, but I like that she usually brings me some soda from the kitchen. They have these tiny cans of soda, but none of them are name brands. Like instead of Coca-Cola, they just have a generic cola. And instead of Sprite, they have a lemon-lime soda.

I like it that my mom fusses over me. Like when I am sitting in my wheelchair in my room, I always get cold, so

I can ask her and she'll put a nice big quilt from my closet on top of me. The nurses will do that too, but sometimes they tell me that it's too hot in the room and I shouldn't have the quilt because I'll get overheated. For some reason, I always feel cold. Except when I feel really hot.

While I am sitting in my room with my mother, a thought suddenly occurs to me. "Do I have any children?" I ask her.

She stares at me in surprise. I guess it was a weird question to ask.

"Why do you ask me that?" she says, her brows scrunched together. "Do you think you do?"

"Probably not," I say. "If I had children, I think somebody would have mentioned them or they would've come to visit me."

In fact, the more I think about it, the more I think that I almost definitely don't have children. If I had children, I would definitely know about them, right? There's no way I could have a son or daughter and just forget that they existed. Plus, I'm sure they would come to visit me.

But part of me is worried that maybe I *could* forget that I had a child. After all, I forgot that my father died. If I have a child and I forgot him or her, I'd feel really bad about it.

"You don't," my mother says.

Thank God.

"Oh, good," I say.

But then another thought occurs to me. I'm thirty-seven years old. I'm pretty old. Shouldn't I have kids by now?

"How come?" I ask.

She stares at me. "How come you don't have children?"

I nod.

She doesn't answer me right away. I think it was a good question. I know sometimes I ask really stupid questions, which I could tell because of the way people smile or laugh when I ask them. Maybe this is a stupid question. But if I am a grown woman and married, it seems like I should've had children by now.

"You wanted to focus on your career," Mom finally says.

So before I got hurt, I was a doctor. Just like Dr. Greenberg, except I was apparently a doctor specializing in skin. That doesn't make a lot of sense to me though. How could you specialize in skin? Skin doesn't get sick. I said that to Amy and she told me that I probably helped people when they had rashes, like the kind that I got on my scalp from all the scratching I did on there. I guess that's an important job.

Well, either way, I don't think it's something I'm going to be able to do anymore.

"It's probably better I don't have children," I say thoughtfully. "Because I wouldn't be able to take care of them right now."

"That's true," my mother says.

It's frustrating that I can't always remember what I was like before I got hurt. When we were in the hallway the other day, they put on this movie about a guy who gets shot in the head during a robbery. Before he got shot, he was this really big jerk, and then after he gets shot, he becomes really nice. So I guess the moral is that it's good to get shot in the head if you are a bad person.

Except I don't really think I was a bad person.

Maybe I was though. After all, hardly anyone aside from my mother comes to visit me. And she sort of has to visit me because she's my mother. I asked my mother about that and she said it was because they all visited me right after I got hurt, and now it's been a long time. Also, a lot of them are really busy with work like I used to be.

I keep trying to remember things that happened before. The memories are still there, but are covered by a hazy cloak. It's like waking up from a dream and trying to remember what happened during the dream. I remember things like having dinner in a restaurant with Clark, or putting these long dangling earrings in my ears, or trying to hail a taxi in the rain. But if I try to grab any piece of it, it's not quite there.

CHAPTER 17
One and a Half Years Before

Believe it or not, I'm still dating Clark.

It's been four months. And between you and me, it's been a really good four months. I'm still not convinced that this man will be the father of my children, but it's not totally out of the question. Stranger things have happened—a man walked on the moon, after all.

Even Kitty has grudgingly accepted him. Sort of. The first month or so, they kept their distance from one another, but now she seems to be treating him like one of the family—constantly following him around and begging for treats as part of her quest to be The Fattest Cat in the Entire Universe. Although Clark doesn't see it that way.

"Your cat doesn't trust me," he said to me. "She's always spying on me."

I laughed. "Spying on you?"

"Yeah," Clark insisted. He was smiling, but I think he was at least partially serious. "She doesn't trust me. She's making sure I'm not up to no good."

"Oh, come on!" I said. "She adores you. That's why she likes to sleep next to your head."

"Right, because she's trying to kill me!" he said. "Charlotte, she sleeps *on my face.*"

"That's a sign of affection."

"Right, well," Clark muttered. "You're going to feel awfully foolish when you wake up to find me smothered by your cat's fat ass."

So, yes. Clark and I have had sleepovers. I'm a woman in my mid-thirties—it's hard to maintain celibacy in a relationship, even if that's what I wanted. And I don't want that. I mean, if you've been in a desert for a year, and you finally come across a stream of water, do you say, "No, I'm going to wait six months before I have any?" No way. You'd take a drink!

I can't help but feel self-conscious during sex. I always flick off the lights before Clark comes out of the bathroom. I wish I were twenty pounds thinner. I wish my breasts were bouncier. I wish my stomach were flatter. For starters.

They say that dating a beautiful woman is expensive for a man. Well, I'm here to tell you that dating a handsome man is expensive for a woman, especially a woman like me, who is not used to putting in much effort with my appearance. It sickens me how much I've dropped recently on clothes and shoes. I don't want to tell you what I spent at the hairdresser last weekend, but I now own every single hair product known to man and my hair is as golden and shiny as the sun. If I can't be skinny, at least I'll have pretty hair.

Also, I have been waxed as hairless as a newborn baby. Well, not completely. I drank a glass of wine to work up the courage for my bikini wax. Dating a handsome man is not only expensive, it's painful too. My Jimmy Choo heels are another perfect testament to that.

I'm not sure if I'm doing it for Clark or for everyone else. I need to become the kind of woman that a man like Clark would date. I'm sick of getting funny looks whenever I go out with him. I know what everyone is thinking: *what does he see in her?* I'd like to pretend I don't care, but I obviously do.

Sometimes I worry that the Charly who just wanted to be myself, screw everyone else, is getting lost.

As I lie in bed next to Clark, sweaty from the activities of the last hour, I try not to think about all that. I allow Clark to draw me closer to him, and I snuggle up against his broad shoulder. Clark's body is always so warm and comforting against mine.

"This is nice," he says.

"Yes," I murmur. And it is. It really is.

I feel his stubble brush against my forehead, and then I hear him whisper the words in my ear, "I love you, Charlotte."

I freeze up. It's the first time he's said that to me. I know I'm supposed to tell him I love him back or something like that, but all I can think to blurt out is, "Why?"

I probably shouldn't have said that. But truly, I'm baffled.

Clark pulls away and stares at me in amazement. "*Why*? How could you ask me that?"

I feel my cheeks turning pink. Yes, I definitely should not have said that. But now it's out there, and I have to explain it. "I just… I mean, the thing is, I'm not very…"

He frowns at me, shaking his head.

"I'm not pretty," I finish.

Wow. I can't believe I just said that. But you know what? I'm not sorry. It needed to be said. It was the elephant in the room the whole time we've been dating.

"Charlotte," Clark says. He squeezes me against him. "You are amazing in so many ways. Not only are you really pretty, but you're smart and funny and sweet."

Well, I'm smart, I'll give him that. My board scores attest to that fact. I don't think I'm particularly funny though. I don't know if I'm sweet either, but I'm not *mean* or anything. I let that Stan Leroy guy down easy.

"I wish you could see what I see," Clark says softly.

He strokes the side of my face. Clark thinks that I am pretty and smart and funny and sweet. I don't think I'm at least three of those things, but whatever. I don't even care anymore. I'm sure this thing will come crashing down on me at some point, but I'm going to stop questioning it. I'm just going to enjoy the ride.

"I love you, Charlotte," he says again.

"I love you too," I whisper.

CHAPTER 18
Sixteen Months Before

I know I'm supposed to be having a romantic dinner to celebrate Clark's and my six-month anniversary of dating, but all I can think about is how itchy I am.

My last patient of the day came in with an itchy rash on his arms and chest that I had initially been led to believe was eczema. By the time I identified it as scabies, it was too late. I was wearing gloves and all, but if I had known there was a chance he might have scabies, I would've gowned up. Hell, I would've put the guy in a bubble.

Now my incredibly handsome boyfriend is sitting across from me, telling me some story about an encounter he had trying to hail a cab, and all I can think about is the tiny bugs burrowing into my skin.

I think I might go crazy.

"You seem a little distracted, Charlotte," Clark says, raising an eyebrow at me.

I can't tell Clark about the scabies. You don't tell the most handsome, sexy man you've ever met that you might have scabies. You just don't.

"Just thinking about work."

Clark nods and smiles. "Anything you want to talk about?"

In addition to being ridiculously handsome (have I mentioned that before?), Clark is incredibly interested in my work. Most people's eyes start to glaze over after a few too many stories about skin problems, but Clark has impressive listening skills. When I tell him about some troublemaker patient or a fight I had with an insurance company, he always makes me feel better about it.

So yes, believe it or not, Clark is a really great boyfriend. I wouldn't have thought it. I had assumed that a man who looked like him would almost definitely break my heart, quickly and painfully. But Clark hasn't shown any signs of it. He's sweet, relatively attentive, and he's understanding about the long hours that I work on top of the fact that I'm training for a marathon. (My knee is so much better.)

Sometimes I wish he weren't *quite* so handsome though. Obviously, I don't mind having an attractive boyfriend, but I just wish he were a little bit less ridiculously good-looking. Especially at times like these, when we're sitting together in a restaurant, and I feel like everyone in the room is wondering how a woman who looks like me ended up with a boyfriend who looks like Clark. Even though I've now lost fifteen pounds, I can't help but think that way.

Our waitress, a girl at least ten years younger than me with shapely legs that put my muscular thighs to shame, comes over to clear away our dinner plates. "Can I interest you in some dessert, Sugar?" she asks Clark.

The waitress has been flirting shamelessly with my boyfriend throughout the entire meal. I'm beginning to wonder if she has some sort of bet going with the waitstaff over whether she can go home with him.

"No, thank you," Clark says to her. To his credit, he hasn't been flirting back.

Our waitress looks disappointed as she walks away. Notice she didn't even bother to offer *me* a dessert. Good thing for her I'm not the one tipping her.

Clark takes a sip from his wine glass, gazing at me over the rim of the glass. I scratch my bare forearm self-consciously. I know the symptoms of scabies take at least two weeks to manifest, but I still feel really itchy.

"Charlotte," Clark says softly, "I just want to tell you how wonderful these last six months with you have been."

"Me too," I mumble.

Maybe I'll go get myself some permethrin cream at the pharmacy on the way home. It will make me feel better about the whole thing.

"I feel so close to you," he goes on. "I never thought I'd feel that way about another person."

"Me too."

Really, you're supposed to tell sexual contacts if you have scabies. Clark is most definitely a sexual contact. But I just can't make myself tell him. I don't want him to think of me as the woman who gave him scabies.

Clark stands up for a minute, and at first, I'm completely confused. Did he realize I was concealing my raging case of scabies from him and is going to walk out on me? But then, instead of walking out, Clark does the exact opposite of walking out.

He gets down on one knee. And pulls a blue velvet box from his pocket.

No. Way.

"Charlotte," he says. He opens the blue velvet box and a gigantic diamond catches the light of the chandelier above us. My friend Bridget knows all about diamonds—the number of carats, the cut of the diamond—but I don't know any of that nonsense. But I've got eyes and I can tell that this diamond is *huge*. I cover my mouth to keep it from hanging open. "Will you marry me?"

Okay, I don't feel itchy anymore.

Everyone in the entire restaurant is staring at us. Even that awful waitress is looking our way and her jaw is dropped open in disbelief.

"Yes," I say quickly. I glance around at the audience we've acquired. "Now get up. Please."

Clark gets to his feet, but he pulls me up with him. He kisses me passionately in front of the entire restaurant, and the room breaks into thunderous applause.

This might be the most romantic thing that's ever happened to me. Well, without the scabies.

———

I can tell Clark is in a good mood this morning because he's whistling. Clark always whistles when he's happy. I recognize most of the tunes he whistles as pieces from Mozart, which seems like an odd thing to whistle. I mean, who whistles classical music?

I recognize at least some of the music from my amazing music appreciation class in high school (thank you, Mr. Lieberman). This morning he's whistling a piece I think is called Requiem as he makes his way out of our bed and into the bathroom. I smile and hum along softly to myself.

I'm going to marry this guy. We're actually going to have a use for the second bedroom.

After Clark takes what sounds to be the longest piss in the history of the universe, he comes out of the bathroom full of energy and presumably ten pounds lighter.

"Let's go out to breakfast," he says, "and then we'll get your ring resized."

The ring he bought me is a bit big. He got my size by measuring one of the rings in my jewelry box, but considering my weight is currently at an all-time low, he overestimated the size. And he adorably wants to go with me to get it fixed.

"Sure," I say.

Clark flicks on the light, and I shield my face instinctively. I washed off all my make-up last night, and I don't want Clark to see the purple circles that formed under my eyes during residency and never went away. And that reminds me—I've got to get my hair retouched—my roots are very visible.

I'm as quick in the bathroom as I can possibly be, then Clark and I take off in the direction of Our Diner. Yes, we have a diner. Initially, we went to a different restaurant every time we went out, but we both love the silver dollar pancakes at the Greek diner two blocks away, so every time we go to breakfast, that's where we end up. Everything is still pretty new between us, so it's nice to have one comfortable habit forming. I can see us going to Our Diner thirty years from now, when we're old and gray-haired. (Well, Clark will be gray-haired. I'll still be honey blond thanks to the hairdresser.)

Clark holds the door open for me. "After you, m'lady."

I smile and push past him, nearly running smack into a man who looks incredibly familiar. His face lights up when he sees me. "Hi there!" he says.

"Hello…" I say, hoping to place him before this gets embarrassing. A patient maybe? A former classmate?

Luckily, he notices my hesitation. "It's Stan. Stan Leroy. You treated me in your clinic for…"

Groin Fungus Guy! Right. How could I forget? Especially after he asked me out and I was forced to reject him.

"Oh, right!" I say. "How are you doing, Mr. Leroy?"

"Can't complain," he replies. He glances over at Clark, and they eye each other curiously.

"This is my fiancé," I say, nodding in Clark's direction. God, it feels weird to say that. I'm sure it will be even weirder to say "husband."

"Oh, congratulations then," Mr. Leroy says, his face falling noticeably. "How did the two of you meet?"

I send Clark telepathic vibes to keep his mouth shut. It doesn't work. He grins with his perfect white teeth. "Actually, I was her patient."

Mr. Leroy's kind brown eyes widen. "Is that so?"

Clark nods. "Great story to tell the grandkids, right?" He leans in to peck me on the cheek. "I'll go get a seat, Charlotte. I'll see you inside."

I want to follow Clark into the restaurant, but I feel like I have to say something to Mr. Leroy. Something to prove to him that I'm not the worst person in the universe, which is sort of how I'm feeling right now.

"Look," I murmur, "the thing about dating patients…"

"No, I get it," Mr. Leroy says quickly. "I understand. You don't have to explain."

"Oh," I say, relieved. "Okay."

"When you said you couldn't date patients, you just meant that you're not allowed to date patients who aren't *attractive* enough to meet your high standards." He raises his eyebrows. "That's it, right?"

Oh God, this really couldn't be any more awkward.

"Mr. Leroy…" I begin.

He holds up his hand. "No, it's okay, really." He shrugs. "The truth is, I don't think I'd want to spend any time with someone like you anyway."

Mr. Leroy pushes past me and leaves the restaurant. I just stand there a minute, a lump rising in my throat. What an asshole. No wonder his wife left him. I'll bet it had nothing to do with groin fungus.

But I still feel like bursting into tears.

I take a deep breath and start to walk into the restaurant to join my fiancé. But before I do, I glance out the door to the diner, and I notice that Mr. Leroy is still standing in front of the restaurant.

Staring at me.

I look away and hurry off to my table.

CHAPTER 19
Fourteen Months Before

Clark and I are in a taxi cab headed downtown. As we navigate through the narrow streets of Chinatown at breakneck speed, Clark reaches out and takes my hand in his. He gives me a squeeze and I squeeze him back.

We skid to a stop at a red light, and I say a quiet prayer that we won't get involved in a fatal (or even non-fatal) collision prior to reaching our destination. As the cab idles at the light, a homeless man approaches us, and without asking, starts wiping down the windshield.

"No!" the cabbie screams at the man. "No! I don't want! Go away!"

The homeless man gives him a thumbs-up and keeps scrubbing. When the light changes back to green, the cabbie zooms off so quickly, the squeegee guy nearly falls on his ass. "Jesus," Clark mutters under his breath.

"I know!" the cabbie says. "Can you believe these guys? No respect." He glances back at us, taking in Clark's dark suit and my off-white knee-length dress. "You two look all nice. You goin' someplace special?"

"You could say that," Clark says, winking at me.

You could definitely say that. In less than an hour, Clark and I will be married.

Married!

I can't believe it either. Only eight months ago, it would have been unthinkable that I'd be in a cab zooming off to City Hall to my own wedding, but here we are. After Clark popped the question, there really wasn't any point in waiting. We're both closer to forty than we are to thirty.

Still, getting married to a guy who I've known less than a year doesn't seem like a Charlotte McKenna kind of move. I've never been the sort of person who does things spur of the moment—if anything, I'm over-cautious. But then again, I don't look like the Charlotte McKenna of a year ago either—I've definitely upped my game recently.

But I still can't hold a candle to Clark. God, he's gorgeous in his dark suit and tie. I thought the attraction would have faded by now, but it hasn't. Not even a little bit. If it were appropriate, I'd jump him right here on the leather seats of this old cab that smells faintly of fast food and cigarettes.

In record time, the cabbie slows to a stop in front of the nondescript white building a stone's throw away from the Brooklyn Bridge. When Clark asked me if I was okay with a small ceremony at City Hall, I couldn't say yes fast enough. Unlike a lot of other women I know, I've never really been into weddings. Let me put it this way: I never wanted my parents to buy me the Bridal Barbie doll. I would have asked for the Doctor Barbie, but those didn't exist when I was a kid. So I had to settle for slicing holes in my dolls' extremities with a scissors and "suturing" them up with needle and thread.

That's not weird, right?

Anyway, I'm thrilled about the small ceremony. Today it's going to be just Clark, me, and the judge. Well, and my mother.

My mother is our witness. I had hoped that Clark's parents would come too, but apparently, they live in Michigan and he doesn't get along with them. I only spoke to them on the phone once when they offered me a stiff congratulations. I couldn't get a straight answer as to why Clark and his parents don't get along. He's really good at changing the subject. He might be better at it than sex.

Clark and I get out of the taxi, and I watch him smooth out his suit, and straighten out his tie. He doesn't seem happy with the knot he's made, so he pulls it open and redoes it. After he's made the second knot, he frowns down at his chest.

"This doesn't look right," he complains.

"It looks fine," I say.

He shakes his head. "Charlotte, can you fix it for me?"

I snort. "You think I know how to tie a tie?"

He raises his eyebrows. "You can sew up someone's face but you can't tie a tie?"

"They're completely different skills."

Clark rolls his eyes then unties his knot so he can redo it one more time. I look up the steps of the building and see my mother waiting by the entrance. She's waving so enthusiastically, she might dislocate a shoulder. She literally could not possibly be happier that her only child is getting married.

"You okay?" I ask Clark as he continues to fiddle with his tie.

"Of course," he mumbles.

"Are you sure?"

Clark looks up at me with those blue, blue eyes. He sighs and his shoulders sag. For a second, I'm terrified he's going to say he can't go through with it. I mean, I would deal with it, but I can't imagine having to break it to my mother. It could very well kill her.

"It's just…" He shrugs a little sheepishly. "I've never been married before. It's kind of… a big deal."

"Are you wondering if you made the right choice?" I ask.

"No," he says, although he hesitates a beat before answering. "It's just…"

I frown at him. "Just what?"

He stares at me for a minute then shakes his head. "Nothing. I'm being dumb."

Hmm. That didn't sound like *nothing*.

Clark reaches out and envelopes my smaller hand in his. "Let's go get married, Charlotte McKenna."

Okay. Let's do it.

Chapter 20
Three Months After

Jamie and I have been separated during Walking Group. Because of the Pea Incident. I guess they don't want to risk him throwing things at me. Luckily, we got a new member in our group to sit next to me.

She's about forty with really pretty, long silky blonde hair because she didn't have to have surgery on her brain like Jamie and I did. I love her hair. I can't stop staring at it.

My hair is still really short since they shaved it. Before they shaved it, I used to have chin-length blond hair, although it seemed longer in more recent photos, like I was growing it out. I know because my mom hung up all these photos of me on the walls of my room. It's supposed to help bring back memories.

"I have to tell you," the woman says to me as we sit in our wheelchairs, waiting for our turn to walk. She has a gravelly voice like she's been talking for a long time and needs some water. "You have the prettiest eyes I've ever seen. What color are they? Purple?"

"Violet," I say. Actually, they just look dark blue to me, but everyone tells me they are violet. So I guess I'll go with that.

"My eyes are the color of mud," she says. I look at her eyes, which are brown. But I guess she's right because brown is the color of mud. "I'm Angela, by the way," she says.

I smile at her. Finally she says, "This is when you tell me your name."

"Charly," I say.

She smiles. Her teeth are a little bit yellow. I know that mine are white from all the photos hung up in my room. At least I have nice teeth. "As in Charlene?"

"No, Charlotte."

"Oh, like the web."

I don't know what she's talking about.

"*Charlotte's Web*," she says. "It's this book for children. About a spider and a pig who become friends. And at the end, the spider dies."

I still have no idea what she's talking about. I never heard of this children's book.

"I don't have any children," I explain.

"Neither do I," Angela says. "That's why I'm here. Because I was taking birth control pills and it made me get a blood clot in my leg which went up to my brain."

"Oh," I say.

Is a blood clot worse than getting shot in the brain? I don't think it is. I'm pretty sure getting shot is the worst thing that can happen to your brain.

Angela adjusts her left arm, which is lying limply on her lap. She doesn't seem to be able to move it, but at least she seems to be able to see things on her left side. I assume she can, because I'm on her left side. "What a mistake," she says. "Stupid birth control. I'd of had a dozen babies instead of this. This is the *worst*."

When it's my turn to walk, I do a little better than I did that first day. I still need both Natalie and Steve helping me, but at least I can take a few steps on the ballet bars. It's some sort of progress at least.

Angela has a bandage wrapped around her left foot that ties up to her calf. When it's her turn to walk, they tie her left arm up in a sling. Natalie helps her to stand up, and makes her left leg move for her, then supports her while she takes a step on her own with her right foot. She has to hang onto the parallel bars, but she makes it all the way down to the end and then back.

When Angela sits down again, she releases the Velcro on the sling with her right hand. Her left arm falls back into her lap and she carefully positions it so that her hand is resting on her thigh.

"What's that sling for?" I ask.

Angela gives me a funny look. "I guess it's for the same thing as yours."

"What do you mean?"

"You have the same thing on your arm!"

"No, I don't."

"Go look in a mirror, honey."

I don't know what she's talking about. I don't have a sling on my left arm.

Or maybe I do? Where is my left arm? It's so hard to find anything on the left. I need Amy to help me find my arm.

"Come on, Jamie," I hear Natalie saying. "It's your turn."

I look over at Jamie. He's sitting in a wheelchair, his arms folded across his chest, staring down at his lap. He's not smiling.

"I don't feel like it," he says, quietly but firmly.

"Don't you want to get better?" she says. She adds, "For your son?"

He lifts his eyes to look at Natalie. "I'm never going to get better," he mumbles. His fingers scrape absently at the staples on his skull. "This is stupid and pointless."

"Come on, Jamie," Angela pipes up in her gravelly voice. "None of us are any good at this. We're all just getting better. You want to get better so you could go home and see your kid again, right?"

Jamie looks around and sighs deeply. I know how he feels. There are times when I don't feel like doing something, but then everyone's around me and telling me I'm going to let everyone down if I don't do it. So I usually end up doing it.

"Okay, fine," he mumbles.

Natalie and Steve take him to the ballet bars. He doesn't do great. He's no better than he was when I first saw him walk a few days ago. Lurching and all over the place. When he makes it down the length of the parallel bars, Natalie needs to help him get back into his wheelchair without falling on his ass.

Jamie drops his head into his hands. "Damn," he says.

Natalie puts her hand on his shoulder but he won't look up. "Jamie, listen to me," she says. "You're going to get better. Dr. Greenberg says based on your brain scan, you've got a really good chance of your ataxia improving."

He still doesn't lift his face from his hands.

"Jamie, look at me," she says.

He slowly lowers his hands. His eyes are red rimmed and wet.

"But you've got to work at it," she says. "You can't give up. Okay, Jamie?"

He nods. "Okay," he whispers.

Again, I know how he feels. There are a lot of times when they tell me not to give up. And I keep going, even though inside sometimes I feel like I want to give up more than anything.

————

Jamie is very quiet today.

They put him next to me in the hallway because they forgot that we are supposed to be separated. I don't think it makes a difference right now though, because he doesn't seem in a pea-throwing sort of mood. I think I'm safe.

Jamie has always had staples in his head, but today they are gone. The incision is still there, caked with old blood, surrounded by shaved hairs. I guess somebody took out the staples. He's healing, at least on the outside.

Despite the fact that I am staring at him pretty blatantly, Jamie doesn't look up at me. He has a tray with a cup of water on it, and he just stares at that, his brown eyes glassy. I wonder why he finds the water so interesting. I stare at it myself for a little while, but I still don't get it.

Dr. Greenberg comes down the hallway, dressed in his white coat, his tie slightly crooked today. Dr. Greenberg always wears interesting ties. Today he has ladybugs on his tie. It seems so weird to me that a doctor would have cartoon bugs on his tie, but it doesn't seem like anyone is bothered by it. Actually, I like it.

I smile eagerly, hoping that Dr. Greenberg will talk to me. But instead he makes a beeline for Jamie.

"Hello, Mr. Knox," he says.

Jamie lifts his eyes briefly but doesn't say anything.

"How are you feeling?" Dr. Greenberg asks him.

Jamie shrugs.

"Jamie," Dr. Greenberg says. "Can you tell me where we are right now?"

My heart leaps. I know this one!

"We're in the hospital," I reply.

Dr. Greenberg smiles at me, although he actually looks sort of annoyed even though I'm pretty sure it's the right answer. "Very good, Charly, but I was asking *Jamie*. Could you let him answer?"

I nod.

"Where are we, Jamie?" he asks again.

"The hospital," Jamie mumbles.

"What kind of hospital?"

I know this one too!

"A rehab hospital," I speak up.

Jamie cocks his head in my direction. "What she said."

Dr. Greenberg lets out a sigh, but I don't know what he's so upset about because I got the right answer. *Again.*

"*Jamie*," he says. "Do you know why you're here?"

Jamie stares at the cup for a long time. Seriously, what is so interesting about that cup? Finally, he says, "Because I fell down the goddamn stairs, and now I can't do anything anymore."

A crease appears between Dr. Greenberg's graying eyebrows. He reaches out and puts his hand on Jamie's shoulder.

"Sometimes," he says, "as your brain starts to get better, one of the first things that happens is you start to recognize how far you have to go. And sometimes that can really get you down."

Jamie shrugs. "Maybe."

"I'm going to give you a medicine to help with that," Dr. Greenberg says. "Are you okay with that?"

Jamie shrugs again. "Sure, why not? Add it to the mix."

Dr. Greenberg removes a folded piece of paper from his white coat pocket, and makes a notation on it. I feel bad for Jamie, because it sounds like he's going to get another medicine. I don't like taking medicines, and I have to take so many of them. That's the one good part about still having the tube in my belly, because if I don't feel like taking them in my mouth, the nurse can just put them down the tube.

CHAPTER 21
Three and a Half Months After

Today my occupational therapist Valerie is working with me on something called grooming. I am sitting up in bed, and there's a tray table in front of me, with a small C-shaped tub of water. Valerie hands me a brush and I grab it with my right hand.

"Okay, Charly," she says. "I want you to brush."

I'm not wearing my helmet because I'm in bed, so I take the brush and I start running it through my hair, or what little is left of my hair. Valerie grabs my wrist and shakes her head.

"Charly," she says. "Is that what you do with it?"

I take the brush and start running it over my eyebrows, which doesn't seem to make Valerie any more pleased. Honestly, I have no idea what she wants me to do. I wish she'd be more specific.

Dr. Greenberg walks into the room, rubbing his hands together. I immediately look over at his tie. It has bats on it. I wonder if it's Halloween.

"How is my star patient doing?" Dr. Greenberg asks.

"Well," Valerie says, "she just tried brushing her hair and eyebrows with a toothbrush, so how do you think?"

"Maybe she thought it's a travel-sized hairbrush?" Dr. Greenberg says, and winks at me.

I know that Valerie doesn't seem to think I'm doing very well, and I like that Dr. Greenberg always seems to stick up for me. He always says that I'm his star patient. Although I'm beginning to think that I'm probably not.

"Are you getting anything out of her left arm?" Dr. Greenberg asks.

"Nothing." Valerie shrugs. "See for yourself."

Dr. Greenberg is right in front of me, but suddenly he disappears! Right into thin air. Maybe he went out the door at the other side of the room. I am certain he must be gone, but then I hear his voice say, "Charly, I'm over here, on your left. Look over here."

I turn my head to the left and I still don't see him. I turn a little more, then little more, then finally I can see the bats again on his tie.

"I see you!" I say.

Dr. Greenberg smiles down at me. "Now I want you to grab my hand with your hand."

I reach over with my right hand and grasp his fingers. His hand feels very warm. I've always liked warm hands. There's an expression that goes "cold hands, warm heart," but that doesn't make sense to me. Why would having cold hands mean that you have a warm heart? Warm hands, warm heart.

"No, Charly," he laughs. "Not with that hand. With your other hand."

Everyone is quiet, waiting for me to do what he wants me to do. But I don't know how to do it. If I could, I would, believe me. He might as well tell me to wag my tail.

"I've seen her move the arm," Valerie says, tucking a strand of her very short brown hair behind one ear. "But I don't think she can do it voluntarily."

Dr. Greenberg nods thoughtfully.

"Also," Valerie adds, "the tone in her left arm is getting horrible. I can barely straighten out her elbow or open her fingers anymore. It's getting harder and harder just to get her dressed."

"Does she try to help you?" Dr. Greenberg asks.

"Sometimes," Valerie says. "But honestly, it's easier if she doesn't. That arm is such a mess. She'd be better off if we just cut it off or something."

Cut my arm off? Oh my God. I didn't even realize that was a possibility.

I suck in a breath. "You're going to cut off my arm?"

I really don't think I want them to do that. Even though I can't find my left arm, I'm glad that it's still there. Of course, if they cut it off, would I even know?

"Of course we're not going to cut off your arm," Dr. Greenberg assures me, patting my right hand. "Valerie was just making a joke, but she shouldn't make jokes like that."

"Yeah," I agree.

"Sorry," Valerie mumbles. She folds her arms across her chest. "Anyway, dressing and bathing aren't getting any easier. She's still basically dependent for all her care. Who's supposed to take care of her when she gets home?"

"We've still got some time to think about that," Dr. Greenberg says. Although I start to wonder how much time I really have here. Where will I go after this? Sometimes it feels like I will be here forever, but I guess I won't. This isn't really a place people live. It's a hospital. Nobody lives in the hospital.

"In the meantime," he says, "maybe you can trial Charlotte with some electrical stimulation to her left arm. It might improve her awareness and help control the muscle tightness."

Valerie mutters something that sort of sounds like "worth a shot." Then Dr. Greenberg starts explaining to me about what electrical stimulation is, but it's hard to listen to him when he's all the way on my left side, and also my neck is starting to hurt from looking at him. So instead of listening, I just go to sleep.

———

Today they are planning on electrocuting my arm. I'm not excited about it, to say the least.

Apparently, it's a whole group of us who sit together and get electrocuted. It's supposed to help my arm to move. I can't even begin to imagine why electrocuting my arm would make it move. I really don't want to do this. I told Valerie that, but as usual, she didn't care.

There are four of us in the group, sitting around a table. There are boxes of equipment stacked in the middle. Angela, the woman from my Walking Group with the pretty blonde hair and smoky voice, is in the room with me. I feel relieved when I see her. Angela is always nice to me.

"Have you done this before?" I ask Angela.

"Sure," she says.

I bite my lip. "What's it like? I mean, what does it feel like?"

"Oh, you know, not that bad," Angela says. "It's sort of like when you're a kid and you stick your fork into the light socket and you get a jolt? It's like that. Makes your hair stand up just a bit."

Oh my God.

Angela laughs her throaty laugh. "I'm just teasing you, Charly. It's not bad at all, I promise."

Angela volunteers to go first, to show me how it isn't so bad. Valerie puts something on her arm that almost looks like the bionic arm that Iron Man has. I'm not into comic books or anything, but I remember Clark taking me to see that movie, *Iron Man*. I remember Iron Man used the device on his arm to shoot people and fly and stuff. I wonder if the device is going to give Angela special powers too. That would be pretty neat. I would like to be able to fly. It would be handy, considering I can't walk.

Valerie flips a switch to turn the device on. I watch, expecting laser beams to shoot out of Angela's arm. Instead, her fingers spread apart.

"Great," Valerie says. "Now make a fist, Angela."

Angela's brow furrows in concentration and I see her fingers slowly start to close.

"Fantastic!" Valerie exclaims.

"No, it's not," I say. "You didn't even shoot anybody with it."

Angela and Valerie both look up at me. Angela laughs, but Valerie just shakes her head.

It's my turn next. At least, it's supposed to be. Instead, Valerie places another arm on the table in front of me and has me watch as she puts the device in place over the forearm and hand. Maybe she wants me to watch another demonstration. I'm not sure whose arm it is, because whomever it belongs to is to my left, but it looks like a woman's arm. There isn't much hair on it, it's sort of swollen, and the fingers are curled up a bit.

"When is it going to be my turn?" I ask Valerie as she adjusts the device on the other person's arm.

"It's your turn now," Valerie says.

"You mean I'm next?"

Valerie sighs impatiently. "I'm putting it on your arm right now, Charly."

"This isn't my arm," I say, confused.

"Yes, it is," Valerie says.

I look over at Angela. She still has the device on her arm, and her fingers are spreading apart. But she's been listening in on the conversation, and she says, "It *is* your arm, Charly, sweetie."

I frown, and look down at the arm again. Maybe it *is* mine. I follow it up, from the hands, to the elbow, to see if it is attached to my body. It's really hard to see things on the left side. I keep trying to use Amy's tricks, *scan left, scan left.*

Oh well. I guess if they tell me it's my arm, it probably is.

Valerie flips on the control. Despite feeling skeptical about this being my arm, I definitely notice a weird sensation as soon as the control turns on. Sort of like a buzzing, like an insect is loose in my body. I watch the fingers on the arm spread apart.

"Okay, Charly," Valerie says, "now I want you to try to make a fist."

I try to make a fist. I really do. I try to send signals down from a brain to my fingers, but it's very hard to make a fist with a hand that you can't really feel, that you're not even entirely sure belongs to you.

My fingers don't budge.

CHAPTER 22
Three and a Half Months After

"Hey, Helmet Girl!"

The voice is coming from my right side. I ignore it, focusing instead on eating my dinner. I'm allowed to eat all solid foods now. Amy says that if I eat enough, they will remove the tube from my belly. I want that so badly. So I need to eat.

"Helmet Girl!"

I feel a ping against my helmet, and a pea drops down onto my dinner tray. I look up and I'm not surprised to see Jamie sitting to my right. He's got another pea in his hand and looks like he's about to hurl it at me. They really need to stop giving him peas.

Apparently, whatever new medication he's been getting has perked him up again. He even did better in Walking Group this morning. He actually managed to walk with a walker, not holding onto the ballet bars, with two people supporting him. That's progress for him. Actually, I'd be thrilled if I could do that.

I put down my fork to glare at him. "Don't call me Helmet Girl. I don't like it."

I expect him to say something obnoxious, but instead he frowns. "I'm sorry," he says. He hesitates. "Your name is Charly, right?"

"Right."

"My name is Jamie," he says.

I don't know why he thinks I don't know his name. I've seen him practically every day for the last two weeks or so. But strangely, there's something really different about Jamie today. He's calmer, less crazy—like his brain has healed itself overnight. Can that happen? I pick up my fork again and take a bite of mashed potatoes. "I know."

"Oh," he says, smiling sheepishly. "I wasn't sure if... well, anyway, I won't call you Helmet Girl again. Sorry about that."

"Thank you."

He looks down at his own food. He has cut-up pieces of meat and a lot of peas, none of which he's made much progress with eating. Seriously, what is up with all the peas they keep giving him?

"You better eat," I warn him. "Otherwise, you'll never get the tube out of your belly."

He makes a confused face and I almost laugh. He really is very cute. In a boy-next-door sort of way. "The *what*?"

"The tube in your belly," I say again. "You have to eat at least half your meals before they'll take it out."

Jamie pushes his tray away from his body. Like me, he's got an alarmed seat belt on his lap, to alert nurses if he attempts to get up. He doesn't touch the belt though.

Instead, he pulls up the hem of his worn T-shirt to reveal the thin layer of dark hair on his lean belly. He stares down at his abdomen. "I don't think I have a tube," he says.

He doesn't. I guess he wasn't hurt as badly as I was.

Jamie releases his T-shirt then gingerly touches the scar on his scalp. "I don't have a helmet either," he says.

"Lucky you." I probably sound bitter. Oh well.

"No way," he says. "The helmet is *cool*. It's better than walking around with your head half shaved and a big red scar."

"It's really uncomfortable though," I explain. "It's hot, and the strap hurts my chin. Sometimes it falls over my eyes so I can't see. And it makes my head feel really itchy and they won't let me scratch."

He squints at me. "Why do you need the helmet, anyway?"

"Because I got shot in the head," I tell him. "And my skull was all cracked and broken, so they took it off. So I have to wear the helmet to protect my brain, because I don't have a skull there anymore."

Jamie's brown eyes widen. "You don't have a skull *at all*?"

"Nope," I say.

Although I think actually that might be wrong. Maybe they only removed half. I think I might have *some* skull left. But the part that I can feel is definitely completely gone.

Jamie stares at me for another minute before he says, "Can I see?"

I glance around the hallway. There are a couple of other patients around, but I don't see any nurses at the moment. They are probably all in patients' rooms, giving medications or changing bedpans. Of course, it's entirely possible they are right next to me and simply standing to my left.

But I have a feeling nobody is here. It's always very quiet around dinnertime.

"Okay," I agree.

I reach for the strap holding the helmet in place. It's pretty hard to work with just my right hand. Actually, I think they've rigged it up to make it harder to remove one-handed because of all the times I've tried to get it off. Jamie watches me intently as I fiddle with it. Finally, I hear a satisfying snap, and my chin strap comes loose.

I slide the helmet off my head. Oh my God. What. A. Relief. It is like a thousand degrees under that helmet. And my head feels so light without it. I feel like I could just float away. That is, if I wasn't seatbelted into a wheelchair.

I don't know why I have to wear that stupid helmet in my wheelchair anyway. It's not like I'm going to fall.

"Wow," Jamie breathes.

"What does it look like?" I ask him.

He raises his eyebrows. "You haven't seen it?"

I shake my head. "I'm always wearing the helmet when I'm looking at myself in the mirror."

Jamie considers my question, stroking his chin thoughtfully. I noticed that he has at least a day's worth of beard growth on his chin. I wonder who shaves him. Considering how shaky his hands are, I doubt he could do it himself.

"It looks like somebody took a bite out of your skull," he says.

"A bite?" I crinkle up my nose. "A big bite or a small bite?"

Jamie grins. "Huge."

I reach for the soft spot in my skull, trying to get a sense how big it is. Now that he mentioned it, the soft area seems massive. God, I probably look like a total freak.

Maybe that's why they make me wear the helmet in the hall. So I don't scare people.

Except Jamie doesn't look scared. He looks fascinated. "So it's just your brain under there?" he asks.

I nod.

He blinks a few times. "Can I feel it?"

I shrug. "Sure, why not?"

Jamie reaches out with his left hand. Usually his arms are all over the place like a drunk person, but I can tell he's being really, really careful right now. Very gently, his fingers graze the soft spot on my head. I barely feel it, before I hear a nurse screaming out, "Charlotte! What are you doing?!"

Apparently, I shouldn't have done that. The nurse makes a huge deal out of putting my helmet back on, and getting the charge nurse to come over to yell at me. Jamie is actually really nice about the whole thing, and keeps telling the nurse that it was his idea and he told me to do it, so they should yell at him. And they do.

He's not so bad though. At least he isn't going to call me "Helmet Girl" anymore.

CHAPTER 23
Four Months After

Walking Group is depressing.

Everyone in the group is doing better than me. Everyone. For some reason, I'm stuck. I can't get past walking on the ballet bars. Everyone else seems like they can use a walker by now.

What's wrong with me? Why can't I do this?

I sit there feeling sorry for myself while Jamie takes his turn walking. If I'm being honest, Jamie isn't doing so hot either. Steve is holding onto his pants and his shoulder, and even though Steve is a really big guy, I can tell it's a lot of work for him. Jamie is maybe a couple of inches shorter and thinner, but it seems like a lot of work to catch him when he loses his balance to the right or the left. Which he does practically every fifteen seconds.

When he finishes his walk, Jamie collapses into his wheelchair next to me. He sighs and rubs his temples. "Well, that sucked," he comments.

"Oh, stop it." Angela rolls her eyes. "You've made a lot of progress just since I've been here."

"Not enough," Jamie mutters.

"Enough for what?" Angela presses him.

"Listen," Jamie says, "you know I've got a kid I've got to take care of. I can't do it if I'm like this."

"Who's taking care of him now?" Angela asks. "His mother?"

Jamie grimaces. "No, my parents are looking after him. His mother... she's not really in the picture anymore. So I'm practically all he's got."

Angela looks like she's mustering up some more inspiring words, but then Natalie comes to help her walk, breaking up the conversation. Jamie just sits there, staring into space as he absently scratches at the scar on his scalp. I bet it itches the same way mine does.

"What's your son's name?" I ask him.

Jamie looks at me in surprise. The distressed look fades from his eyes, and a smile touches his lips. "Sam."

"How old is he?" I ask.

"He's six," Jamie says. He adds, "He's great. I... I really miss him."

I frown. "Kids can't visit here?"

"They can, but..." Jamie sucks in a breath. "He can't see me like this. I mean, I don't want him to."

I know if Angela were with us, she would say he was being silly. But I completely understand. I watch as he scratches again at the scar on his scalp. The hair is already starting to grow back around it. At least he'll *look* normal again soon. Unlike me.

"How did you get hurt?" I ask.

"I fell down a flight of stairs," he says. "There was a broken step." He cocks his head thoughtfully. "That's what they tell me, anyway. I don't remember anything about it. I don't remember anything from the entire day that it happened. And for like two weeks after. It's sort of weird to have such a big gap in my memory."

"Was it at your house?"

"It was at a bar," Jamie says.

"Were you drunk?"

"What? No!" He seems offended then thinks better of it. "Actually, I guess that's a reasonable question, since it was at a bar. But I wasn't."

"You should sue the bar then," I suggest.

Jamie laughs. "Unfortunately, I can't. It was my bar."

I stare at him. "You own a bar?"

I've never known anyone who owned a bar before. It's kind of cool, actually. I don't say that though.

"Me and my brother Brad, yeah," he says with a shrug.

Angela plops back in her wheelchair just in time to hear the tail end of our conversation. She releases her left arm from the sling she's wearing and leans towards Jamie. "You own a bar?" she asks him. She sounds impressed. "I had no idea you were that cool. I bet it was a total chick magnet."

"Yeah," Jamie says flatly. "It was a total chick magnet. That's why I haven't had a date in over a year."

"*You* haven't had a date in a year?" Angela snorts. "I don't believe it. First, you're adorable. Second, bartenders always have girls throwing themselves at them."

"Yeah, well…" Jamie shrugs. "I'm not a cool bartender. I'm just a nerd with a degree in accounting and business. I take care of all of what my brother calls 'the boring stuff.' I only bartend when my son is in school, when the place is practically empty. The kind of women who drink at two in the afternoon are not the kind of women I want to date."

Angela grins. "So when we get out of here, will we get drinks on the house? For me and Charly?"

"Angie," Jamie says, "if I get out of here and get back to work, everyone in this whole goddamn hospital can have drinks on the house."

"I'd like a White Russian," I say. I'm joking, obviously. I'm pretty sure there's no way I can drink alcohol the way I am now.

"And I'd like a shot of bourbon," Angela says.

"Also," I say, "I'd like to meet your son."

Jamie looks surprised by my comment then he suddenly gets all quiet and distant. I feel bad, because I know he's taking those pills because he's sad, and I'm not supposed to make him more sad. But I really would like to meet his son. I bet he's really cute, like Jamie is. I wish I had children, although I guess it's better that I don't considering what happened to me. Then I would miss my children as much as Jamie misses his son.

"Charly," I hear Natalie saying. "It's your turn to walk. Do you want to try the hemi-walker today?"

The hemi-walker is what Angela uses when she walks. She can't use a regular walker because she can't move her left arm at all and you need two arms to control a walker. The hemi-walker is a half-sized version of a regular walker that you just grip with one hand. It seems impossible to use. Maybe Angela can do it, but I don't think I can.

Actually, scratch that. I know I can't.

"I don't think I can do it," I tell Natalie.

"Steve and I will help you," Natalie says in her chipper, cheerleader voice. I can almost see her turning cartwheels and waving her pom-poms in the air. "We won't let you fall."

I shake my head. "I can't."

"Come on, Charly," Angela says, shaking her fist at me. "You can do this. You got this, girl."

I look over at Jamie for support. I figure if anyone realizes I'm not capable of doing this, it's him. But he's just smiling at me.

"Hey," he says, "look at what a mess *I* am. If I can walk with a walker, anyone can."

I'm obviously being bullied into this.

Both Natalie and Steve join forces to help me. They help me to stand, and I immediately get the now familiar unstable feeling that I get every time I stand up. I don't know where the left side of my body is, which makes it very difficult to balance. Impossible, really. And it's noticeably harder to walk with the hemi-walker than it is to walk holding on to the ballet bars. The ballet bars provide a lot more support. The hemi-walker feels like it might slip right out from under me.

"I want to sit down," I say to Natalie. I haven't taken even one single step yet. "I think I'm going to fall."

"You're not going to fall," Natalie insists. "I'm holding you up, and Steve has your left leg. There's no way you could fall."

"I think I'm going to fall!" I repeat more insistently. My heart is pounding in my chest. Why can't they see that I'm not ready for this? Maybe I'll never be ready. I'm just not making progress like everyone else is. I should just give up right now. Resign myself to the fact that I'm not going to walk again.

"You can do it, Charly!" Jamie yells. I don't know why he's yelling, because he's only about one foot away from me. I can hear him just fine without him yelling.

I feel beads sweat breaking out along my forehead. I really don't want to do this.

"Yay, Charly!" Angela chimes in.

I don't know how they do it, but somehow Jamie and Angela manage to get everyone in the whole room to start chanting my name. *Char-ly! Char-ly!* Even that old guy who barely opens his eyes through the entire group gets in on it. I have to admit, it makes me feel really good to have everyone in the room cheering for me. I can't remember the last time anything like that has happened to me. That's not to say that it hasn't happened, but I just don't remember it. Then again, I don't remember a lot of things.

Gripping the hemi-walker as hard as I can, I take a step with my right foot. Steve moves my left foot for me, and then I take another step with my right. Before I know it, I've walked across the entire room, and that's when everyone bursts into applause.

"We knew you could do it, Charly!" Jamie calls.

I sure didn't.

CHAPTER 24
Four Months After

My mother and I are in my room and we're watching this show called *Jerry Springer*. It's interesting, because one of the people who is on the show is a woman who was shot, like I was. Except she was only shot in the leg, so she's obviously not as badly hurt as I am. She was shot by her sister because she was sleeping with her sister's son's father. I think so, at least. It's a little hard to follow.

Her sister is on the show also, and she's trying to apologize to the woman for having shot her. The woman is crying, and saying she's not sure she could trust her sister anymore. I think she's right not to trust her sister, because her sister shot her.

It makes me wonder if when we figure out who shot me, I'm going to have to go on television and forgive them.

"Did they figure out who shot me?" I ask my mother.

I have the dream about the night I was shot maybe once a week. Every time now it's the same—the gunshot, and the whispered voice in my left ear: *You deserve this*. It's scary, and it's also frustrating. If only I could see on the left, I could see who it was that shot me. But my left side is a blank, just like in real life.

She looks at me with a frown. "They think it was probably a burglar, but they haven't been able to find him."

Except why would a burglar tell me I deserved to be shot?

"Maybe it was someone I knew?" I say.

My mother's frown deepens. I'm lying in bed and she's sitting next to me, so she has to reach across me to grab my call button. She uses it to change the channel. "You shouldn't be watching this."

"But I want to know if she forgives her sister," I protest.

"Of course she will," my mother says. "This is television."

The next show is a sitcom. I think I recognize some of the actors on it, but I don't know what show it is, which makes it very hard to follow. I wish she would put *Jerry Springer* back on. I like that show.

After a few minutes of watching the sitcom, Dr. Greenberg walks into the room, and my mother quickly shuts off the television. She sits up very straight, adjusts her blouse, and brushes some gray hairs away from her face. Sometimes I think she has a little crush on Dr. Greenberg. It would be nice if they went out. I don't think my mother has dated much since my father died.

Dr. Greenberg waves at us, and comes close enough that I can see his tie. It has little dogs on it, interspersed with tiny bones. The tie makes me smile.

"How is everything going, Dr. McKenna?" Dr. Greenberg asks me.

Even though I know I am a doctor, almost nobody calls me that around here. It actually feels very weird when they call me that, even though I worked as a doctor for many years. Dr. Greenberg is the only one who sometimes calls me "Dr. McKenna." And only rarely.

"Okay," I say. Then I add, "I'd really like to know if that woman forgives her sister for shooting her."

Dr. Greenberg looks puzzled. My mother rolls her eyes and says, "We were watching *Jerry Springer.*"

Dr. Greenberg throws his head back and laughs, and I can see fillings on his teeth. He doesn't have perfect teeth like I do. Actually, I sort of like that about him.

"How have you been holding up, Mrs. McKenna?" Dr. Greenberg asks my mother.

"There are good days and bad days," she says. "Sometimes Charlotte seems almost back like her usual self, and is sharp as a tack. But other times, she hardly talks at all and doesn't even seem to know who I am."

Dr. Greenberg nods. "That's not abnormal. Her brain is still recovering. The neurons that are still alive are healing, and the healthy ones are making new connections to make up for what she lost. It's a very slow process, but she's really making great progress."

"Yes..." my mother says, although she sounds uncertain.

"However," Dr. Greenberg says, "that wasn't what I asked you. I was asking how *you* are holding up, Mrs. McKenna."

My mother smiles without showing her teeth. "You know, good days and bad days," she says. "I'm just trying to figure out what's going to happen after her time here is over."

A crease appears between Dr. Greenberg's eyebrows. "Yes, I know that's an issue. But it's probably best we don't discuss it in front of your daughter." His voice raises several notches. "Anyway, I've some great news for Charly. Apparently, you've been eating very well and I've been given the go-ahead to remove your feeding tube."

I'm going to get the tube out of my belly? I can't believe it! That's the best news I've ever heard in my entire life!

"Is that okay with you, Charly?" he asks.

I reach down with my right hand and pull up the hem of my gray T-shirt, revealing the tube I've had for as long as I can remember since I got hurt. It pokes out around four inches above my belly button, and the skin surrounding it is an angry red. Just lifting my shirt irritates it, and makes me wince with pain.

"Take it out," I tell him.

Dr. Greenberg laughs. "I guess that's a yes. We don't have to do it this minute though—"

"I want it out *now*," I say firmly.

"And *that's* the old Charly," my mother says.

Dr. Greenberg goes outside my room to put on a yellow gown, and a pair of blue gloves. I watch him open up packages of gauze on the table by my bed.

"How do you get it out?" I ask him.

"Pull really hard," he says.

I'm not sure if I like the sound of that.

It doesn't matter though. I want this tube out, even if he has to slice it out of me with a knife while I'm still awake. So I don't resist as he lays one hand on my bare abdomen, and grips the tube with his other hand. "One, two, three!"

Oh my God. Oh my God, this hurts so much. I am going to die before this stops hurting.

I hold my breath and squeeze my eyes shut, trying to hang in there. Finally, I hear a pop, and the pain diminishes, although I still feel it.

"Holy shit, that hurt!" I yell.

Dr. Greenberg holds up the tube. He points out the end that was inside of me, which looks like a little mushroom. The mushroom is much bigger than the hole that it came out of. It's sort of like I gave birth to it. Not that I would know, since I never gave birth.

"That's the last tube," Dr. Greenberg says. "Charlotte McKenna, you are officially tube-free."

They'll have to fight me if they want to put it back.

CHAPTER 25
Four Months After

The only visitor I get is my mother, while Jamie mostly gets visited by his father. Jamie's father is here a lot, maybe three or four times a week. He seems really nice, like Jamie is. Lately, they've been talking a lot about the bar that Jamie owns with his brother. I get the feeling that Jamie doesn't trust his brother to be able to manage on his own. He keeps saying things like, "Brad can't even balance the register."

Of course, I have a feeling that right now, Jamie couldn't do it either. Except he doesn't seem to realize that.

Jamie's father always shows up right when we're finishing dinner. Exactly six o'clock. Today is no exception. Jamie and I are sitting in the hallway, finishing the last of our food. Except not really. Jamie has dropped about half of his meal on his chest and lap. And I probably haven't eaten anything on the left side of my tray yet.

"Hey, Dad," Jamie says.

"Hi, Jamie," his father says. The first thing he does is lean over Jamie and start cleaning food off of his chest.

Not that it really matters. As he brushes off the food, Jamie's father smiles at me. "Hi, Charly."

I don't actually remember Jamie ever introducing his father to me, but he must have because somehow his dad knows my name and always says hello. It's nice that he always talks to me. This way, it feels sort of like I have a visitor too.

"Is Brad handling the tax returns?" Jamie asks. "You know, if he brings it to me, I could…"

"Relax," Jamie's father says. "We hired someone to take care of it."

Jamie's eyes widen. "How much are they charging? Because my medical bills—"

"Jamie, stop worrying about this," his father says in a stern voice. "Just get better, and we'll worry about it later." He pulls up a free chair that's in the hallway for visitors, and sits down next to Jamie. I heard him mention once that he has bad knees, so he doesn't like to stand too long. "Your mother is here, by the way. She's on her way up."

Jamie frowns. "Who's watching Sam?"

His father hesitates. "She brought Sam."

Jamie's eyes widen. "No," he says, shaking his head. "*No.*"

"Jamie…"

Jamie looks about as upset as I've ever seen him. His face is really red, almost purple.

"Dad," he says in a low voice. "I told you I don't want him to see me right now."

"You're being ridiculous, Jamie," his father says. "Sam asks about you every day, when he's going to get to see you. It's not right. You're so much better now, and—"

"I still can't *walk*," Jamie hisses at his father.

"Well, who knows when that's going to happen," his father says. "What if it *never* happens? I mean, how long do you expect to go without seeing him?"

Jamie just shakes his head. It's obvious it's much too late anyway, because there's an elderly woman walking down the hallway, hand-in-hand with a little boy. The second the boy catches sight of us, he drops the woman's hand, and starts running towards us. "Dad!" he screams so loudly that I jump.

The boy is about half the size of an adult, with brown hair and brown eyes like Jamie's, but he's got this adorably round face. Not that Jamie isn't cute and all, but his son is much cuter, although obviously in a different way. When he gets closer, I can see that he has freckles streaming down the sides of his nose. He throws his arms around Jamie, who hugs him back with equal enthusiasm. The whole scene makes my chest ache.

"I missed you, Daddy," he says. I think that's what he says, at least. His voice is all muffled because his face is buried in Jamie's shoulder.

"I missed you too, kiddo," Jamie says. "A whole lot."

Even though Jamie said he didn't want to see his son right now, he looks *really* happy to see him. Sam starts talking to Jamie about what's been going on with him, and he's talking so rapidly that it's a little bit hard for me to follow. I wonder if Jamie is going to introduce me to his son. I know he said that he would, but I can sort of understand why he wouldn't want his son to meet a weird woman wearing a big helmet. I would forgive him if he didn't introduce me.

"—And grandma made chicken last night for dinner, but I didn't like it, so we went to McDonald's and I wanted chicken nuggets, but she said I couldn't because I didn't want to eat chicken," Sam is saying. "But chicken and chicken nuggets are completely different. Chicken is white and doesn't taste good, and chicken nuggets are brown and crunchy."

"I completely agree," Jamie says. He glances over at me and doesn't even hesitate. "Hey, Sam. This here is my friend Charly. She really wanted to meet you."

Sam breaks off his monologue about chicken and looks at me with really wide eyes. I'm absolutely certain he's going to ask me about the helmet, but instead he says, "Your eyes are purple."

"Violet," I correct him.

"They look pretty," he says. I smile at him. For a moment, I think I'm off the hook, but then he says, "Why are you wearing a helmet?"

I look over at Jamie, wondering if he wants to explain it himself. But Jamie just looks embarrassed. So I guess it's up to me.

Obviously, I don't want to tell a little boy that I was shot in the head. That seems like it might traumatize him. So I say instead, "There's an ice hockey rink out back and I was going to play some ice hockey soon."

Sam's eyes get even wider. "There's ice hockey here?" He couldn't have looked any more excited if I told him the North Pole was out back, and Santa was busy making Christmas presents with his elves in the parking lot. "I want to play! Can we go play, Dad?"

Jamie looks at me and rolls his eyes. "No, maybe another time."

"I want to play *now*," Sam insists. He grabs Jamie by the hand. The wheels on Jamie's chair aren't locked, so he rolls a few inches before he can grab the wheels to steady himself. Sam looks annoyed. "Get *up*, Dad!"

Jamie's father puts his hand on Sam's shoulder. "Sam, what were we talking about on the way over? I told you that your dad is still sick and he can't play with you right now."

"I'll be better really soon though," Jamie says to his son. "And first thing when I get out of here, we'll go play ice hockey. I promise."

I feel like Jamie probably shouldn't make promises to his son that he definitely can't keep.

Sam pouts, his adorable little mouth curling into a frown. Finally, he says, "Can Mommy take me?"

There's an awkward silence as Jamie's brown eyes fly open. He stares up at his parents. "He hasn't seen Karen, has he?"

Who is Karen?

Jamie's parents exchange looks. His father says to his mother: "Why don't you take Sam to Jamie's room. We'll be there in a few minutes."

I can see Jamie's cheeks turning red again. He looks even more upset than he did when his father told him that Sam was coming. As soon as his son is out of earshot, he hisses at his father, "He saw Karen?"

"She heard about your accident," his father says. "She just wanted to see Sam. She'd like to help."

"She's an irresponsible junkie!" Jamie snaps.

His father glances at me and frowns. "James, keep your voice down."

I've noticed that whenever Jamie's father is upset with him, he calls him "James." The same way my mother always calls me "Charlotte" when she's upset at me.

"I just don't trust her," Jamie says, more quietly this time.

His father sighs. "You haven't seen her in a long time. She's really gotten her act back together. She's like a completely different person." He pauses. "She's hoping you'll be willing to work out… an arrangement. »

"What did she want?" Jamie asks. "Visitation rights?"

His father shakes his head. "She mentioned joint custody."

Jamie's mouth falls open. He stares down at his lap, his eyes glassy. "Never. She will never, ever…"

"Jamie," his father says in a gentle voice. "When you come home, you're still going to need a lot of help. If Karen can take Sam part of the time, I think that would make things a lot easier for all of us. Your mom and I aren't so young anymore, you know."

When Jamie speaks again, his voice is low but I can hear every word: "She'll have to kill me first."

CHAPTER 26
Four Months After

Today I'm doing physical therapy in the hallway with Natalie. I'm sitting in my wheelchair, and she's standing in front of me, her hands on her hips and her shiny brown hair pulled into a high ponytail that swings behind her head. Natalie is skinny but she's very strong. When she helps me walk during my Walking Group, I can see the wiry muscles bulging in her arms below her scrub top.

"Today," Natalie says, "we're going to work on wheelchair mobility. I'd like you to get better at pushing your own wheelchair. I think that would be better for you than a power wheelchair."

Natalie looks very young, but she seems so confident all the time. Like she's been doing this for a million years.

"Why do we need to do that if you're teaching me how to walk?" I ask.

A tiny crease appears between Natalie's eyebrows. "Walking is good exercise," Natalie says, "but you have to realize, Charly, you're not going to be walking well enough when you leave here. You're going to be primarily using your wheelchair to get around when you go home. Probably for a while. You know that, right?"

"Oh," I say. I *didn't* know that. I try not to let on how much this disappoints me. Despite how awful I've been doing my Walking Group, I still assumed I'd be walking at the point that I left here. "For how long?"

Natalie shakes her head. "I can't predict that."

At least the answer isn't "forever."

Natalie straightens up and gets real close to me. "Okay, Charly," she says. "Put your hands on the rims of the chair."

I do as she says.

"No," she says. "Put *both* hands on the rims."

"I am," I insist.

"You have your right hand on the rim," she observes. "But not your left. Put your left hand on the rim."

I hate my left arm. I hate it when people ask me to do things with it that I can't do. I hate it when it gets in the way. I almost agree with Valerie that I'd sort of like to cut it off. Then at least people would stop nagging me about trying to use it when I can't.

Because I know I'm not going to be able to do it the normal way, I pick up my left hand with my right, and attempt to place it on the left rim of the chair. This is not very easy for a number of reasons. First, I can't see the left rim—it's in that endless chasm that makes up the left side of the universe. It's also sort of hard to see my left arm. When I touch it with my right hand, I can't really feel it, not in a normal way, and it often feels very stiff and hard to move.

Right now, I get my hand on my left arm, and it will not budge. Not only that, it seems to be pulling away from me, which it doesn't usually do. I wonder if that's a good sign.

"Charly!" Natalie exclaims. "What are you doing?"

"Putting my left arm on the rim of the chair," I say.

"That's *my* arm!"

Oh. That explains a lot.

Natalie sighs and steps away from me, studying me for inspiration. Finally she says, "You're not going to be able to push this chair with your left arm."

Yeah, I could've told her that.

Natalie kneels down and removes the right footrest from my chair. She then instructs me to push with my right hand and use my right foot to help guide the chair. I keep my left arm safely tucked in my lap and my left leg in the foot rest. It actually works fairly well, and I find myself moving further than I have gone in a long time under my own power.

"You're doing great!" Natalie tells me.

I go faster and faster. I want to make it down the entire stretch of hallway. I want to go faster. I want to feel wind running through my hair, even though I don't have hair anymore, and what little hair I have is covered by a helmet. I'm almost there, almost at the finish line, when all of a sudden…

The wheelchair stops short.

For no reason whatsoever. I get thrown forward, and the wind is knocked out of me. I probably would've fallen to the floor if I didn't have a belt across my lap.

"What happened?" I ask, baffled.

"You ran into a wall on the left," Natalie says. She smiles and rubs my shoulder. "You don't have to go so fast, Charly. And watch out for obstacles on the left. This isn't a race."

A race.

Something in Natalie's words jogs my memory. I close my eyes for a second and remember a photo hung up in my room. A photo of myself, my short blond hair tied back in a ponytail, my skin wet with sweat, the number 237 pasted on my tank top.

"I used to run marathons," I say.

"Yes," she says quietly. "Your mother told me."

I can feel myself running, my feet pounding against the pavement, my helmet-less hair flapping in the wind. I used to love it.

"Do you think I'll be able to run marathons again?" I ask.

"Sure," Natalie says. "Even if you can't run, there are people who could push you the length of the marathon in your wheelchair. So you can definitely be a part of it."

That really isn't the same thing at all. But that's okay. I don't think I wanted to hear the real answer to my question anyway.

CHAPTER 27
Four Months After

I feel so tired today.

My body feels so heavy. My arms feel like they weigh a thousand pounds each. My head weighs one ton. The effort of keeping it on my shoulders is just too much for me.

I don't really feel like eating right now, even though my lunch tray is right in front of me. When they came to get me to walk this morning, I didn't feel like doing that. I told them no. All I want is to go back to bed.

That guy who always sits next to me in the hallway is sitting next to me now. I forget his name. It starts with a "J", I think. He's trying to talk to me. I'm too tired to talk though. I'm too tired to even tell him that I'm too tired to talk. I wish he would stop talking to me and just let me go back to sleep. I wish somebody would take me back to my room and put me in bed.

The doctor comes over to us to talk. I can't remember his name either. I'm having trouble remembering names today. Why does everyone have to have a different name? It's so hard to remember. Everyone should have the same name.

Maybe the doctor can bring me to bed. I might be too tired to ask him though.

"Dr. Greenberg," says the guy next to me. Oh right, the doctor's name is Dr. Greenberg. I need to try to remember that. I wish I weren't so tired. "There's something wrong with Charly today."

The doctor raises his graying eyebrows. He has smiley faces on his tie. They dance around before my eyes. "Is there? Why do you say that?"

"She's not talking," the guy says. He looks worried. He has a little crease between his eyebrows. He's very cute. I wish I could remember his name. "She hasn't said a word since she got out into the hallway, and she's not eating her lunch."

The doctor smiles. I forgot his name again. Dammit. "Well, Jamie, I'm sure you know that Charly isn't the most talkative person."

"She always talks to me," the guy insists. "*Always.*" He takes a breath. "The first thing I remember clearly after getting hurt is sitting here in the hallway, talking to her."

I stare at smiley faces on the doctor's tie. They look blurry for some reason.

"Charly's recovery is going to be slower than yours," the doctor says to him. "Her injury was much more severe. She's going to fluctuate day-to-day."

"*No,*" the guy says, shaking his head. "There's something wrong, Doc. I *know* it."

The doctor steps toward me. The smiley faces become clear for a minute, then become blurry again. I just need to sleep, just a little bit. Please. *Please.*

"Charly," the doctor says. "How are you feeling today?"

I'm feeling tired.

Did I say that out loud? I'm not sure I did.

"Charly." The doctor is shaking my shoulder now. "Look at me. Look at my face."

"I'm tired," I finally manage to say.

I feel the doctor's fingers touch my forehead. I don't know why his fingers are so cold. They are like ice. Cold hands, cold heart.

"I think you have a bit of a fever," the doctor tells me. "We're going to take you back to your room and do some tests."

I'm going back to my room. I get to go back in bed. I'm so happy. I can finally sleep.

"Is she going to be okay?" the guy next to me asks.

"Don't worry, Jamie," the doctor says. "She's going to be fine. I promise."

Of course I'm going to be fine. Just as soon as I can get some sleep.

———

I'm dreaming. It's that dream I always have but so much more vivid this time. Like it's almost real. Like I can almost touch it.

I'm coming home from work late in the evening. I step out of the elevator, into the dimly lit hallway. It's very quiet, and makes me wish we had a doorman who I had to make inane small talk with. I hear the muted thumps of my feet hitting the carpeted floor in the hallway outside my apartment. I reach my door, last apartment on the right. I put my key in the lock.

The door swings shut behind me as my left hand absently feels around for the light switch. I flick the switch. *Let there be light.*

Then I see it. The gun pointed straight at me. My blood turns to ice. I want to scream, but I can't.

I hear the explosion.

For a moment, everything is black. Well, not entirely black. Crimson, actually. Like my corneas are coated in a layer of blood.

Then the crimson fades away and I'm staring up at the ceiling of my apartment. I recognize the crack that sort of looks like a dinosaur. I meant to get the ceiling repainted. I've just been too busy. I'm always so busy.

I try to get up, but I can't move. My body doesn't seem to work anymore. I feel sick, dizzy. There's something really wrong with me. I'm injured. Actually, I think I'm dying. I think this might be the end.

And that's when I hear the footsteps. Heavy shoes rising and falling on the wooden floor. The footsteps stop right next to my left ear. I try to see the shoes, to identify them, but I can't. My left side has dissolved into a giant void.

I can here the floorboards creak as the person bends down next to me. I may be dying, but I'm not dead yet, and I suspect this person intends to finish the job. I try to turn my head, to capture my left side. But all I can grasp is more ceiling.

I try to remember Amy's instructions: *turn left, scan left.* But it's as useless now as it is during our sessions.

The person leans in closer to me, so close that I can feel hot breath on my neck. And then I hear a husky voice speaking to me, right in my ear:

"You deserve this."

And then I wake up. Drenched in sweat that isn't from my fever.

CHAPTER 28
Fourteen Months Before

When I was younger, I really never gave much thought to getting married.

I guess I assumed I'd meet some nice guy in medical school. We'd date for a few years then get married. And after finishing residency, we'd have two children. Or at the most, if he *insisted*, maybe we would have three. Definitely not four children. What on earth would I do with four children?

Needless to say, I didn't meet my future husband in medical school. The boys in my class seemed so immature, too focused on partying and joking around, and when I decided on dermatology, I knew I had to work harder than anyone in order to secure a spot. Dermatology is incredibly competitive. So my social life in medical school was practically nonexistent. At the time, it didn't seem like that big of a sacrifice.

By the time I finished my internship, I had a bit more free time to consider dating, but by then, it seemed like "all the good ones" had been taken. Or more likely, there were no good ones in the first place. Not for me, anyway. I started to feel like maybe I was one of those people who was just never meant to couple off.

It didn't bother me so much. I mean, sometimes it did. When there would be a wedding or some other event, and I didn't have a plus one. But in general, I was fine. I'm not a particularly social person. I had friends. I had a great job that I genuinely loved. I didn't feel sorry for myself or cry myself to sleep at night. I was fine with being single.

And now I'm holding hands with my handsome husband as we wait to check into our room at our honeymoon suite in the Bahamas. It's surreal. I keep looking over at Clark and reminding myself he's my husband. He's in no way the husband I would have pictured for myself, even in the days when I believed getting married was a given. I've always been maddeningly realistic, and I imagined my husband would probably have some male pattern baldness or a bit of a gut. I never in a million years thought I would ever be married to such a handsome man. Who's also a lawyer, for God's sake.

Jesus, I can't believe this guy is my husband. What the hell?

Clark gives my hand a squeeze. I love the way my smaller hand gets lost in his big one. "I can't wait to get to our room," he says.

"Me too," I tell him, squeezing his hand back.

I may not be as charismatic and likable and *gorgeous* as Clark, but for some reason, he seems to really like me. I mean, he married me, so he must. Right?

Sorry, it's just a little bit hard to let go of those insecurities. Even after I lost the twenty pounds I wanted to lose. Because it turns out I really needed to lose thirty pounds.

The hotel concierge, a dark-skinned man with an easy smile whose badge identifies him as Pierre, hands over our room keys. "Congratulations," he says warmly. "I just confirmed your reservation for three weeks."

Great. We've only just checked in and already there's a screw up I have to fix.

I clear my throat. "I'm sorry, there's been some mistake. The reservation is only for two weeks."

"It's okay, Charlotte," Clark says, laying his hand on my shoulder. For not the first time, it strikes me as odd that he still calls me Charlotte, even though all of my friends and family call me Charly. Even my work colleagues call me Charly. It's sweet though. He wants to have a different name for me than everyone else does. "I changed it to three weeks."

I frown at him. "But I only have two weeks off from work. There's no way I could take more time off than that. I've got patients scheduled."

"Yeah, I know." Clark smiles sheepishly. "But I thought I'd stick around here another week. I changed my return flight home."

He did *what*?

I am completely stunned. *Stunned.* I don't know what upsets me more, that he did this without telling me, or that he intends to spend an extra week alone on our honeymoon. That's a weird thing to do, right? It's not just me, right?

"What about your job?" I ask him.

"Oh yeah," Clark says. He glances over at Pierre, who is still standing there, overhearing every word of our exchange. "I quit my job."

"You *what*?"

Suddenly, I can hardly breathe. I feel Clark's hand on the small of my back. "Charlotte, can't we discuss this later?"

I look up at Pierre. Admittedly, I don't want to have this conversation in front of Pierre any more than he does. "Fine."

The bellboy helps us upstairs with our luggage. I know I should be in total bliss right now. I mean, I'm on a honeymoon in the Bahamas with my handsome husband. It's every woman's dream. Instead, I feel like I'm going to throw up.

I just can't believe he lied to me like that.

When we get up to our hotel room, the bellboy lingers at the door, and I realize he's waiting for a tip. Clark is already in the bathroom, so I suppose it's up to me. I have no idea what to tip a bellboy. I reached into my purse and pull out five dollars, and hand it over.

"Thank you, Miss," he says. He hesitates for a moment then says to me, "Miss, I have to tell you, you have the most unusual and beautiful eyes I've ever seen. Are they violet?"

I lower my eyes, embarrassed. "Just blue," I mumble.

"Exquisite," the bellboy says.

I suspect he's complementing me to squeeze more money out of me for his tip. That's sort of a rotten trick.

Fine, I'll give him an extra dollar.

After the bellboy leaves, Clark stays in the bathroom just about forever. If this is some sort of scheme on his part to make me forget how furious I am with them, it's definitely not going to work. I sit on our queen-size bed, staring at the wall, thinking of everything I want to say to him. I don't even turn on the TV. I don't want any sort of distraction from my anger.

Eventually, Clark comes out of the bathroom, wearing nothing but a Speedo. The lean muscles on his chest that first attracted me to him bulge enough to almost make me forget my anger. *Almost.*

"So," Clark says with a crooked grin, "do you want to hit the beach?"

"No," I say. "I want to talk about the fact that you quit your job without telling me."

Clark rolls his eyes. "It's not that big a deal."

"It *is* a big deal," I insist. "I'm your wife and you're supposed to discuss these decisions with me."

In all honesty, even though I'm still really angry, it gives me a bit of a thrill to refer to myself as his *wife*.

"Well, you weren't my wife when I quit," he points out.

"When did you quit?"

"A month ago."

I almost choke. He's been keeping this from me for *an entire month*? What the hell? This just keeps getting worse and worse.

"I'm starting my own law practice, Charlotte," Clark says. "You know that's always been my dream. I've always wanted to be my own boss. I hate having to wear a tie and always groveling to some asshole."

"So you're not even going to *try* to join another practice?" I say.

"What did I just tell you, Charlotte?" Clark's voice has taken on an inpatient edge. Like I'm stupid for even asking. "I *hated* that job. Quitting was the best thing I've ever done in my entire life."

"So what's your plan exactly?"

"Well," Clark says thoughtfully. "I was going to rent myself a little office, and then start advertising online for clients. There are plenty of lawyers who work independently. I don't need a big firm to be successful—if anything, they were holding me back."

I've heard him mumble about not loving his job, but this is all news to me. Then again, we've only been together for eight months. Which suddenly doesn't feel like nearly long enough.

"Did you rent an office yet?" I ask.

"Not yet." He raises his hands defensively. "Look, I needed a break. I've got a list of places I'm checking out."

"And do you have any clients?"

Clark frowns. "I can't get clients if I don't have an office yet."

Yes, exactly.

"You should have told me," I say, attempting to keep my anger in check.

"It didn't concern you though," Clark says. "I would've done it whether or not I was with you."

"You would have?" I shoot back. "You really would've quit if you didn't have my income and savings to support us? What money would you have used to rent the office?"

Clark winces. I hate myself for saying that, but I can't help but feel it's true. I make a lot of money working full-time as a dermatologist, and I've got savings and investments on top of that. It's enough to support both of us very comfortably. And I happen to have noticed that Clark loves my spacious Central Park-adjacent apartment and definitely appreciates the finer things in life.

Also, even though he's secretive about his finances, I get the feeling he doesn't have much in the way of savings. He's not exactly financially savvy. I really don't believe he would've quit if he didn't have me. I don't know if he *could* have quit if he didn't have me.

That said, maybe it wasn't the best choice of words. I feel like a huge bitch right now.

"I'm sorry," I say softly. "I want you to be happy. I really do. I just feel like you should consult me before you make any big decisions."

Clark nods. "You're absolutely right. I'm really sorry. Next time I have a big decision to make, we'll make it together. Okay?"

Clark leans forward and I feel his strong arms encircle my body, and then his lips against mine. I've always thought that Clark and I had amazing kisses. I used to believe it was some sort of amazing chemistry the two of us had together.

But now, for the first time, I start to wonder if maybe it's not about us at all, and maybe he's just a very good kisser.

CHAPTER 29
Thirteen Months Before

Clark may have a lot of good qualities, but now that we're living together and married, I'm definitely becoming aware of some of his bad qualities. For example, his laundry never makes it into the laundry basket. He can drop his laundry on our bed, the bathroom, our sofa, or even in our kitchen, for God's sake, but not once in the laundry basket. One time I found a dirty sock next to the laundry basket, nearly touching it, and I applauded him for getting it that close.

Another bad quality of his is that he's lazy. God, is he lazy. Soon after we got back from our honeymoon, I asked Clark while he was sitting on the sofa, watching television, when he was going about renting some office space. He didn't take it well.

"I *just* got back from a trip, Charlotte," he said.

"You just got back from a *vacation*," I pointed out. "In the Bahamas."

Clark shut off the television and turned to me. "Look," he said. "The thing is, I'm short on funds right now. So I don't know if I'm going to be able to afford any office space. But, you know, I'll make it work."

"Without an office?" I shook my head. "Clark, you're my husband. We can pay for an office. It's not a big deal."

Clark avoided my eyes. "I don't know if I'd feel right about taking your money."

"Don't think about it that way," I said. "This is an investment in our future."

So I ended up going online and looking up office space listings. Everything in Manhattan was out of control expensive, but Brooklyn wasn't too bad, so I printed out some of the more reasonable listings. And yesterday, Clark proudly informed me that he had found a space to rent out.

"Do you want to come see it?" he asked me.

"Of course!" I said.

The office is in Brooklyn Heights, in a slightly decrepit brown building that doesn't look like anywhere I'd like to be late at night. We took a taxi to get there, and I plan to call a taxi to get home as well. But Clark is a man, and it's not such a bad neighborhood that I'd worry about him here, at least during the daytime hours. And I definitely don't see Clark burning the midnight oil.

The office itself is in a suite he shares with another attorney. He explained that the furniture all came with the office: the rusty file cabinet, the splintery wooden desk, and the creaky wooden chairs. I decide that for Clark's birthday, I'm going to buy him a really nice, expensive desk for the office.

"What do you think?" Clark asks me.

"Looks great," I say.

"It's all because of you, you know," he says as he envelopes me in his arms. "I never would have had the nerve to go off on my own if not for you, Charlotte. You're, like, my inspiration."

I'm also his bankroll. But no. I shouldn't think that way. Like I told him, he's my husband. This is an investment in our future. Together.

"So are you putting an ad in the paper?" I ask.

Clark groans. "Charlotte, I *just* got the office."

Some investments are better than others.

———

I know this is going to sound weird, but I feel like lately, I've been seeing Stan Leroy everywhere.

Ever since that day he confronted me at the diner, I feel like I've been seeing his face out of the corner of my eye. Then I'll turn and he's gone. It's the strangest thing.

I went into our patient records and looked up his address, and he doesn't live anywhere near me. Yet I did see him at that diner, so maybe he knows someone around here. Or maybe I'm not actually seeing him at all, and I'm just going insane.

While I'm picking up food from a Chinese restaurant to bring home for dinner, the guy behind me in line keeps staring at me in a really unnerving way. He's definitely not Stan Leroy, and the man isn't scary-looking or anything (although I'm trying not to look), but the whole thing is really bothering me. I keep stumbling over my order of chicken with broccoli for me and moo shu pork for Clark, and have to ask the cashier to keep repeating what he was saying.

"Okay, what's the name on that order?" the cashier asks me.

"McKenna," I say.

No, I haven't changed my name since getting married. I've been Charlotte McKenna for thirty-six years. My medical license is under that name. Changing my name would be like changing my entire identity at this point. It's just not worth it.

I step aside to wait for my order, when the guy who's been staring at me finally says: "Charlotte, is it?"

I whirl around to study my would-be stalker. He's maybe in his forties, dressed in a suit and tie like he just came from the office. To be honest, he doesn't look all that frightening. My first guess is that he must be a patient. I can't tell you how many times I run into patients in public, and they expect me to remember them. As if that mole check was *so* incredibly memorable. Usually I have to fake it.

When he notices the look on my face, the man puts out his hand for me to shake. "Kenneth Landers," he says. "I used to work with Clark at Gregory and Patterson. You guys recently got married, didn't you? I heard about it on Facebook."

Oh my gosh, it's one of Clark's colleagues. That is *so* much better than a patient. I've hardly met any of Clark's friends, and I'm not sure if I've met even one person he worked with before.

"That's right," I say, taking his outstretched hand. "It's nice to meet you."

"Likewise," Landers says. "Don't worry, I'm not offended you didn't invite me to the wedding."

I blush. "It was a really small ceremony. Just the two of us in City Hall."

"And you were okay with that?" Landers raises an eyebrow. "Wow, Clark really is a lucky man."

"Thank you," I say, suppressing the urge to roll my eyes at the cliché.

He grins. "We've all been dying to meet the beautiful woman who finally made an honest man out of Clark. I can't say I blame him."

This time I really do roll my eyes. "Thank you," I say again.

"So how has married life been?" Landers asks me.

"Great," I tell him, glancing over to see if my food is ready. It isn't. "I feel bad I never got to see the practice."

Landers laughs. "Well, that's okay. I don't think they'd ever let Clark back in there after what he did when they let him go. God, it's been over a year and people still talk about it all the time. Because of him, they never fire people at the start of the day anymore."

What? What is he talking about?

"*Excuse* me?" I say.

Landers raises his eyebrows. "You mean Clark never told you about his epic last day at G & P? Oh man."

"I'm afraid I missed that story," I say weakly. "But… you said it's been a *year* since he's worked there?"

Landers frowns thoughtfully. "No, I'd say probably a little more than a year."

My brain fills up with so many questions, it might explode. *I* might explode. When Clark and I met, he told me he was working for G & P. That was the job he apparently quit right before we got married. Except now it seems like he hasn't worked there in over a year. And oh yeah, he got *fired*.

No *wonder* Clark never introduced me to anyone he knew from work.

I'm going to *kill* my husband. I will murder him. I will murder him so bad that they won't be able to identify the body.

"Order for McKenna!" the guy behind the counter calls out, right in my ear. For God's sake, I was standing right in front of him.

"Thank you," I say through my teeth. I look in Kenneth Landers's direction and force a smile. "It's been so nice meeting you. I... I have to get going."

"Nice meeting you too," Landers says. "Hey, maybe we could get together sometime. My wife would love to have you and Clark over at the house. We're out on the island."

"Sounds great!" I say with forced enthusiasm. "Just send Clark an email about it."

Yes, that will ensure that I never see Kenneth Landers again for the rest of my life.

I walk home, clutching the pungent brown paper bag of Chinese food in my fist. I've completely lost my appetite. Honestly, I feel like I'm going to throw up. How much do I really know about Clark Douglas? It seems like half of what he told me about himself has been a lie.

And why hasn't he let me meet his parents? What's that all about? I initially accepted that it was simply a strained relationship, but now I wonder.

When I get upstairs, Kitty greets me at the door. She meows loudly to let me know she's starving. Apparently, Clark never bothered to feed her while I was at work. Even after all this time, Kitty has never entirely warmed up to Clark, and vice versa. I should have listened to Kitty in the first place. Even my cat has better sense about men than I do.

As I dump a can of Kitty's gourmet cat food into her bowl, I hear Clark turning off the water in the shower. Why is he showering in the middle of the evening? Is there something that he's washing off of himself?

No, I can't let myself think this way.

I'm standing rigidly in the middle of the living room, still clutching the Chinese food, when Clark emerges from the bathroom, a towel wrapped around his waist, whistling Eine Kleine Nachtmusik. I can see all the well-defined muscles in his chest and I have to admit, my anger fades slightly. He may not work hard, but he always at least makes time to work out. He runs a hand through his wet hair and grins at me.

"Perfect timing," he comments.

I take a deep breath, my heart slamming in my chest. "When was the last time you worked at Gregory and Patterson?"

Clark stops mid-stride. I could tell from the look on his face what the answer to my question is. "A little while ago," he says carefully. He's obviously trying to figure out how much I know.

"Define 'a little while,'" I say through my teeth.

Clark laughs unevenly. "What kind of question is that?"

I drop the paper sack of Chinese food on our coffee table so aggressively that I practically throw it. I fold my arms across my chest. "The kind of question you can't answer, apparently."

Clark doesn't say anything for at least a minute. Finally, he sighs and runs his hand through his wet hair. "Who told you?"

"Kenneth Landers."

Clark frowns.

"I ran into him at the Chinese restaurant," I explain.

"Right," Clark mumbles. He sinks down into the sofa, running a hand nervously through his hair again. He looks up at me with those blue, blue eyes. "Charlotte, I'm so sorry I lied."

I don't join him on the couch. "How about you tell me the truth?"

"Like, what part?"

"Like *all* of it!" I plant my hands on my hips. "Start with why you got fired."

"I just couldn't keep up, Charlotte," he says weakly. "The pace they expected at G & P was ridiculous. I mean, they wanted us to bill for two hundred hours a week. I was always a week behind. They gave me a few warnings, but I just couldn't perform at the level they wanted. So they fired me."

"Okay…" I say.

"I thought it was really, really unfair," Clark continues. "I was super pissed off about the whole thing and I wanted payback. Everyone knew that old man Patterson was fooling around with his receptionist every afternoon during their three o'clock 'conference call.' So I decided to schedule a little meeting with his wife at three-fifteen. Well, you can guess what happened."

I wince. "Wow. That's gutsy."

"And dumb," he says, shaking his head. "Patterson blackballed me so that no law firm in the whole city would touch me. I basically ruined my whole life for a little bit of revenge."

"Christ," I say. "So how have you been paying the bills?"

"I had savings," he says. "And I did freelance work when I could get it. Friends, neighbors, stuff like that. But… it was tight."

I bite my lip. "So how come you never told me?"

"Are you *kidding* me?" Clark shakes his head again. "You're like this gorgeous, successful, intelligent *doctor*, and I'm supposed to tell you that I'm an unemployed slob? You wouldn't have given me a second look."

"That's really unfair," I say. "You should've told me the truth. I would have been fine with it."

"Bullshit," Clark practically spits. "You would have judged me the same way everyone else did!" His face is bright red now. "Why do you think my parents don't speak to me anymore? Because I'm always a screw up, always begging them for help, never good enough. And they're right. They're *right*."

There are tears in his eyes now. I see patients cry all the time, but I've never seen Clark cry. But he seems dangerously close right now.

"I wanted to be good enough for you, Charlotte," he says, more quietly this time. "I was ashamed of myself. I was so scared that if you knew the truth, I would lose you."

"You wouldn't have lost me."

Clark puts his elbows on his knees and buries his face in his hands. "I love you so much. I'm so sorry that I lied. I wish I could take it back."

God, I can't believe I'm considering forgiving him for this. But then again, we're *married*. What am I supposed to do? Divorce him because he got fired?

Clark lifts his face to look at me. It's so hard to resist him.

"Charlotte…" He holds out his hands to me.

Really, is it so awful that he was trying to impress me? It just went a little too far.

CHAPTER 30
Four and a Half Months After

I spend three days in bed.

That's what they tell me anyway. I barely remember most of it. All I remember is lying in bed, feeling sleepy and confused, and wanting to be left alone. And the nightmares. Every night, the nightmares.

It turns out everything was because of an infection in my urine. Now I'm on antibiotics. One more pill to add to the mix.

One nice thing about being sick was that I got to stay in my room and didn't have to sit in the hall, being gawked at by visitors and nurses. Now I'm better, so I'm stuck out in the hallway again. It looks the same and different. Sort of like when you go back to your old high school for a visit after you graduate, and it's all the same hallways and classrooms, but the faces are mostly different.

Of course, if I were at a high school, the faces wouldn't be nearly this old.

The worst thing is that I don't see Jamie everywhere anywhere. Maybe he's gone home. That would make me incredibly sad.

I am chewing a mouthful of green beans when I hear a voice yell my name: "Charly!"

It's Jamie! Jamie! I would know his voice anywhere. I see him being pushed in his wheelchair by a large, burly man in scrubs. His face is all lit up and he's grinning at me. I feel suddenly overcome by the urge to reach out and hug him, but that wouldn't work out for so many reasons.

Jamie cranes his neck back to look at the man who is wheeling him. "Hey, Lou," he says to the guy. "Stop. Put me next to Charly."

The guy frowns. "I thought you said you wanted to eat lunch in your room."

"No," Jamie says, shaking his head vigorously. "I want to eat out here. Next to Charly."

The man starts to push Jamie's wheelchair past me, but Jamie stops him. "No," he says again. "On her *right* side. I've got to be on her right side."

It's nice when somebody knows you very well.

When Jamie is positioned on my right side, the man goes off to fetch his food for him. "You look a lot better," Jamie says to me.

"You look better too," I tell him.

Jamie laughs and raises an eyebrow. "What's that supposed to mean?"

"Your hair is growing back," I point out. His hair is at least a centimeter long and dark brown in color. "You can barely see the scar anymore."

Jamie touches the healing scar on his scalp self-consciously. "Yeah?"

"You look almost normal," I say.

"Gee, thanks," Jamie says, rolling his eyes, but he's smiling.

Something suddenly occurs to me. That man was ready to take Jamie back to his room for lunch. I always thought Jamie used to sit in the hallway for the same reason as me: because he couldn't be trusted alone in his room.

But obviously that isn't the case. Jamie is allowed to eat alone in his room. He's actually *choosing* to be out here.

If I had that choice, I would *never* stay out here. Not in a million years.

"Did I miss anything while I was gone?" I ask him.

Jamie shakes his head and smiles. "You know we couldn't have any fun without you." He hesitates for a minute and his face gets all serious. "I was worried about you, Charly. Really worried. I'm glad you're okay."

Then Jamie does something that really surprises me. He reaches out and grabs my hand and gives it a squeeze.

The only hands I've held recently have been my mother's tiny, arthritic fingers. Jamie's hand is large and strong. And warm. Warm hands, warm heart, right? After that one squeeze, he hesitates for another second, then pulls his hand away just before that man reappears with his lunch.

———

There's a man who keeps shuffling his way back and forth across the hallway. He's maybe in his fifties and he has thinning brown hair that seems sort of weird and unnatural. He's wearing a hospital gown and instead of shoes, he's got on those thick socks with pads on the bottom so he doesn't slip. He has a white bracelet around his ankle that flashes a red light every minute or so.

"It's so he doesn't escape," Jamie says from my right side.

I look at him and frown. "What do you mean?"

"You're looking at his ankle, right?" Jamie says. "That thing around his ankle sets off an alarm if he tries to leave the unit. I heard it go off yesterday."

I look down at my own ankles. I don't have a bracelet on my ankle. Unless it's on the left ankle, which is always a possibility. I check Jamie's ankle, and he doesn't seem to have one either. "Why don't we have one of those on?"

Jamie rolls his eyes. "Gee, do you think one of us is going to make a run for it?"

No, I guess we aren't. If either of us tried to run for the door, we would be on the floor before we got a quarter of the way there. I'd be on the floor after one step. Jamie might make it a little further, but not much.

The man keeps looking at me every time he paces back and forth. It's making me kind of uncomfortable. I wonder if he's staring at my helmet. I guess I wouldn't blame him.

Finally, after what must've at least been his hundredth time across the floor, he pauses right in front of me. Now that he's standing in front of me, I can see there are bruises all along the right side of his face. He's got a shiner on his right eye and the eye itself is all bloodshot. He squints at me.

"Dr. McKenna?"

I feel the wind knocked out of me. *Nobody* calls me Dr. McKenna. Not anymore. Not here. Who *is* this guy?

"Yes…" I glance over at Jamie, who is staring at the guy and frowning, his forehead all bunched up in a way that makes him look really cute.

The guy's face lights up in a smile. "I can't believe it's you!"

I don't know exactly what to say to that. "It's me," I confirm.

His face gets real serious. "You're a genius, Dr. McKenna. I really mean that. You saved my marriage." He takes a deep breath. "I just wanted to say thank you. Thank you *so* much."

I suddenly get a vaguely familiar warm feeling. I remember patients coming up to me, thanking me for what I had done for them. I remember how good it used to feel.

"Oh," I say. I still have no idea who this guy is. But I'm still happy I helped him. "You're welcome."

Jamie is still frowning at the guy. "What did Charly… I mean, *Dr. McKenna* do that saved your marriage?"

Thank you, Jamie, for asking that.

Beaming, the guy points at his head. "She gave me this hair transplant. Totally revived my sex life."

I look at the guy's weird hair, which seems to be sprouting out of his head in odd tufts. Did I really do that to him? Jesus.

"I wish I could give you something," he goes on, "to show you how grateful I am to you."

"That's all right," I say. I add, "Really."

The guy seems like he's going to say something more, but then he just pauses in front of me for what seems like an eternity. Finally, he shuffles away and starts pacing back down the hallway.

"I can't believe I did that to his hair," I whisper to Jamie. "If that's really what I did for my career, maybe I shot *myself* in the head?"

Jamie clasps his hand over his mouth, stifling a laugh. I'm glad I made him laugh. It seems like whenever I make somebody laugh these days, it's rarely on purpose. Jamie looks like he's about to say something else, but then his mouth falls open.

"Charly," he says quietly. "I hate to tell you this, but it looks like that guy gave you a little present after all."

I have no idea what he's talking about, but then he nods in the direction of the floor. I follow his eyes to a spot right in front of me, where the man had been standing. Right where his feet had been is a small pile of feces.

Maybe I really did shoot myself in the head.

CHAPTER 31
Four and a Half Months After

I have officially graduated from my Orientation Group. I can consistently tell you my name, where I am, what the date is, and what the name of the President of the United States is. (Although I still don't know what he ate.)

My new group is called Thinking Skills Group. I'm not entirely sure what it is, but I have to agree that I definitely need help with my thinking skills. My thinking skills are not so great right now. Also, Angela is in the group too, and she told me that it's a lot of fun. And it doesn't involve my hand being electrocuted, so that's a plus.

We meet in a cozy room that barely allows room for our wheelchairs around a small wooden table. There are four of us in the group: Angela, another female, and a man. The female looks to be around in her seventies or so, but the man is really old. He's possibly the oldest man I've ever seen in my life. His wrinkles have wrinkles. He's wearing a Yankees cap, but appears to be completely bald except for two or three scattered tufts of white hair protruding from his scalp.

Amy left the equipment for the group back upstairs, so she leaves the four of us alone to retrieve it. She's probably forgotten then I'm not supposed to be alone, but I do have an alarming seatbelt on my lap. Although I'm pretty sure I could be out of my chair and flat on my face before any staff member could reach me. Fortunately, I have no desire to be flat on my face.

"This is Charly," Angela tells the other two members of the group. "Charly, this is Helga and Dr. Vincent."

Helga smiles at me. Her graying hair is in a bun and she has a wide gap between her front two teeth. "I know you," she says in a thick German accent. "I always see you in the hallway talking to the cute one with the shaky hands."

Angela laughs. "That's Jamie. He has a *massive* crush on Charly. It's adorable."

I feel my cheeks grow warm. "No, he doesn't."

"And what's even more adorable," Angela says, "is that Charly doesn't realize how crazy he is about her."

"He isn't," I mumble.

"Well, I don't blame him," Helga says. "You are obviously a very beautiful woman. I love your eyes. Are they violet?"

"Just dark blue," I mumble.

"She's not that pretty," Dr. Vincent speaks up in a crackly mutter. Even his voice sounds ancient. "She doesn't even have any hair!"

"*Sie dumm fuhrt!*" Helga snaps at Dr. Vincent. "You don't need hair to be beautiful. Anyway, I'm sure it will grow back."

Angela nods in the direction of Dr. Vincent. "Up until he had a stroke, he's been working as a psychiatrist," she says. "Even though he's ninety-three years old."

"I'm a doctor too," I tell him.

"Really?" Dr. Vincent raises his eyebrows. Despite how little hair there is on his head, his eyebrows are completely overgrown and threatening to protrude on his vision. "What sort of doctor?"

I bite my lip and look at Angela, who just shrugs. "I don't really remember," I start to say, but suddenly it comes to me: "I'm a skin doctor."

"What happened to you anyway?" Dr. Vincent asks me.

"You don't ask her a question like that!" Helga yells at Dr. Vincent.

Dr. Vincent spreads his hands apart. "Why not?"

"Because it's not polite," Helga insists. She gives me a confidential look. "Dr. Vincent and I both had schematic shocks."

"What's that?" I ask.

"She means we had ischemic strokes," Dr. Vincent says. He rolls his eyes. "My thinking skills are working fine, thank you very much. Now you tell me why you're here, Charly."

Before Helga can defend me further, I say, "I was shot in the head."

Helga clutches her hand against her chest. "*Ach mein gott!*" she cries out. "Who would do something like that to you?"

I shake my head. "The police don't know who it was."

"It was probably somebody you knew," Dr. Vincent says, stroking his wrinkled chin thoughtfully. "Most women are murdered by somebody they knew."

"She was not murdered, *dummkopf!*" Helga says.

"I assume," Dr. Vincent says, "if somebody shot her in the head, they meant to kill her."

"My mother thinks it was a burglar," I say.

"Maybe it was your husband," Dr. Vincent suggests.

"*Ach mein gott!*" Helga cries again. "How can you say such a thing?"

Dr. Vincent shrugs. "Who else would it be?"

"He never visits her," Angela confides to the others. "I haven't seen him even once. Not even once."

"Where is your wedding ring, *meine liebste*?" Helga asks me.

I shake my head. I don't know where my left hand is and even if I did, I don't think I'm wearing my ring.

"My husband and I were jewelers for forty years!" Helga announces. "You show me your ring and I will tell you if your husband is a good man."

Dr. Vincent snorts at Helga. "Do you remember anything at all?" he asks me, his overgrown eyebrows knitting together.

I shake my head no. "Nothing. Except…"

All three of my groupmates are looking at me with interest. I wish I had something interesting to tell them.

"It's just this dream I keep having," I say. "It's a dream, but it feels more like a memory somehow. But... I don't know, it was too fuzzy. Something was happening on my left side and I just couldn't see what it was."

Angela nudges Dr. Vincent. "What would Freud say about that kind of dream?"

"A dream that you are dying is a sign of inner changes or transformation," Dr. Vincent says thoughtfully. "Of course, the Freudian interpretation goes out the window if you were recently shot in the head."

Amy interrupts our conversation when she returns to the room carrying a stack of games and appearing slightly breathless. She drops them on the table in front of us. Some of the games look vaguely familiar, maybe from parties or TV shows. Maybe this group won't be so bad.

"What have you been talking about?" Amy asks us.

"We're trying to figure out who shot Charly in the head," Dr. Vincent explains. "It was either her husband or a burglar."

Amy's eyes widen and she proceeds to lecture us about how we shouldn't talk about these kinds of things. Although I don't really see why not. It seems like the police are never going to figure out who shot me. My only hope is to try to remember.

———

And I have that dream again. About the night I got shot.

It's night. Outdoors, it's chilly. Raining. My boots slosh against the marble floor in our lobby when I step inside. "Hey, Charly," says Annie, my neighbor from two flights up. I nod and smile back at her.

My boots are quieter on the carpeted floor in the hallway outside my apartment. I fit my key in the lock of my apartment door.

Then the explosion. Followed by crimson.

I can't get up. I can't move. There's somebody in the apartment with me, somebody who means to hurt me. I sense them, on my left side. I try to turn my head, try to see who's there. But I can't see them. I can only hear the voice echoing in my head:

"You deserve this."

And then I wake up.

CHAPTER 32
Eleven Months Before

When Bridget invited me over to her apartment for lunch, somehow I got the idea that we were going to eat lunch. I'm not sure how I made that mistake.

Back in the old days, lunch with Bridget usually meant going out to a Greek diner, where we would agonize over whether we should get a healthy salad or else the burger that we *really* wanted. (The burger. Always the burger.) Then we'd go shopping or maybe hit the movie theater or just reminisce about our college roommate days. Either way, we'd end up spending a long, lazy afternoon together.

Unfortunately, ever since little Chelsea came along, our afternoons together seem to revolve around the baby. Lunch with Bridget actually means my watching Chelsea eat mashed turkey dinner. Which is obviously super fun for me.

It's interesting to see how frazzled my best friend has become since the birth of her daughter. Her apartment has always been immaculate—filled with expensive, uncomfortable furniture, and without a speck of dust on the coffee table. But now there are stains on everything—

milk, food, and something brown that I don't want to ask about. Even Bridget is stained. She's wearing baggy jeans and a tank top that has crusted food in the bottom right corner. The old Bridget wouldn't have walked around with food on her shirt, and she definitely wouldn't have put ugly, soft plastic edges on the corners of her coffee table.

Chelsea, who has a bib protecting her ridiculously impractical frilly, pink dress, seems nonplussed by the idea of eating turkey in purée form. I can't say I blame her. Just the sight of it is so revolting that it almost kills my appetite. Which is good, because I'm pretty sure I'm not going to get any food during this alleged lunch.

"Please, Chelsea," Bridget begs her little daughter, "please just take one bite for Mommy…"

Chelsea presses her little pink lips together tightly. She's cute, only because I'm not the one who's force-feeding her.

Bridget drops the baby spoon and sighs. "We're trying to introduce meat, but it's not going well."

"Really," I say.

"The worst thing," Bridget says, "is that her poop has been a complete disaster since she started eating meat. I thought it was bad when we introduced solids. You should see what it looks like now."

"Really," I say. What would be a polite way to change the topic? To anything besides Chelsea's poop.

"Actually," Bridget says, her eyes brightening, "I took a picture of Chelsea's poop yesterday because it was just so amazing." She starts reaching for her purse. "Do you want to see?"

Has my best friend *completely lost her mind*? "That's all right."

Bridget's face falls. She's probably been waiting to show me the poop photo all day. Thankfully, she doesn't push the matter further.

"Do you want to go out and get some food?" I suggest. "Like, for ourselves?"

"Oh, *no*," Bridget says. "Charly, look at me! I still haven't lost my baby weight."

"So what are you saying?" I crinkle my nose. "Have you given up eating?"

"When we go out, we always overeat," Bridget points out. "You know it's true. I mean, you're skinny as a rail so you can afford to eat a bacon cheeseburger, but I can't."

I'm not skinny as a rail. Far from it. I'm actually still ten pounds above my goal weight. But that doesn't mean I've stopped eating.

"How about you and Clark?" Bridget says with a sly smile. "Are you guys going to try for a baby soon?"

I cross and uncross my legs. Maybe I should try to change the topic back to Chelsea's poop. Maybe it's not too late to see the photo. "We haven't really talked about it…"

"You want kids though, don't you, Charly?"

I watch as Bridget wipes off Chelsea's face, and Chelsea stretches out her little arms to be picked up. Bridget picks her little girl out of her highchair and cuddles her, messy dress and all. Chelsea wraps her chubby little arms around Bridget's neck.

Don't tell my mother, but I think I do. I want a child.

I didn't think I would. I had always been one of those women who assumed I would have children one day, but wasn't particularly excited about it. But now that I'm married and practically all my friends either are mothers or are trying for a baby, it's been on my mind more and more. Whenever I see a woman pushing a baby carriage down the street, I get a little ache in my chest.

Although luckily, I haven't gotten to the point where I have the slightest interest in seeing a photo of a nine-month-old girl's poop.

"I guess so," I say. "I mean, I think so."

"Well, what are you waiting for?" Bridget says. She raises her eyebrows at me. "Charly, we're in our late thirties!"

I frown at her. "Thirty-six is not late thirties. It's *mid* thirties."

"Bullshit," Bridget argues. "Anything after thirty-five is late thirties by definition."

I'm not entirely sure that's true. But then again, obstetricians consider anything over thirty-five to be advanced maternal age. Right now, I'm advanced maternal age and I haven't even started *trying* for a baby yet.

"Steve and I are going to try for a second as soon as Chelsea is one year old," Bridget says. "You and Clark should start trying right now."

Bridget is right, of course. But somehow I have reservations about trying for a baby with Clark. Ever since that revelation about his employment, I haven't entirely been able to trust my husband.

But I know that's silly. There's no reason in the world why Clark and I shouldn't start trying for a baby. That's what you do when you get married, right?

CHAPTER 33
Eleven Months Before

Clark has been really stressed out lately about his new practice. He's got a few cases now that aren't going great, and he's been putting in a lot of hours. Clark stressed out is not pleasant, as I found out. He just paces around the house and snaps at me whenever I try to talk to him. With the amount of pacing he's done in the last few weeks, he's probably paced the equivalent of a marathon.

And our sex life has pretty much dwindled to zip. I guess Clark used up all his energy with pacing.

I think the two of us both needed a break from the pacing, so we decided to take a night out to unwind. Clark somehow got us reservations at a swanky restaurant called WD 50, which specializes in something called molecular gastronomy. I don't entirely know what that means, but Clark is eating something called a deconstructed Eggs Benedict. I'm eating shrimp grits. Not shrimp and grits, just shrimp grits. Basically, it's grits made out of shrimp, with pickled jalapeño and bright shreds of green onion. It's amazing, actually.

I haven't decided whether or not it's a good thing that we've only just received our main course and Clark is on his fourth glass of wine. I'm glad he is loosening up a bit, but this might be a little bit too much loosening up. Also, he's looking for our waiter to get a refill.

"This was a *great* idea, Charlotte," Clark says, as he downs the last few drops of pinot noir.

"Well, you were the one who got us reservations," I point out.

Clark winks at me. "Very true."

I take his hand across the table. He holds my hand for a moment then goes back to eating. "I think you're too wrapped up in your practice," I tell him. "Maybe there are some other things you can think about instead."

"Maybe." Clark shrugs. He picks up my glass of wine (my first) and steals a sip. "What sorts of things? Were you thinking about a trip somewhere?"

"Not exactly," I say. I take a deep breath. "I was thinking maybe we could start trying for a baby."

Clark starts to choke on my wine. A few droplets of purple end up on his white shirt. "A baby? Now? Are you out of your mind?"

"Clark, I'm thirty-six years old," I remind him. God, I sound just like Bridget. Oh well. "When am I supposed to have a baby if not now?"

"I didn't even think you *wanted* a baby," Clark says shaking his head. "You're so caught up in work. When would you even have time?"

I wince. In previous relationships, men had always complained that I was too caught up with work. Clark had never said anything like that to me before. He had always seemed thrilled that I had a job that I loved.

"We could hire a nanny," I say. "And I can cut back on work a little bit."

Clark shakes his head again. "How are we supposed to afford that?"

"I've got enough savings," I say. "It will be fine."

Clark just keeps shaking his head.

"Before we got married, you said you wanted kids," I remind him.

"Right," he says. "I do want kids. Someday."

"I'm thirty-six years old," I tell him again. "How long am I supposed to wait?"

"Thirty-six is young," Clark says. "You're only in your mid thirties."

"No," I say. "I'm in my *late* thirties."

Now I really do sound like Bridget.

Clark waves his hand in dismissal. "So what? Women have babies in their forties all the time now. I think waiting till forty is completely reasonable."

"I don't want to wait till I'm forty," I say. It's like I'm deciding at this moment. I hadn't been certain about the whole child issue, but I am now. I don't want to wait till I'm forty. "It might be too late by then."

"You always have to have it your way, don't you?" Clark grumbles.

What the hell is that supposed to mean?

I stare at Clark, feeling the resentment creep over me. I don't want to sit here and have dinner with him anymore. I'm this close to storming out the door of WD

50. I certainly don't have much of an appetite anymore for shrimp grits.

A waiter breaks our heated silence when he comes by our table and refills Clark's wine glass. Clark lifts up his newly filled glass, swishes the liquid around for a moment, and takes a long drink.

"Listen," he says. He reaches across the table and takes my hand in his. "You're right. I want to have a baby too, and we're not that young. How about... a year? We start trying in one year."

I smile across the table at him. "Yeah?"

"That will be perfect," he says. "My practice will have stabilized by then, and we'll be married for over two years when the baby comes."

"Sounds perfect," I say.

I actually feel kind of relieved that he doesn't want to start trying right away. I'm scared of the idea of becoming a parent too, and this will give me a little time to adjust to it. And to get to know my husband better before we burden ourselves with a child.

"But," Clark adds, a smile playing in his lips, "you have to promise me that we're going to have a boy. And that we're going to name him Clark Junior."

"Oh no," I say. "She's going to be a girl and she's going to be Charlotte Junior."

"Hmm," Clark says. "What about some combination of the two? Clarotte? Oh, I've got it—Chark!"

"Brilliant!" I laugh.

I dig back into my shrimp grits. One more year until we start on the road to parenthood. Maybe I can run another marathon.

CHAPTER 34
Four and a Half Months After

"So are you ever going to get your skull put back on?" Jamie asks me.

We're sitting together in the hallway, like we do every night. We just finished eating dinner, and an aide has cleared away our trays of food. I still can't get over the fact that Jamie could go back to his room if he wanted, but instead he's staying out here with me. He's got to be out of his mind.

"I guess so," I say. At least, I hope so. I really don't want to have to wear a helmet for the rest of my life. Then again, my skull was pretty much destroyed by the bullet. Can they make a new skull? Do we have that kind of technology yet?

"When?"

"I have no idea," I say. I touch the helmet, which feels suddenly very itchy. "Hopefully soon."

"I hope so too," Jamie says. He grins at me. "I want to see what your hair looks like."

I can't help but remember what Angela said yesterday in Thinking Skills Group. About how Jamie has a crush on me. I wonder if that could be true. After all, he does stay in the hallway with me when he doesn't need to...

But no, I'm pretty sure he doesn't. He couldn't possibly.

Jamie scratches absently at the scar on his scalp. I've noticed he does that a lot. "Does it itch a lot?" I ask him.

He blinks in confusion. "Does what?"

I gesture at his head. "The scar."

"Oh." Jamie laughs and touches his scalp self-consciously. "Yeah. Like crazy."

Another thing that we have in common.

Jamie is looking at me, still smiling. He's got that look like he wants to say something, but whatever it is, he isn't saying it. He's just sitting there quietly, looking at me.

Then I suddenly see the smile fade from Jamie's face. One second he's smiling, the next he looks completely horrified. His eyes widen, and I see a vein stand out in his neck that I'd never seen before. He's not looking at me anymore, but at something past me.

"Karen," I hear him say in a choked voice. "What the hell are you doing here?"

Then I see her appear. In that sudden way that people appear when they approach me from the left side.

So this is Karen. As terrible as my memory is these days, I remember who Karen is. She's the mother of Jamie's son.

She's young. Younger than I thought she would be, far younger than I am. Maybe mid-twenties, late twenties at most. She's very tall, probably nearly as tall as Jamie is, and he's above average height for a man. She has long, wavy black hair, and she's very thin. The cheekbones on her face look sharp, like they might hurt if you nuzzled against her. And she's pale. Like she hasn't been out in the sun in years. The purple lipstick she's wearing makes her look like a vampire.

I can't help but notice that she doesn't look anything like I do. Or at least, the way I did before. If this is Jamie's type then I am definitely not Jamie's type.

"Jamie," she says quietly. "We need to talk. I keep calling you, but you won't pick up."

"There's nothing to say," he practically spits at her. "So why don't you get out of here. Before I call the security guard."

"God, don't be so dramatic," Karen says. She blinks her black-lined eyelids. "Look, if you don't want to talk to me, then you're going to have to talk to my lawyer. But I prefer not to do things that way."

Jamie sucks in a breath. "You're wasting your time, Karen. You're never going to get custody of Sam. Never."

"Who's supposed to take care of him?" She raises her eyebrows. "*You?*"

"I've been doing a pretty good job of that for the last five years," he retorts.

Karen folds her arms over her chest. She's so thin that she has zero in the way of bust. At least I've got *that* over her. "Your nurse told me you can't even get dressed by yourself."

Jamie's mouth drops open and his face turns pink. "That's not true. And anyway, she had no right to talk to you."

I'm pretty sure it *is* true. I watch Jamie eat every day, and even though he's a lot steadier, I'm willing to bet he still needs help getting dressed.

"Your parents aren't so young," Karen points out. "When you go home, do you expect that they're going to take care of both you *and* Sam? You *need* my help, Jamie. And I want to see my son again."

"I absolutely don't need your help," Jamie says. "I'm fine. I'll be completely fine."

"You're fine?" Karen snorts. "Prove it to me then. Get up and walk down the hall for me. If you do that, I'll go away and never bother you again."

Jamie's face turns an even darker shade of red. He can't do it. Not if she gave him half the day. Maybe with a walker he could manage. But without it, he'd fall on his face for sure. I know it, he knows it, and apparently, Karen knows it too.

"It doesn't matter," Jamie says through his teeth. "I'm not turning my son over to a drug addict."

Karen glances at me. I guess it occurs to her that I might not be completely brain-dead and that I've heard their entire conversation. She lowers her voice a notch. "I'm clean now, Jamie," she says softly. "I swear to you, I'm completely sober now. I would never do anything to endanger Sam."

Jamie just shakes his head at her. "I don't believe you."

"I'd like us to be friends, Jamie," she says in a calm voice. I notice for the first time that her eyes are bright green, contrasting sharply with her ebony hair and dark make-up. "I want to work out a way for both of us to be a part of Sam's life without bringing lawyers into it and making everyone unhappy." She leans forward and looks him in the eyes. "But either way, I assure you, I'm going to see my son again regularly. Whether you like it or not."

Karen is very lucky that Jamie can't walk. Because if he could, I'm pretty sure he would've gotten out of this chair and wrapped his fingers around her neck.

CHAPTER 35

Four and a Half Months After

The next day in our walking group, I can tell that Jamie is still mad about what happened yesterday with that woman Karen. He's really quiet, first of all. He hardly talks to Angela or me much, which is unusual for him. He just sits in silence, watching everyone else walk.

When it's finally his turn, he says to Natalie, "I want to walk without the walker today. Let's try it with just a cane."

Natalie looks like she doesn't think it's a good idea. I saw Jamie walk yesterday, and I don't think it's a good idea either. "I'm not sure if you're ready for that," Natalie says.

Jamie looks up to meet her eyes. "I'm ready."

Natalie obligingly fetches a cane for him. It's pretty supportive for a cane. It has four prongs at the base instead of just one. He's able to stand on his own without a problem, but the second he starts walking, you can see how bad his balance is. But it's a lot better than it used to be. Natalie has to hang onto him and catch him a few times, but he manages to make it across the room and back without coming close to falling.

When Jamie collapses back into his wheelchair, he looks pleased with himself for the first time that day.

Angela squints at him. "What's your hurry?"

"I need to be able to walk again," Jamie says. "Like, ASAP."

She raises her eyebrows. "And why is that?"

"Because if I don't get out of here soon," he says, "my son's mother is going to try to sue me to get custody. She came by yesterday evening when Charly and I were having dinner in the hallway and started threatening me."

"Charly!" Angela snaps at me. "You saw Jamie's ex-wife and you didn't even tell me? What did she look like? Was she hot?"

"Kind of," I admit, while Jamie rolls his eyes.

"Who does she look like?" Angela asks. "I mean, like, what celebrity?"

I can't think of any celebrity that Karen resembled. Actually, it's sort of hard to think of any celebrities in general. Finally, I say, "Morticia Addams."

Angela bursts out laughing, while Jamie shakes his head. "That's low, Charly," he says, although he's smiling. "Really low."

"She was also really young," I add. "I mean, *really* young."

"So you like them young, do you, Mr. Knox?" Angela teases him. "Very interesting…"

Jamie groans. "She's twenty-eight years old, you idiots."

"Suuuuure she is," Angela snorts. "So tell me, who's hotter: Morticia or Charly?"

Jamie's face turns almost as red as it did last night. "Angie, quit it. Anyway, I can't even think about Karen that way anymore. She's evil."

Angela grins at him. "I take it that you and your ex-wife are not on good terms."

Jamie winces. "She's not my ex-wife... we were never married. We were never even dating, not really. We just hooked up a bunch of times before I realized she was an alcoholic and a drug addict."

"That's what you get for picking up women at your bar," Angela says with a wink.

Jamie rolls his eyes. "Yeah, thanks for the tip, Angie."

"So I guess it wasn't a planned pregnancy?" Angela says.

Jamie snorts. "Are you kidding? I didn't even realize she was pregnant until a year and a half later when I got slapped with a paternity suit."

"Ouch," she says.

"Yeah, it wasn't great," he sighs. "Actually, it completely messed up my life at the time. I was living with a woman and that fell apart. She didn't like that I had a kid she never knew about or the fact that I wanted to be part of his life. But I was adamant about that. I mean, I didn't want to have a son that I didn't even *know*. So we worked it out that Karen had custody, but I got visitation rights."

"So what happened to make you hate her so much?" Angela asks the question I've been dying to know the answer to.

"I came in one day to pick Sam up," Jamie recalls. "I found him toddling around the floor with uncapped needles lying around. Karen was unconscious in the bathroom. I called the police, and she ended up going to some inpatient drug rehab program. And I got full custody."

"So you had sole custody of your son for the last five years?" Angela asks him. "Wow, I bet your social life sucks."

He hesitates. "Okay, yes, it does. I mean, it *did*. But that's not the most important thing. I'm not about to compromise Sam's safety. She's been wanting joint custody for the last year claiming she's clean, but I don't buy it. So I've been fighting her."

"Does Sam like her?" I ask him.

"Well, yeah, of course he does," he says. "She's his mom…"

Jamie trails off then, looking into the distance. He bites his lip.

"Does she have proof that she's clean now?" Angela asks him.

Jamie shakes his head. "Yes, she does. But… I mean, this is my kid we're talking about. Even if she's sober now, what if she doesn't stay that way?"

"Or what if she falls down a flight of stairs and cracks her head open?" Angela retorts.

Jamie glares at her. "You know what, Angie? You're being really annoying. Why can't you just blindly be pissed off on my behalf?"

Angela shrugs. "I speak the truth. If you don't want to hear it, then don't listen."

"I thought she was really just way too skinny, Jamie," I volunteer. "I bet she gives really uncomfortable hugs. Sam probably won't like her as much as you."

Jamie's face relaxes, and he smiles at me. "Thanks, Charly. I knew I could count on you to be on my side."

He seems much more upbeat after that, until the next time he walks, when he practically falls flat on his face.

Chapter 36
Four and a Half Months After

Have you ever heard of a game called Taboo?

We play it in Thinking Skills Group today. I sort of remember playing this many years ago. Each person gets a card, and that card has a word on it that you have to make the other players guess. Pretty simple, as long as you don't have brain damage. Which, of course, we all do.

"It's your turn, Charly," Amy tells me.

She hands me the box of cards, and I select one with my right hand. The word at the top is "clown." I suddenly feel a little bit confused about the rules of this game.

"You want the others to guess the word at the top," Amy says to me when she notices my hesitation. "And you can't use any of the five words at the bottom."

"Okay," I say.

I stare at the word "clown," thinking about it for a minute.

"Charly?" Amy says. "Go ahead."

Obviously, I'm taking too long.

"This kind of person wears a lot of white make-up on his face," I say. "He also has a red nose and is in the circus.

Also, the Joker and Ronald McDonald are this kind of person."

"It's a clown!" Helga cries out excitedly.

"That wasn't very hard," Dr. Vincent complains.

Amy sighs. "Charly, you weren't supposed to use any of the words at the bottom, but you used *all* the words at the bottom."

"I thought that was what I was supposed to do," I say, frowning.

Amy just shakes her head. "Helga, why don't you have a turn?"

Helga takes the box of cards and discards at least five of them before she settles on a card.

"Okay," Helga says. "This is something that happens to women at some point in their lives, but it might not be a good thing."

"A stroke," Angela speaks up. She laughs at her own joke.

"Her period?" I guess.

"Oooh, I know," Helga says. "When it happens, she has a big party and wears a white dress."

"A wedding," Dr. Vincent says quickly.

"Helga," Amy says gently. "You used one of the words that was taboo."

Helga frowns and throws the card down. "I don't like this game," she says. "It's too hard."

"I don't like it either," Dr. Vincent chimes in. "I'd rather try to figure out who shot Charly in the head."

So would I.

"Dr. Vincent," Amy says patiently. "I told you that we're not going to talk about that. We don't want to traumatize Charly."

"It won't traumatize me," I say. "I want to know more than anyone else who shot me in the head."

Plus it's way easier than playing Taboo.

"Do you remember any more of your dream, Charly?" Dr. Vincent asks me.

I close my eyes. I can see the living room of my old apartment. I can hear that voice over my head: "You deserve this."

It's so familiar. If only I could see the person on the left. Stupid brain.

"It was a man," I say. "I know that much. If he'd only move to my right side, I could see him."

"Maybe in the dream, you could ask him to move?" Helga suggests.

"And while you're at it," Angela says, "You can ask him not to shoot you."

"Alright," Amy says, placing the box of cards resolutely in front of Dr. Vincent. "We need to get back to the game."

I close my eyes again, trying so hard to remember. I'm worried that part of my brain is simply gone and I'll never remember.

CHAPTER 37
Four and a Half Months After

Dr. Foster is the psychologist here. That means he's supposed to talk to us about our feelings. Even though it's his job, I'm not sure he's particularly good at it. I probably talked to Dr. Foster half a dozen times, but I've never felt like opening up to him. Maybe it's not his fault though. Maybe it's me.

Today we are having a group talk therapy session in the gym. The group is called "stroke group," even though I didn't actually have a stroke. It currently consists of only three people: me, Angela, and a young guy named Alex. The three of us each sit in wheelchairs, although I know I've seen Alex walk without support.

I remember when Alex came in, Angela whispered to me that he had a stroke from doing too many drugs. Looking at him now, I believe it. He keeps fidgeting in his seat, running a shaky hand through his long dark hair. His skinny arms are covered in tattoos—literally, covered. There's hardly a millimeter of un-inked skin. He looks like he'd rather be anywhere but here, which is something I can certainly sympathize with.

"Why don't we begin?" Dr. Foster suggests. He sits facing the three of us, perched in an armchair, as a psychologist should. He's mastered that part, at least.

"Could I have a drink of water first?" Alex asks.

"Certainly," Dr. Foster says, rising from his chair.

"Don't," Angela warns him in her smoky voice. "It's a trick. He can't have water."

"Bitch," Alex hisses at Angela.

Dr. Foster frowns at Alex. He rises out of his seat and checks the tag hanging from the back of one of the handrails of his wheelchair. He shakes his head. "She's right, Alex. You're on water restriction because of your blood sodium level. I can't get you water."

"But I'm thirsty!" he nearly yells.

Alex's face turns bright red. He looks like he might leap out of his chair and start sucking the saliva out of our mouths.

"You need to focus on other things besides being thirsty," Dr. Foster advises him.

Alex squares his jaw. "I'm only allowed one liter of fluid per day," he says. "Do you know how much one liter of fluid is?" He doesn't wait for an answer. "Neither do I, because this is *America* and we don't use the metric system here. But let me tell you something, it's not much."

"I understand," Dr. Foster says. He looks at Angela and me. We don't seem nearly as thirsty. "Maybe it would be better to begin with someone else today. Angela, how are you feeling today?"

"Super," Angela replies, rolling her eyes.

Dr. Foster amps up his caring shrink face. "Anything in particular bothering you?"

Angela shrugs. "Just… you know, thinking about the future."

I wait for Dr. Foster to prompt her, but he doesn't. He just looks at her, waiting. Angela doesn't seem to be taking the bait though.

"While we're waiting for her to talk," Alex says, "can I get some water?"

He leans forward eagerly in his wheelchair. Dr. Foster shakes his head at him and he falls back dejectedly.

"My boyfriend came to visit yesterday," Angela finally says. "Happy?"

I saw Angela's significant other during lunchtime yesterday. He had a mullet and dirt ground into his fingernails. But Angela's face really lit up when she saw him. I don't think I've ever seen her that happy.

"How long have the two of you been together?" Dr. Foster asks.

"Twelve years."

"That's a long time," he comments. "Longer than a lot of marriages."

"Longer than I've gone without having water," Alex throws in.

"*Anyway*," Angela says, shooting Alex a look. "Bobby told me that he thinks I should come home from here, and he'll take care of me."

Dr. Foster raises his eyebrows. "And what's wrong with that?"

Angela gives him a look like he's an idiot. "Bobby is my *man*. He's not going to still want me if he's helping me on the toilet."

"And what's the alternative?"

Angela shrugs. "I guess there isn't any. I don't have anyone else."

It's hard to feel sorry for Angela. She might not have anyone besides Bobby, but I would kill to have even one person who would be willing to take me home and take care of me. I have a husband, apparently, but he seems to have absolutely no interest in me. And it's entirely possible that he was the one who put me here in the first place.

Dr. Foster pushes his spectacles up his nose. "So if Bobby were the one who had a stroke, you wouldn't help him?"

"Of course I would," Angela says, shaking her head. She frowns at him. "You're twisting my words, Doc."

"Listen, Angela," Alex says. "If somebody cared about me enough to get me some water, I wouldn't start thinking about it too much and wondering how it would work out. I would just take the water, you know what I'm saying?"

"You're saying that I should let him help me," Angela acknowledges.

"No!" Alex barks at her. "I'm saying that nobody cares about me enough to get me some goddamn water!"

With those words, Alex leaps out of his wheelchair. There is a sink for hygiene in the corner of the room, and before Dr. Foster can stop him, he turns the sink on and sticks his face underneath, his tongue hanging out, lapping up the precious water.

It takes three people to get him away from that sink.

———

I'm sure if you gave Valerie a choice between dressing me and dressing a corpse, she'd pick the corpse. Even a corpse that was stiff and decomposing. I bet she wouldn't even have to think it through before deciding.

I'm not sure how the simple act of putting on a shirt has turned into such a battle. Basically, it's Valerie versus My Body. And while Valerie always wins, My Body definitely puts up a valiant effort.

"Stop *pushing* me," Valerie says through her teeth as she fights to get my right arm through the shirt sleeve. That's my good arm, so it should be easy. But it isn't.

My mother is watching. She frowns at the site of our struggle at the edge of my bed. "Why does she always lean so much to the left when she sits up?"

Valerie looks relieved to temporarily abandon her quest to put on my shirt. "She doesn't know where her midline is," she explains. "When she's tilted to the left, she thinks she's sitting upright."

Mom squints at me. "Charly, do you think you're sitting up straight?"

"Yes," I admit. Even though I know it's the wrong answer.

"Jesus," my mother says.

"So what happens," Valerie continues, "is whenever I try to correct her by moving her to the right, she feels like she's tilted to the right and is going to fall, and she starts pushing me with her good arm so that she can move back to the left."

Mom shakes her head. "How do you fix that?"

"Mirrors can sometimes help," Valerie says. "The idea is that if she sees herself in the mirror, she'll realize that she's tilted to one side. But her vision is so bad on the left side, it doesn't help her very much."

"So what else can we do?"

Valerie shrugs. "Hope that her brain heals."

Well, that doesn't seem to be happening anytime soon.

As Valerie continues to dress me, I tell myself over and over again that I am not going to fall to the right side. Even if I feel that way, I know that I am really sitting up straight. But it's very hard not to believe in your own sense of balance.

"Charly, stop pushing me!"

And the battle continues…

CHAPTER 38
Nine Months Before

I try to run when Clark isn't around. I know it sounds silly, but I don't want my husband to see (and smell) me when I'm all hot and sweaty. Yes, I know I get hot and sweaty during other activities. But I can't really do anything about that.

I get back to my apartment from a five mile run, feeling high on adrenaline. My knee is completely better. I could have run ten miles, except I wanted time to doll myself up before Clark got back from the office.

Don't tell my mother, but I went running at Central Park. She hates it when I run there—she's convinced I'll almost certainly be raped and murdered. But seriously, what's the point of living near this amazing park if I can't run there? I stick to more crowded paths, for the most part. Even though it's much nicer to run in solitude.

Before heading upstairs, I stop to check the mail. It's the usual mix of bills, medical mail, and junk mail. Honestly, I don't mind spam in my email, but junk mail seems like just a horrible waste of trees. It makes me sad. Medical mail is the worst though. A large bulk of it is journals. I honestly don't understand how I receive so many medical journals, since I have no recollection of requesting any of them. They end up in a huge pile on my coffee table, making me feel guilty about the fact that I never, ever read them until I crack and throw them all out. And then there are the invitations to conferences and other continuing medical education activities—I swear, I could be traveling three hundred and sixty-five days of the year and not manage to go to half of those conferences.

And finally: insurance. The American Medical Association wants more than anything in the world for me to have good life and disability insurance.

In the stack of mail, there's only one item I can't identify, which is an envelope with no return address. My name and address have been typed in. Intriguing. Is it possible that I've gotten one piece of interesting mail?

I rip open the envelope right in the mail room. I pull out a torn sheet of typewritten paper. I scan the writing and realize it's a divorce decree.

And my stomach sinks.

I grab my mail and head upstairs, shaking in spite of the sweat I worked up during my run. I ride up in the elevator, willing it to make it upstairs before my legs give out from under me.

When I get to the apartment, I'm relieved to see that Clark is home early. He's sitting on the couch, watching television, when he's *supposed* to be working on an upcoming case, but I'm too upset right now to be annoyed at him.

"Clark," I say.

Clark looks up at me and grins. "Hey, there. You look all cute and sweaty."

I ignore his remark and plop down next to him on the couch. "Look what I got in the mail."

Clark takes the torn piece of paper from me and studies it for a minute. "I don't get it," he finally says. "It's a divorce paper."

"Right," I say. "And look at the names."

"Kyle Barry and Regina Barry," he reads. He shrugs. "I have no idea who they are."

Right. I don't suppose he would. "Remember that day you came to my clinic and that guy was threatening me?" I say.

"Of course," Clark says, brightening. "I saved you, remember?"

"This is him," I say. "Kyle Barry. He was threatening me because he thought his wife was going to leave him because I cured her psoriasis. And I guess she did."

Clark looks down at the paper again. "So… I don't get it. Why would he send you this? Do you think it's a threat or something?"

"Maybe…" I shiver and hug myself.

"It *is* kind of creepy," Clark admits. "Do you think we should call the police?"

"And tell them what?" I say. "That I got a ripped divorce paper in the mail? It's not like it's got a threat written on it. Or it's covered in blood."

"Do you want me to call this Barry guy?" Clark offers.

"No!" I yelp. "God, no. That will just make it worse."

Clark drops the paper down on the couch between us. I slide away, afraid to even let it touch me.

"I think he's just trying to scare you," Clark says. "He's a dick, and he wants to freak you out. And it's obviously working."

He's right.

"If you don't want to call the police, I think you should try to forget about it," Clark says. "This guy's all talk. Seriously."

"Okay," I say quietly.

Clark gives me a pointed look. "Charlotte, you don't look like you're going to forget all about it."

I glance down at the ripped paper and remember how frightened I felt when I was face to face with Kyle Barry. But then again, if he were actually going to hurt me, he probably wouldn't send me a letter to warn me about it.

Would he?

"I'll be fine," I say.

CHAPTER 39
Nine Months Before

When I get home from work, Clark is sitting in his usual spot on the couch, watching *Modern Family* in jeans and a T-shirt. He glances up when I walk into the living room, then reaches for the remote to shut off the television. Which he actually almost never does. I wonder what the special occasion is where I get priority over the TV.

"Hey," Clark says. He's grinning at me. "I'm glad you're home. I want to show you something."

Sounds like a present. Is it an anniversary I'm not aware of? I smile back at him. "Sure."

Clark hops off the couch, and heads for my desk, which is in the corner of the living room. Kitty even emerges from her current hiding place to see what all the fuss is about. Kitty and I watch as Clark slides open the top drawer, then pulls out the contents. I've never seen one before in real life, so it takes me a minute to recognize what he's holding as a gun.

I almost faint. Is he freaking *kidding* me?

"You bought a *gun*?" I almost scream at him. Kitty hisses in Clark's general direction. She's totally on my side.

"Yeah!" Clark is bouncing on his heels, excited about the deadly weapon he's introduced into our home. "It's a GLOCK 19. The guy at the gun store told me it's a good starter gun."

Starter gun? Does that mean he thinks there will be *future* guns?

"Why did you buy a gun, for Christ's sake?" I'm still almost screaming.

"Well, you seemed so worried about that threatening letter you got the other day," Clark says. "I thought this would reassure you. To have some protection in the house."

"This does *not* reassure me," I say. "You know that having a gun in the house puts members of the household at higher risk for being shot themselves, right?"

Clark rolls his eyes. "It's not like we're a couple of redneck idiots. We'll be careful."

I look over at the weapon in his hand. It looks so *real*—so much like a gun. Which I guess makes sense because that's what it is. It's black and has a trigger and everything.

"Honestly," Clark says, "I can't believe you never bought a gun yourself. I mean, you're a single woman, living all alone right by the park. You don't even have a doorman. You really ought to have a weapon."

"I have knives."

Clark raises his eyebrows. "You really think you'd stand a chance during a break-in with a *knife*?"

I fold my arms across my chest. "Clark, I'm *not* shooting anyone. I don't even know how."

He shrugs. "It's easy. You just point the business end at the person you want to shoot, and pull the trigger. It's not brain surgery." He grins. "Or dermatology."

I don't return his smile. "You know, that drawer doesn't even lock."

"So we'll get a lock," Clark says. "It's not like we have a kid who's going to stumble across the gun."

"What about Kitty?"

Clark stares at me. "Are you saying you think your *cat* is going to open your desk drawer, take the gun out, and accidentally shoot us?"

When he says it that way, it doesn't seem incredibly likely.

"Look," Clark sighs, "you didn't want to go to the police when you got that threatening letter. I'm just trying to help here." He pauses. "I think you need to give the gun a chance."

"Fine," I say.

I am getting rid of that gun. As soon as I figure out how to dispose of a gun and work up the nerve to actually touch it, that gun is gone.

CHAPTER 40
Five Months After

One of the buttons on my shirt has inexplicably come undone in the process of getting cleaned up from lunch. It's possible that my mother snagged her finger on it as she was brushing food from my shirt. It's also entirely possible that the button was never done in the first place. I can't say I'd notice for sure if I've had my shirt hanging open the entire day. It seems very obvious now though, but at least my mother and I are alone in my room.

Buttons are a challenge for me, especially the small kind that's on my shirt. Have you ever tried doing up a very small button with only one hand? It's not easy. I can do it, but it could take me fifteen or twenty minutes.

Unfortunately, my mother isn't that much better at it. She has arthritis in her fingers, so helping me with my buttons is both challenging and sometimes painful for her.

We both look down at my open button. I think we're both trying to decide if it's worth it. Finally, my mother sighs, and starts trying to do the button for me. It takes her a few minutes, but she gets it closed.

"Mom," I say. "I need to use the bathroom."

"*Now*?" she asks me.

I shouldn't have to dignify that with a response. She knows when I say I need the bathroom, it always means *now*. Like, immediately. This is something I have struggled with the entire time I've been here. They offer me the bathroom every two hours, but a lot of the time I don't need to go. But when I get the urge, I've got five minutes to get to the bathroom. Maybe ten.

That's why I still have to wear briefs. Because unless I'm getting therapy at the moment, it's pretty challenging for a nurse to make it inside and help me to the bathroom before I lose control.

If I were a man, it would be so easy. They all just have these little jugs that they pee in.

"Yes," I say. "Now."

My mother gets up to go find a nurse, and now the countdown has started. I have a feeling that she's not going to find anyone in time. It's the change of shift right now, so all the nurses are busy.

Before my mother can get out of the room, she stops short at the sight of a figure standing at the door entrance way. There is a scary looking man with a shiny bald skull wearing a black suit with a dark shirt and a black tie. My breath catches in my throat at the sight of him.

"Detective Simpson," my mother says, looking surprised. "What are you doing here?"

This man is a policeman. Maybe this has something to do with who shot me. I feel a shiver go through my body.

"I wanted to talk to Charlotte," Detective Simpson says. "Actually, both of you." He pauses. "We think we have the guy who shot you, Charlotte."

Is he serious? After all this time, they really have him? How is that possible?

I shiver again, thinking about the ominous voice coming from my left side. *You deserve this.* Maybe I don't want to know who shot me.

No, of course I do. I just can't believe they caught him. It doesn't seem possible.

My mother's eyes widen. She frowns and the crease between her eyebrows deepens. "You... have a suspect?"

The detective nods. "Charlotte," he says. "Does the name Kyle Barry mean anything to you?"

Somehow it does. It tugs at the outside of my consciousness, like a word just on the tip of my tongue. "I think so..."

"He threatened you in the waiting room at your office," Detective Simpson says. "It was quite a long time ago, but one of the receptionists at your clinic suddenly remembered him. We thought it was a long shot, but we showed his picture to your neighbors, and one of them identified him as someone they had seen in the building. Also, he used to work as a locksmith, which explains how he got through Charlotte's locks."

"Is that all you have?" my mother asked. "Seems a little... what's that word they use in law shows? Circumstantial."

The detective smiles dimly. "Yes, I would have agreed. But there were a few unidentified partial prints in

Charlotte's apartment, and they matched up to Barry's. Including one on the gun itself, which had been wiped down."

"He sent me a threatening letter," I say suddenly. "I remember."

"Right," Detective Simpson says. "Your husband mentioned a letter that he said was sort of threatening and that's why he bought the gun. But he couldn't remember the name on it or find the original. So we didn't have much to go on."

"I threw it out," I admit. "It... got me really scared."

"Anyway," he says, "he was actually pretty hard to track down—he had traveled to another state. Clearly, he was hiding. When we confronted him with the evidence, he broke down and confessed to everything."

"Wow," my mother murmurs.

"The only thing we're missing," the detective says, "is a positive ID from Charlotte. I was hoping you would allow me to show her a picture..."

"She doesn't remember what happened, Detective," my mother snaps. "I'd rather you didn't upset her."

"It's okay," I speak up. "I... I'd like to see."

My mother just shakes her head. Detective Simpson advances toward me, and despite the fact that I gave him permission to do so, I flinch self-consciously. He smiles at me. "It's okay, Charlotte," he says. "This will only take a few minutes."

I just stare at him.

His eyes soften. "You're looking very well. I'm glad you're feeling better than the last time I saw you."

I nod.

Detective Simpson reaches into his jacket, and for a second I'm certain he's going to pull out a gun. In that second, whatever small bit of control I had over my bladder vanishes. I feel the warmth spreading across my groin. I know I have to say something, but I can't in front of this stranger. I'll just have to wait and get cleaned up later.

Instead of a gun, he pulls out a small photo album. He places it down on the tray in front of me. "Can I show you the pictures, Charlotte?"

I nod again.

He shows me a book of faces. Male faces, men who look scary, like thugs. They have scary-looking eyes and scars, and noses that look like they might have been broken. I shudder with each photo I look at.

"I know this is probably hard for you," Detective Simpson says to me. "But I want you to try your best to identify the man who shot you."

"But I don't remember it," I protest.

Detective Simpson frowns, but keeps turning the pages. "Do your best."

I turn through the pages, looking at photo after photo of men staring back at me. Wide noses, small noses, large foreheads, thick eyebrows. Blue eyes, hazel eyes, brown eyes...

Brown eyes.

For a moment, I'm no longer in my hospital room. I'm back at my apartment. I jiggle my keys in the lock, and then open the door. And then I see him in my living room. Dressed in casual clothes that would've gotten my unobservant neighbors to hold the door open to let him in. He's sitting at my desk, his face gleaming with sweat, his bald head shimmering under the lights I flicked on when I entered. He smiles at me. *Hi, Dr. McKenna*, he hisses. *Remember me?*

And then I see the gun pointed at my face.

I feel a cold sensation come over me. I can still see Kyle Barry's beady brown eyes staring at me, biting into me. I look down at my hands and I see that they have started trembling. Bile rises up in my throat, and I retch.

"Charly!" my mother gasps. "Are you all right?"

"It was him," I manage, placing my hand on the picture of the bald, burly man in the photo. "He's the one who shot me."

"That's Kyle Barry," the detective confirms.

They've got him. After all this time, they've got the bastard that shot me. And with that realization, I throw up all over the detective's photo album.

CHAPTER 41
Five Months After

Today I have a family meeting scheduled to discuss the future.

My mother and I are meeting with Dr. Greenberg and my therapists to figure out What Will Happen to Charly. I am terrified, to say the least. I know I haven't done as well as everyone hoped, and I can't even imagine my mother taking care of me by herself. She can't even help me to the bathroom on her own. So my options are limited.

We're having the meeting in a small conference room just outside the rehab unit. My nurse brings me outside the room to wait for everyone to arrive. I do my best to sit patiently in my wheelchair. I start feeling restless, but I've learned from experience that if I move too much or start playing with the belt on my lap, an alarm will go off. If the alarm goes off, that means I can't be trusted alone. And more than anything, I want everyone to trust me to be alone.

So I just mostly play with the hem of my sweatshirt. It's an old shirt that I've had since college, and all the elastic in it is stretched out. It's not exactly what you'd call attractive, but it's comfortable, and it zips up, so it's easy to get on while wearing my helmet. There's a little hole at the bottom of it, and I can easily fit my finger inside.

"Hello, Charlotte," a voice says from behind me.

I turn my wheelchair around, and immediately, I get this feeling like I was punched in the chest. This time, I can easily recognize the incredibly handsome man standing in front of me. It's Clark, my husband.

"Hi," I say in a hoarse voice.

"It's really good to finally see you again," he says softly.

"Yes," I manage.

"I missed you," he says.

"Yes," I say again. Then I add, "I missed you too."

Have I really missed him though? Or better question, has he really missed me?

"You look great," he says.

I don't look great. By any definition of the word "great," I don't look great. I am dressed in sweatpants and a sweatshirt that are least two sizes too big, and I have a giant helmet perched on my skull. I'm pretty sure I also have a big white splint on my left hand, but I'm not sure because I don't know where my left hand is.

Clark really does look great though. I always forget how handsome he is. His chestnut hair is so thick and luxurious, I can almost feel my fingers running through it. His eyes are as blue as the waters of Aruba. Even though he's just wearing a casual plaid shirt and jeans, they fit him perfectly.

"Thank you," I say.

"Your voice is getting closer to normal," he says.

I squeeze my knee with my right hand. What does *that* mean? I feel the sweat break out in the back of my neck. "What's wrong with my voice?" I blurt out.

"Oh," Clark says with a shrug. "The last time I saw you, your speech was all slurred. But it's much better now. And you put back on all the weight you lost. And then some."

Oh my God, is he telling me that I've gotten *fat*? Have I? It does seem like my clothes have been getting tighter recently. And the nutritionist paid me a visit yesterday, which I thought was weird. But Jamie and Angela never said anything about it. Not that I would've expected them to.

"What are you doing here?" I ask him.

Clark seems surprised. "I'm here for the family meeting." He winks at me. "I'm your family, am I not?"

"Right," I say. I still feel confused about the whole thing. Why is Clark here today? Who asked him to come?

I start to ask him, but then I suddenly feel self-conscious about my speech. And then my mom and the therapists show up, and we all go into the room together. I guess I'll figure it all out eventually.

Dr. Greenberg sits at the head of the table in the conference room, and I'm next to him, with my mother beside me, and Clark across from me. Amy, my speech therapist; Valerie, my occupational therapist; and Natalie, my physical therapist are sitting at the other end of the table. All three of them keep casting curious looks at

Clark, I guess because they haven't seen him before. Amy seems to be shooting him the stink eye.

"Before we begin," Clark says to the people around the table, "I just want to introduce myself. My name is Clark Douglas, and I'm Charlotte's husband. I haven't been around much because my work has kept me busy, but from now on, I'm going to be around a lot more."

"We certainly appreciate that, Mr. Douglas," Dr. Greenberg says. His tie has pictures of balloons on it, which is somehow comforting to me. He clears his throat. "I'd like to start the meeting by thanking everyone for showing up. I know we all care about Charly very much, and want the best for her."

Everyone in the room nods in agreement. My mother puts her hand on my right hand, and gives me a squeeze.

"I'd also like to say," Dr. Greenberg continues, "that Charly has made huge progress since she's been here. I think we all remember what she was like when she first was admitted to the hospital."

Everyone remembers except me. And maybe Clark, since he wasn't around.

"However," Dr. Greenberg goes on, "at this point, we are beginning to feel that Charly's progress is slowing down, and her insurance will not continue to cover her stay here."

I look over at Amy, who is shaking her head. "It's not right," she says. "Charly is doing great with me. She's getting better at reading, and her speech is so much better than it was before."

"I agree," Clark says eagerly. I guess he's glad to have something to contribute. "She sounds light-years better than last time I saw her." He looks at Amy and winks at her. "You've done a wonderful job."

Amy gives Clark a look. "Thank you," she says quietly.

"Charly is *not* making great progress on my end," Valerie speaks up. "Her neglect of the left side is really a huge barrier and it hasn't improved at all. She completely ignores her left side when she's dressing and bathing herself. She fights me when I try to dress her. Basically, I have to do all the work and then some. And now her muscles are getting tighter on the left side, which makes it just that much harder."

Dr. Greenberg nods, not looking surprised at all. I know Valerie thought that I wasn't doing a good job, but to hear her say it in front of everything makes me feel terrible. It sounds like she's talking about some sort of bratty child. It's not like I can help what my stupid body can and can't do.

"What do you think, Natalie?" Dr. Greenberg says to my physical therapist.

"I have to agree with Valerie," Natalie says. She sounds sadder about it than Valerie did. "As she said, the left neglect really makes things hard. Walking is really difficult for her, because she doesn't have any control over her left leg. She's definitely going to be using her wheelchair when she leaves here as her primary mode of mobility. And even that she has trouble with. She isn't able to use her left arm to wheel the chair at all."

"What about a power wheelchair?" Dr. Greenberg suggests.

"Oh God," Natalie says. "That would be a disaster. She's already bumping into things in the manual wheelchair. She'd be dangerous in a power wheelchair. She's better off in the manual wheelchair and letting somebody else push her."

"And what about using the bathroom?" Dr. Greenberg asks Valerie.

Valerie shakes her head. "She can't do it on her own. At all. Like, not any part of it. She needs somebody to help her move to the toilet. She doesn't even wash her hands properly afterwards."

Dr. Greenberg looks thoughtful. "And Amy," he says. "Do you think that Charly can be left alone when she gets home?"

Amy doesn't meet my eyes. "No. She can't. Not for more than a few minutes."

Despite the fact that Amy has been my biggest cheerleader, that comment hurts me most of all. I've tried so hard to prove to everyone that I could be alone safely. I can't believe she would say that.

It's not true. It's *not*.

Dr. Greenberg turns to my mother. "I think you can see, Mrs. McKenna," he says, "that Charlotte is going to need a great deal of help when she gets home. It's my understanding that you don't feel that you can provide that help."

My mother shakes her head. "I wish I could," she says, her voice trembling. "But I have arthritis and a bad back. I just... I can't..."

Dr. Greenberg nods. "It's all right, Mrs. McKenna. There are other options for Charly. We can use her disability insurance and savings to hire someone to help her, but my understanding is that it may be beyond your financial means. Alternately, we can look into a nursing home in the area."

I've been feeling increasingly sick through this meeting, and now, when Dr. Greenberg mentions a nursing home, it's like a hand tightening around my throat. "I don't want to go to a nursing home," I say. I'm scared that I'm about to cry. I don't want to cry in front of everyone here.

Everyone in the room is really quiet. It occurs to me that everybody knew about this except for me. Everyone knew that this was eventually going to happen, that I was going to end up in a nursing home. They've just been waiting to tell me about it, shielding me from the horrible inevitable truth.

"It won't be as bad as you think, Charly," Amy says. "You're still going to get physical therapy there. It would just be an hour or two instead of three hours a day. It really won't be that much different."

How could she say that? I'm going to be in a *nursing home*. And I'll probably be there for the rest of my life, because what exactly is going to change in the near future? I've been doing my best, and I'm just not getting better. Valerie said it all.

"Oh, Charly," my mother says, grabbing my hand in hers. "Please don't cry. I swear, I'll come visit you every day."

Dr. Greenberg magically produces a tissue from inside his pocket. He hands it to me and I wipe my eyes. Or at least, I wipe my right eye. I think maybe I get at my left eye too. Who knows? "It really is for the best," he says.

And then, when it seems like I couldn't feel any worse, Clark speaks up, "I'll take her home with me."

The room goes completely silent. Everybody is staring at Clark. I stop wiping my right eye so I can stare at him too.

Dr. Greenberg is the first to break the silence. "Excuse me?"

"I said I'll take her home," Clark says. He smiles crookedly. "She *is* my wife, after all. I don't know why you're all acting so surprised."

Amy glares at him. "You've never seen her in therapy. You have no idea what you're offering."

"She's my wife," Clark says again. "And I intend to take care of her while she's sick." He cocks his head to the side. "I think it was in our marriage vows or something."

Everyone in the room keeps staring at Clark. I can't believe this. Clark is going to take care of me. He's going to save me.

CHAPTER 42
Five Months After

There's a porch attached to the hospital where patients sometimes sit with their families. I haven't been there in a while, because it's been winter and it's just too cold. But today is the first really nice day of spring, and after Clark leaves, my mother suggests taking me there.

At first I'm not sure. I'm so comfortable in my own unit, around the people I know. I get scared at the thought of people passing by on the street, and maybe seeing me. But then my mother reassures me that the porch is invisible to passersby on the street. And it really is a beautiful day.

My mother wheels me to the porch, because I still haven't gotten the hang of wheeling my chair without bumping into the wall on the left side. I'm definitely better at it. But I'm still terrible. It's so frustrating when I think that I'm just heading straight, and then all of a sudden I slam into a wall.

When we get to the porch, I'm surprised to see that Jamie is already out there. His father is with him, and so is his son, Sam. I guess Jamie got over his embarrassment at the idea of Sam seeing him in the hospital. Sam seems so hyper, running back and forth across the porch, and then jumping back and forth across the porch on one foot. It makes me feel a little bit sad watching him somehow. I wish I could jump on one foot. I wonder if that's something I'll be able to do again. Probably not.

Jamie's face lights up when he sees me. "Hey, Charly," he says. "You remember my son, right?"

"Of course I do," I say. Although with my memory the way it is, it's entirely possible that I might not have remembered him. But I do.

"Daddy," Sam says, hopping between his feet. "Can we play catch?"

Jamie hesitates only a moment before he says, "You got a ball?"

Sam nods eagerly. "Yeah. Mommy bought me one this morning."

I expect that Jamie will fly into a rage at the mention of Karen like he did before. But he doesn't. He seems to completely take it in stride that Sam was visiting with his mother this morning.

"Okay," he says. "Let's play."

While Sam runs off to locate the ball in Mr. Knox's bag, Jamie leans in to talk to me quietly. "I'm letting Karen have a trial of visitation," he explains. "She's agreed to submit to random drug testing. If it goes okay, we can split custody."

"Wow," I say. "You seemed really angry at her. I didn't think you'd agree."

"Yeah…" He heaves a sigh. "I'm not thrilled about it. But… she *is* his mom, and… well, I think we can all agree that I could use some help right now."

Sam comes up with a white wiffle ball. I'm not particularly surprised that Jamie has a lot of trouble aiming the ball. His throws all seem to miss Sam by about two feet. Luckily, Sam doesn't seem to have too much of a problem with chasing down the ball. The kid has endless energy. It makes me worry that Jamie isn't going to be able to keep up with him after he gets out of here.

"You have the worst aim I've ever seen," I say to Jamie.

Jamie looks in my direction. He smiles. "Oh *really*? Well, I'd like to see you do better, Dr. McKenna."

I hold out my right hand, and Jamie places the ball inside. As he hands over the ball, his thumb rubs briefly against the side of my palm. At first I think it's probably an accident, but then he winks at me and I wonder.

"All right," Jamie says to Sam. "Charly is going to throw you the ball, and attempt to completely humiliate me by being awesome at it. Maybe you should back up."

He's teasing me. I can tell he doesn't think I'm going to be able to throw the ball very well. I draw back my arm, cock my wrist, and hurl the ball at Sam. Even though Sam isn't much better at catching the ball than his dad is at throwing it, the ball lands squarely in his hands.

Jamie raises his eyebrows at me. "Holy shit," he says. Then he glances at his son, and quickly says, "I mean, great throw."

"Charly played softball in high school and college," my mother speaks up. "She's always been a really great athlete." Although I can tell she seems a little surprised as well.

"Is that so?" Jamie asks. He actually looks pretty impressed.

"Apparently," I say with a modest shrug.

"Again!" Sam orders. He tosses the ball at me, but he's off by about a foot, and I'm terrible at catching things anyway. My depth perception is completely off.

We spend the better part of the next hour on the porch playing catch. It's the most fun I've had in a long time. Maybe years.

CHAPTER 43
Five Months After

"How did the meeting go yesterday?" Angela asks me during our Walking Group.

Jamie is taking his turn walking right now. He's doing way better now than he was before, when we both started in this group together. He can walk pretty well with the cane right now. He has to lean heavily on it, and sometimes he loses his balance so that Natalie has to catch him, but right now, he manages to make it all the way across the gym without a problem.

I'm jealous.

"It went well," I say. "Actually, my husband was there. I'm going to go home with him when I leave here."

Angela raises her eyebrows. "Your husband? Are you still with him?"

"Of course I'm still with him," I say.

Angela gives me a pointed look. "He hasn't been by here once the whole time I've known you."

I clear my throat. "We've had some problems. But I think we fixed them. Anyway, I want to go home with him."

Jamie falls back into his wheelchair just in time to hear the end of our conversation. I see a couple of beads of sweat on his forehead because it's still an effort for him to walk across the gym and back. He frowns at me. "Home with who?"

"My husband," I say when Angela is silent.

Jamie's eyes widen. "Your *husband*? But I thought that you and I…" His voice trails off. "I mean, I didn't even think you were with him anymore."

Humph.

"I don't know why everyone keeps saying that," I say. "I never said I wasn't with him."

"Then why doesn't he visit you?" Jamie asks, the volume of his voice now several notches higher. "He hasn't been here *once*, has he?"

"He *does* visit me," I say, even though it's not really true. "You just haven't seen him."

Jamie frowns, but he doesn't say anything else. I don't know why he cares anyway. Jamie and Angela are both going to walk out of here. I won't. They really shouldn't be judging me.

"Is this Walking Group?" a voice from behind me asks. "I'm looking for Charlotte."

I recognize Clark's voice before I even turn my head. He's dressed casually, in jeans and a T-shirt, and he looks so healthy compared with the rest of us. Angela turns to look at him, and her eyes start bugging out.

"Is that your husband?" she hisses at me, grabbing my arm. She shakes her head. "Charly, you never told me how hot he was!"

I shrug, but secretly I feel sort of pleased. I raise my right hand to wave at Clark. "I'm here," I say.

Clark glances awkwardly around the room then walks over to where I'm sitting. "Valerie told me to come fetch you," he explains.

"For what?"

"She wants to start teaching me how to take care of you," he says. He shrugs. "I guess they feel you need to leave here sooner rather than later."

"Okay," I say. A week ago, that would've really scared me. But now that I know I'm going home with my husband, it doesn't bother me nearly as much.

Clark seizes the handle of my chair and pushes me out of the gym, and down the hallway to my room. I am getting slightly better at pushing the chair myself, but it's a slow process, and half the time I bump into a wall. I don't want Clark to see me hitting the wall. So I just let him push me.

Valerie is waiting in my room. When I come in, the first thing she does is look down at her watch and roll her eyes. "Well," she says, "the only thing we have time for is to do a transfer, considering you're forty-five minutes late to our session."

I feel my cheeks get hot. "I am?"

"Not you," Valerie says. She's looking at Clark.

"I'm really sorry about that," he says. "Something really important came up."

Valerie just shakes her head.

The first thing Valerie demonstrates is how to transfer me out of the wheelchair into my bed. I can't really help with that, so it's lucky she's very strong. The first thing she does is remove the right armrest of my chair and both leg rests. Then she stands in front of me, with my knees between her knees, bracing me. She bends forward, and I grab onto her shoulder with my right hand, and she puts my left hand on her shoulder. She grabs onto my pants then basically lifts me out of the chair and onto the bed. I can't really help at all, aside from hanging onto her with my right hand.

Once I'm sitting on the bed, I feel like I'm upright, but I suspect that I might be leaning to the left by the way Valerie keeps holding on to me. She helps me get back into a lying down position. And then we're done.

"Easy as pie," Valerie says. Except I think she might be being sarcastic, because there's a line of sweat at the top of her forehead. Plus Valerie is sarcastic a lot. I can only tell sometimes.

Valerie gets me back into the wheelchair, then she steps aside to let Clark have a turn doing the transfer. He looks really nervous, but like he always does when he's nervous, he acts extremely confident, like he's done this a million times before.

Clark braces my knees with his like Valerie did, then I put my right hand on his shoulder. His shoulder feels so broad and strong compared with Valerie's. It makes something stir inside me, something long forgotten. I check Clark's face, to see if maybe he's feeling the same way, but he's just looking down at my lap.

I feel Clark's fingers lace into the waistband of my sweatpants. "Okay, now lift," Valerie instructs him.

I feel myself rising into the air, but I don't feel secure like the way I did when Valerie was lifting me. I feel anxious, like he might drop me. I tighten my grip on his shoulder, but at the same time, I feel my left arm slide off him.

"You have to brace her," Valerie says.

"I'm doing it," Clark insists.

I feel myself falling to the left side, and my heart starts to pound as I realize there's nothing I can do to prevent this from happening. But fortunately, Valerie is there to support me, and I make it to the bed without incident.

"If you don't brace her," Valerie says, "you're going to drop her."

"I *was* bracing her," Clark says.

Valerie squints at him. "Are you seriously not aware that you almost dropped her?"

"We would've been fine."

Valerie sighs and shakes her head. They practice the transfer back to my chair, and then back to the bed again. The second time, Clark does much better. Or at least, he doesn't almost drop me.

"That's all we have time for today," Valerie says. She looks at him pointedly. "Next time, hopefully you can come on time."

Clark nods. "For sure."

Valerie nods back at him. She looks down at me, lying in bed. "Charly, you have another hour until your next therapy. Do you want to stay in bed?"

Despite the fact that Valerie and Clark did all the work, I feel exhausted. "Yes," I say.

"Okay," Valerie says. "Let me take your helmet off for you."

Valerie reaches down and undoes the strap under my chin. I feel a rush of relief as that heavy helmet lifts from my skull. I immediately reach up to scratch my head, but then remember I'm not supposed to and lower my hand again. If they see me scratching, Valerie will put the helmet back on.

I look over at Clark, who suddenly seems very pale under his tan. Actually, he is not so much pale as slightly green. "Charlotte," he gasps. "Your head... I didn't realize that it looked..."

"She's missing half her skull," Valerie says. "How did you *think* it looked?"

"I don't know," he mumbles. "I just thought..."

I see a few beads of sweat break out on his forehead. Then he whirls around and races in the direction of my bathroom. I hear him retching.

Valerie rolls her eyes at me. Usually she's rolling her eyes about me to someone else, so I like the change.

"Quite a gem you've got there," she comments before she spritzes her hands with alcohol and leaves the room.

Clark emerges from the bathroom a minute later, walking slightly unsteadily. He won't even look at me.

Somehow I think of when I showed Jamie my skull. He didn't seem fazed at all. But then again, his own head was covered in staples.

"Listen, Charlotte," Clark says. "I've got to go. But I'll be back tomorrow morning."

"You promise?" I ask him. My voice sounds tiny, like I'm five years old.

"I promise," Clark says firmly.

Then he gives me a little awkward wave. He doesn't try to hug me or kiss me, and it occurs to me that he hasn't done either of those things since I got hurt. He doesn't even seem to want to *touch* me unless he has to.

I watch my husband race out of the room as fast as he can go.

CHAPTER 44
Five Months After

Clark is supposed to come the next morning at eight a.m., and this time he's only ten minutes late. Valerie, fortunately, predicted this, and scheduled us for an extra fifteen minutes at the end. So really, as she explained, he's early. Except not really.

As soon as Valerie walked into the room, I asked her if she would put my helmet on. Even though I hate that helmet, I don't really want to be without it when Clark is here. I don't think I could bear it if he got that look on his face again

I'm still in bed when he arrives, which is part of the plan. Valerie is supposed to teach him how to help me get dressed. I'm not sure if "help" is exactly the right word though, considering I can't do any of the dressing process myself. Basically, she's teaching him how to dress me. That's more accurate.

Clark is wearing a T-shirt and jeans, and looks incredibly fit. He doesn't look like the sort of man who should be learning how to take care of his disabled wife. He looks like he ought to be out there on a surfboard or something with a fit blonde supermodel. Especially with the tan he's sporting.

I'm really lucky he's here for me.

"Okay," Clark says, rubbing his hands together. "What do we do?"

"We'll get her pants and socks on while she's in bed," Valerie says, "then we'll sit her up to put on her shirt."

Right now, I'm wearing a hospital gown, which is stained with the remains of my breakfast (oatmeal). I can't wait to get out of it. Valerie pulls back my blanket then hands my socks over to Clark to put them on. Once those are in place, Valerie starts lifting my gown up, but I stop her with my right hand.

"What's wrong, Charly?" Valerie asks.

So somehow I'd forgotten until this very moment that I was wearing a brief. I know, how could I forget, right? But I did. And the idea of my handsome, virile husband seeing me in what is (let's face it) essentially a diaper is too mortifying for words. He can't see me this way. He *can't*.

Except what am I supposed to say? Clark just volunteered to do all my care after I leave here. So how can I possibly get around this?

The answer is that I can't.

"Nothing," I mumble.

Valerie flips up my gown, revealing the blue plastic briefs underneath, secured in place with four pieces of tape. I can't even look at Clark. And just when I feel like I couldn't possibly feel any more humiliated, I hear Valerie announce, "This is wet. She needs to be changed."

Clark, who has apparently been playing Angry Birds on his phone this whole time or I don't know what, gasps, "She's wearing a *diaper*?"

Valerie frowns at him. "We prefer not to use that word. She's not an infant."

"But that's what it is…" Clark shakes his head. "She really needs that?"

"Obviously," Valerie replies impatiently. She clucks her tongue at me. "Charly, didn't you realize you were wet?"

"No, I didn't," I mumble. I wish I could crawl under the bed and just disappear. Why can't Clark just accept this and move on? Besides, if he's around me all the time to help me to the bathroom, I might not need the briefs when I get home.

Thankfully, Valerie changes me herself before instructing Clark on how to put on my pants. Sweatpants, that is. I wonder if I'll ever wear anything besides sweatpants. Maybe shorts. Maybe a skirt. Anything would be better than sweatpants. I really hate sweatpants.

Valerie helps me sit up on the bed. Since I'm already wearing my helmet, she's selected a zippered hoodie sweatshirt for me to wear. I can get my right arm through the sleeve easily, but the left is tricky. Valerie lets Clark struggle with it a bit, and I can hear him grunting on my left side.

"God, this arm is impossible," he mutters. "How do you do this every morning?"

"You get used to it," Valerie says.

"Couldn't we just leave her in the gown?"

"Sure," Valerie replied. "I mean, why bother ever changing her clothes at all? It's not like she's going anywhere important."

"Exactly," Clark says.

Even *I* realized she was being sarcastic that time. I'm pretty sure Clark completely missed it though.

Clark manages to get my arm through the sleeve, but he seems very put out by the whole thing. Honestly, I'm beginning to worry that Clark had no idea what he volunteered himself for.

I feel like he's one more revelation away from throwing up his hands and walking away forever.

———

In the afternoon, I have physical therapy with Natalie, and Clark sits in for that session as well. Lately, during our one-on-one sessions, Natalie and I have spent more time working on wheelchair mobility rather than walking, since I get to do walking during my group, and anyway, she's told me repeatedly that I'm mostly going to be using the wheelchair when I get home. But today, Natalie gets me up with my hemi-walker and starts walking me across the hallway.

"She's been doing much better with walking," Natalie tells Clark, after I've done about ten steps, with Natalie supporting me on my left side, and holding me up by the waistband of my pants. I feel like I can't control my left leg, but a lot of the times it just moves forward on its own volition. It's sort of weird. Other times, it doesn't budge, and Natalie has to nudge it forward.

"Yes, she's doing great," Clark says in this overly enthusiastic voice. The kind of voice you'd use to tell a five year old that their fingerpainting was a masterpiece.

After another ten steps, Natalie and I are both exhausted, so she asks Clark to fetch my chair, and I collapse into it.

"Obviously, she's going to mostly be using the wheelchair," Natalie says. "But this is great exercise."

Clark nods. "Sure…"

"Unfortunately," Natalie says, "her insurance will only pay for a wheelchair or a walker, not both. So we'll get the wheelchair paid for, and you'll have to pay for the walker out of pocket."

Clark frowns. "Why do we have to buy a walker at all?"

"I just explained to you…"

"Yeah, for exercise, right." Clark shakes his head. "So let me get this straight. I'm going to be getting her out of bed in the morning, bathing her, dressing her, helping her to the bathroom, making her food, giving her medication. And on top of that, you expect me to try to basically drag her across the room so she gets some 'exercise'?"

Natalie's lips form a straight line. "Exercise is incredibly important. For her bones, her general health—"

"Her general health?" Clark raises his eyebrows. "I think it's a little bit late to be worrying about that, don't you think? I mean, look at her."

I hate the way he's talking about me like I can't understand him, like I'm not sitting *right there*. I want to tell him that he's being a jerk, but the truth is, he has a good point. He *is* going to be doing a lot for me. And he's right that it does seem like a waste of time to be focusing on walking when it's not something I'm going to be doing a lot of.

Don't get me wrong, I love walking with Natalie. Even though I'm terrible at it, it makes me feel almost normal again even though I fully recognize that I don't look normal. But I have to admit, it's not entirely practical.

"Look," Clark says to Natalie. "I think it's great what you guys are doing for her here. But let's be realistic. At home, she's going to be in the wheelchair a hundred percent of the time. That's just the way it has to be." He looks down at me and smiles, "Charlotte, you're okay with that, aren't you?"

I force a smile to my lips. And I nod.

CHAPTER 45
Five Months After

The worst time to need the bathroom is during the nursing change of shift. It happens at eight in the morning and four in the afternoon. The change of shift means that the nurses are busy signing out to one another, too busy to take a patient to the bathroom. No matter how badly I have to go.

But it's not like I can control when I have to go.

At about a quarter after eight, I feel the urge come over me. Number two. I jam my thumb vigorously into the red call button, as if that would make a difference.

About ten minutes later, it's too late.

By now, I'm used to it. That's what the briefs are for, after all. No, I don't like being cleaned up after wetting myself or worse, but the nurses here are nice and don't make me feel bad about it. The only reason I care today is that Clark will be here any minute to practice dressing me with Valerie. I really would prefer if he didn't find me sitting in my own shit.

I know I should be practical. When we get home, Clark is going to be cleaning me up on a daily basis. But like I said, I'm certain once I get home the accidents will be less frequent. Clark is my husband. I want him to still feel attracted to me, not grossed out.

About five minutes after I relieve myself, Clark walks into the room with Valerie. Just my luck, it's the one day he's actually on time. They don't smell anything, but they will soon.

Clark is dressed casually as usual, in a T-shirt and jeans. But somehow, he looks especially handsome today. I can't help but notice. It reminds me about the fact that it's been a really long time since I've had sex. Hell, it's been a really long time since I've kissed a man. Or been physically close to a man who wasn't doing physical therapy on me.

I expect that at some point Clark and I will resume a more intimate relationship. I know that might take some time and adjusting though. I'm not going to push the issue. I can be patient.

"Okay," Valerie says, rubbing her hands together. "We're going to work on lower body dressing today. Sound good, Charly?"

Now might be a good time tell them about my accident. I should probably tell them, just to warn them. But I can't make myself say it. Especially considering how good Clark looks today.

Valerie takes my silence as a positive response. She pulls back the covers from my bare legs, and Clark winces. "Christ," he says. "Don't they have razors here, Charlotte?"

The truth is, until that second, I hadn't even realized that it had been months since I shaved my legs. It hadn't even occurred to me. There were so many other things to be embarrassed about besides a little hair on my legs. I didn't think I was *that* horribly hairy.

But now that I'm looking where Clark is looking, I can see he has a point.

"You're welcome to shave them," Valerie says.

Clark snorts. "No thank you."

Maybe I can get my mother to shave my legs.

And oh God, what about my eyebrows? I haven't had my eyebrows done in such a long time. They probably look terrible. And what about that one hair under my chin that I always have to pluck? That hair must be like six inches long by now! It's practically a ponytail.

My hair-related thoughts are interrupted by the stench that suddenly fills the room. And I remember that I have much worse things to be embarrassed about than a single hair.

It's horrible. Particularly horrible today, for some reason. Not that fecal matter ever smells *good*. But there is some sort of spectrum. And today is a bad day. Maybe it's something I ate.

"Oh my God!" Clark gasps, clenching his palm dramatically over his face like there is poisonous gas in the room. "What *is* that?"

"Charly," Valerie scolds me, shaking her head. "Why didn't you tell me you had an accident?"

"I didn't realize," I lie.

Valerie looks skeptical. "Seriously?"

I shrug.

Valerie shakes her head. "Well," she says thoughtfully, "it's a good opportunity for Clark to learn incontinence care." She turns to my husband. "Let's get her cleaned up."

Clark pales under his tan. "What? I don't want to do *that*."

Valerie puts her hands on her hips. "Mr. Douglas, if you can't get your wife cleaned up after she has an accident, how do you expect to take care of her?"

It's a really good question. A really, *really* good question.

Clark just stands there, open-mouthed, for a minute. Finally, his shoulders sag. "Okay," he says.

Valerie rolls me over and instructs Clark on how to get me cleaned up. I'm glad Clark is behind me so I don't have to see his face. I'm sure he's less than thrilled about the entire thing.

But he's doing it. That's love, I'll tell you. I feel bad that I ever doubted him.

When I am dressed and settled into my wheelchair, I can finally look Clark in the eyes again. Except I'm noticing he's having some trouble looking *me* in the eyes. He seems very focused on the whiteboard overlooking my bed.

"So," Clark says, more to Valerie than to me, "if we're all done, I really should get going."

"Would you like to sit in on Charly's Walking Group?" Valerie offers.

Although it's pretty obvious what his answer is going to be, I still feel disappointed when he shakes his head. "I really have to get going."

"That's okay," I say quickly, not wanting to let on how I'm feeling. My care is so high maintenance, the last thing I want to be is emotionally high maintenance.

I raise my head to look at him. This is the point when a normal husband would probably give his wife a kiss on the lips goodbye. But when Clark leans in, he just brushes his lips against my forehead. Like I'm a child or an elderly aunt.

I guess it will take time to get back to where we were. Good thing I've got plenty of time.

Chapter 46
Two Months Before

Back in the old days, a woman might discover her husband was cheating by finding lipstick on his collar while doing his laundry. Or maybe she'd smell an unfamiliar perfume on his clothing. Or she'd overhear him talking flirtatiously on the phone.

But this is the twenty-first century and I first start to suspect Clark of cheating because of a text message.

Usually I wake up at six in the morning and am out the door by seven, but yesterday, our morning clinic was pushed back due to some sort of carpet cleaning adventure, so I decided to sleep in until a luxurious eight o'clock. I woke up feeling deliciously well-rested, and only slightly resentful of a still-snoring Clark lying next to me in bed.

After I got out of the shower, I heard Clark's phone buzz with a text message. I swear, I wasn't trying to spy on him or anything. I just wanted to see if it was something important that I needed to wake him up for. I picked up his iPhone, still attached to the charger, and saw the message on the screen:

Is she gone yet?

There was no name attached to the number. And no further messages aside from that one.

I didn't pry any further. Well, I couldn't. Clark locks his phone and I don't know the code to unlock it. Otherwise, I'm pretty sure I would have scoured every message on his phone.

I never said a word about it to Clark, but I was distracted all day, thinking about that message. It was *all* I could think about. Maybe there was some benign reason somebody could be asking Clark if I had left the apartment yet, but in my head, I couldn't think of anything that made sense aside from a girlfriend on the side.

Bridget agreed to let me come over after I was done with work, and I was practically tearing my hair out by then. Bridget looked comparatively calm in her new uniform of ripped sweatpants and a T-shirt stained in baby food.

"Is she gone yet?" Bridget repeats, mulling over the phrase, while she opens a can of something she called "baby ravioli" for Chelsea.

"He's cheating on me, right?" I say.

"Not necessarily," Bridget says. "Maybe he's getting the apartment cleaned?"

"No," I say. "I'm the one who deals with the cleaning woman."

"Maybe he's planning a surprise party for you?" Bridget suggests.

I just look at her.

"Okay, fine," she sighs. She dumps the can of ravioli on Chelsea's tray. Chelsea picks up the slimy little noodles with her chubby fingers and shoves them in her mouth happily. "You really think Clark would cheat?"

I think back to Clark's revelation about having been fired over a year ago. "Yeah. I think he's definitely capable of it."

Bridget is silent for a minute, thinking. Finally, she says, "Hey, how do you know that 'she' even refers to you?"

I frown. "Who else would it be?"

Bridget shrugs. "It could be anyone. I mean, what if it has something to do with work? Like, maybe 'she' is a client? Or a judge?"

"Maybe," I say. "Or maybe 'she' is me and his girlfriend is texting him to see when she can come over."

"Maybe," Bridget agrees.

I feel like crying. How did my marriage fall apart so quickly? I should have known I wasn't capable of having a decent relationship with a guy. I should have just stuck with my instincts and stayed single forever.

"I'm such a loser!" I blurt out. "I can't even get my husband to be faithful for more than a few months!"

"Oh, Charly," Bridget sighs. She throws her arms around me, and pulls me into a hug. I've never been a huggy sort of girl, but I let her do it this one time. I really need a hug right now.

"Should I confront him?" I ask her, wiping away the beginning of tears with the back of my hand. I refuse to cry over this.

"Definitely not," Bridget snorts, pulling away from our hug. "Why would you give him a chance to deny it and hide the evidence?"

I shrug helplessly. "So what am I supposed to do?"

Bridget gets this devious look on her face. Of all the people I know, Bridget is the last one I'd ever want to cross. Of all the men she dated before her husband, the ones who broke up with her always regretted it, and not because they were sorry they let such a great girl get away.

"Okay, Charly," she says, "I'm going to tell you exactly what to do…"

———

If feels almost ridiculous to be here. Real people don't go to see private investigators.

I feel like I ought to be in black-and-white, smoking a cigarette with a filter, blowing elegant smoke rings. Instead, I'm sitting in a tiny office, in front of Mark Spinelli's coffee-ring-stained desk, which is overflowing with stacks of papers. Spinelli himself is fat and balding and has a yellow blotch on his button up plaid shirt. He's not exactly my idea of a noir private investigator. But he came highly recommended on Yelp.

I contacted Spinelli two weeks ago. I explained my suspicions to him, and wrote out a check as a deposit. He seemed disturbingly comfortable with the idea of spying on my husband.

"You said you had information for me," I say. My heart is pounding as I clutch my purse to my chest.

I really hope that information is: *your husband is not cheating on you.* That's probably too much to hope for. That sort of information could be conveyed over the phone.

Spinelli nods grimly. "I'm afraid you were right to be suspicious, Mrs. Douglas," he says.

Crap.

Ever since I discovered that text message, I've been hoping I was wrong. I've been watching Clark for any signs that he's cheating on me. I actually googled "signs your husband is cheating on you." He wasn't really showing any of the signs—he doesn't make private phone calls, he hasn't had any unfamiliar scents on him, and I wouldn't know if he deletes his text messages because he doesn't allow me access to his phone. Although the fact that I can't access his phone might be suspicious in itself.

"Are you sure?" I ask. Please don't be sure.

"Oh yes," Spinelli says with maddening confidence. "I've confirmed that your husband is definitely in some sort of romantic relationship with a Miss Haley Matthews."

"Haley Matthews?" The name doesn't sound familiar. Which is a good thing, I guess. At least he's not cheating on me with a friend.

He slides a manila envelope across the table. "I've got pictures, in case you're interested."

I stare down at the plain yellow envelope. I can't believe there are pictures in there of my husband doing God knows what with another woman. Oh God, I wonder if they're having sex in the photos.

"Mostly they're just kissing," Spinelli says, answering my unasked question. He must do this a lot.

I lean back in my creaky chair, feeling suddenly dizzy. This can't be happening. It can't.

"You're *sure*?" I ask again.

"Damn sure," Spinelli says. "You get yourself a good divorce attorney right now. I got a list of names if you want it."

I'll just bet he does.

Jesus. The last thing I want to worry about right now is a divorce. I thought that part of my life was taken care of. I was married. We were going to try for a baby soon. How could it all be over?

I have to see it for myself.

I snatch the envelope off the table and rip it open. Half a dozen full color photos spill out onto my lap. I pick up the top photo and study it for a second.

It's Clark with another woman. He's standing very close to her and his hand is on her back. The photo is blurry, but I can tell that the woman is probably ten years younger than I am, and nearly as tall as Clark, with long, glossy black hair, and the high cheekbones of a supermodel. She's gorgeous—the sort of woman I always thought that Clark ought to be with.

I toss that photo onto Spinelli's desk and I look at the next photo. In this one, they're kissing. I'm not going to go into details, but let's just say this girl isn't his sister.

As I look at the photo, the whole world around me starts to go black. Spinelli, his cluttered desk, his entire office disappears and all I can see is my husband kissing this beautiful woman. I feel a pulsation in my skull, like there's something in there that could burst any second. As I grip the photo, it starts to crinkle in my trembling hand.

"Are you okay, Mrs. Douglas?" Spinelli asks me, his thick eyebrows furrowed together.

And then I'm back. I'm in Spinelli's office again, and I just found out my husband is a lying, cheating son of a bitch.

I just can't wait to get out of here so I can go take everything Clark owns out of my apartment and burn it.

CHAPTER 47
Two Weeks Before

I think I'm drunk.

Or if I'm not, I will be soon. I'm on my third glass of wine. I'd prefer to be swigging whiskey or something like that, but all we have in the house is wine. I'm not a big drinker, and Clark only drinks red wine, so there you have it. It does seem a little ridiculous though that I am feeding my anger for the most important conversation of my life by *sipping pinot noir*.

He's late. I had no idea that he got home so late every night. What was I thinking? That he sat home every night, just twiddling his thumbs, waiting for me to come home? Obviously not.

It makes so much sense how he was able to get away with cheating on me. I'm never home. I'm at work, or am running, or I'm out with friends. He could get away with anything right under my nose. And I guess he did.

I sit at my desk, staring at the door with all my concentration. Kitty attempts to cheer me up by rubbing against my leg, but it doesn't help. Not this time. I shake my leg to get her to leave me alone, and I end up kicking the leg of the desk. I hear something rattle loudly.

I slide open the desk drawer and see Clark's gun inside.

I was so angry with him when he bought that gun. But now, looking at the black revolver lying peacefully in the desk drawer, I'm not angry. In fact, the gun gives me a sense of comfort.

No, not comfort. *Power.*

I carefully lift the gun out of the drawer, my heart pounding in my chest. It's heavier than it looks. I wonder if it's loaded. I have absolutely no idea how to tell if it's loaded, and I'm worried any attempts to figure it out will result in my accidentally firing the gun into my foot or something. I'm just going to assume it's probably loaded.

I aim the gun in the direction of door, imagining Clark standing there. And just for a minute, I imagine pulling the trigger.

The sound of the key in the lock jars me out of my fantasy. I quickly place the gun down on the desk and wait for Clark to let himself inside. Kitty, sensing an imminent confrontation, makes a dash for the kitchen.

"Charlotte!" Clark seems shocked to see me sitting there. "What are you doing here?"

Any other day, it would've been an innocent comment. Today, his words make me want to strangle him.

Or shoot him.

"I live here," I remind him. "Or have you forgotten?"

Clark shrugs off his dark jacket, slightly damp with rain. "You're just never home this early, that's all. I didn't expect to see you."

"Who were you expecting?" I ask. I lower the boom: "Haley?"

Clark freezes. Despite everything, I sort of wish I had a camera so I could record the look on his face. It's actually almost amusing. I can tell he's trying to maintain his composure, but failing miserably. "Who?" he manages.

"Haley Matthews," I say. I don't budge from my seat. "Isn't that the name of the girl you're sleeping with? That's what the detective said."

Is he going to deny it? I almost hope he does. I'm so ready to whip out the photographs. Instead, his eyes lower and he finally notices the gun lying on the desk in front of me.

"Charlotte," he says, a slight tremor in his voice. "Why do you have the gun out?"

"What's wrong?" I place my hand on the barrel of the gun before he can attempt to make a grab for it. "Does my having a gun make you nervous?"

Despite everything, it's actually very gratifying to see how downright frightened he looks right now.

"Can we just…" He takes a shaky breath. "Can we put the gun away? Please?"

My fingers close and tighten around the pistol. "No, Clark," I say. "No, I don't think we can."

"So what are you going to do?" He shakes his head at me. "Are you going to *shoot* me? For Christ's sake, Charlotte, I made *one mistake*. That's it. You're going to kill me over one mistake?"

Clark is looking at me with those blue, blue eyes. Would I really shoot him? No, of course I wouldn't. That would be crazy.

Of course, I'm kind of drunk right now. And definitely a little more than angry.

But no, I wouldn't shoot him.

"Please put the gun away, Charlotte," he begs me. "Please, honey. Put it away and I'll tell you everything. I promise."

There's a voice in my head screaming not to put the gun away, to hold it tight in my hand and not let it go. But the sensible, sober part of me knows that I can't have a reasonable conversation with my husband while I'm threatening him with a pistol. So I take the gun and slide it back into the drawer.

Clark watches me. When the drawer snaps shut, his shoulders sag, and he sinks down onto the sofa. He buries his face in his fists, and I can see that he's shaking.

"Charlotte," he murmurs. "Charlotte, I'm so sorry…"

He lifts his face, and I can see that his eyes are wet. Is he *crying*? Is that bastard *crying*? How come he's the one crying when I'm the one who got cheated on? This is such bullshit.

I fold my arms across my chest. "You're *sorry*? Is that all you have to say for yourself?"

Clark rubs his face with his hands. He looks up at me with pathetic blue eyes, and I have to admit, my heartstrings get tugged ever so slightly. "Charlotte, you're *never* home. I got lonely."

"So that's your excuse for messing around my back?"

"No." He shakes his head. "There's no excuse. I made a horrible mistake. I don't blame you if you hate me."

Damn. He is really taking the wind out of my anger.

"Do you hate me?" he asks, in this soft, sad voice.

I don't know what to say. Do I hate him? An hour ago, I might've said yes. But at this moment? I don't know. I guess not.

I definitely don't feel like blowing his brains out anymore.

"It's over," he says firmly. "I swear to you, it's over. It's been over for the last few days. I couldn't take it anymore. I hated myself. I felt like the worst guy in the whole world."

I want it to be true. I want it to be true so badly. I don't want a divorce. I want to stay with Clark.

God, I don't know what to believe anymore.

"My new practice is stressing me out," Clark says. "I know that's not an excuse, but… I need to take a break from it all." He smiles up at me, a little tentatively. "I was just thinking that what I'd really like is… is to start trying for a baby."

I stare at him. "A what?"

"A baby." He gives me a hopeful little smile. "I want to have a baby with you. I feel like I'm ready to be a dad. I'm sick of waiting."

He's playing me. He must be. He's saying all the things I want to hear. He knows how much I want a baby right now, and he knows his only chance of being forgiven is to give me the thing I want the most. I know exactly what he's doing and I'm far too smart to fall for this.

At least, I hope I am.

"Aren't you sick of waiting too, Charlotte?" he asks.

My mouth feels dry. "I…"

The truth is, Clark is my last chance to have a baby. If we get divorced, by the time I find another person willing to procreate with me, it really will be too late. I'm not sure if I can make peace with that fact.

Clark reaches out his hand to me. "Will you please give me another chance, Charlotte? I love you so much."

The other truth is that I *do* still love Clark. I can't turn off my love for him just because I found out he cheated. He made a mistake. Everyone makes mistakes. That's why pencils have erasers, right?

"I need to think about it," I croak.

Clark nods. "I understand. Do you… want me to leave?"

Part of me does want him to leave. But then again, if he leaves, will he go stay with *her*?

"You can stay in the guest bedroom," I tell him.

Clark nods again. "I'm going to make this right," he promises.

CHAPTER 48
Five Months After

I was never the sort of person who liked to nap. When I was up for the day, I just wanted to be up. Napping always made me feel disoriented, like I wasn't sure what time it was.

It's funny how napping has now become my favorite activity.

First of all, I'm tired all the time, to varying degrees. There's a medication I'm taking that's supposed to make me less tired, but I guess it's not working. Or not working enough, at least. And anyway, I'm always disoriented no matter what. May as well work in a little sleep. Not like there's anything better to do around here when I'm not in therapy.

Meals make me the most tired. The second I eat, I immediately want to sleep. This morning, I wake up very early for breakfast, eat too much, then pass out again soon after. Jamie told me once he does the same thing. He calls it his "morning siesta."

I wake up from my nap to the sound of whispers from the corner of my room. The room is still dark, so I give my eyes a chance to adjust, and I can make out the image of my husband, sitting in the corner of the room, talking on his cell phone.

"Yeah, she's still asleep," Clark is saying into his phone. "That's half of all she does now. Sleep."

Well, he's got my number.

"I know, I'm dreading it," he continues. "It's rough but… it's worth it. For sure."

I don't know to whom Clark is talking, but he's obviously talking about me. And he's saying it's worth it to take care of me. For sure, he said. Well, that's comforting.

"Look," he says, sounding a little bit angry. "You're not the one in debt. This is a lot of money we're talking about. What do you want me to do? Go back to scraping around for wills or divorces just to pay the bills?"

What?

"I know," he says, quieter this time. His voice is gentle now. "Believe me, I don't want to do this. But it's the best option right now… anyway, I should go. She'll probably wake up soon." Then he adds, "I love you."

It's too much to hope for that he's talking to his mother or something innocent like that. I feel *sick*. My husband is cheating on me. He's practically doing it right in front of my face.

"Charlotte!" Clark says, smiling when he sees that my eyes are open. He doesn't seem the least bit concerned that I overheard his conversation as he walks across the room to stand by my bed. I guess he overestimates my brain damage. "You're awake. And I'm on time, see?"

"You're cheating on me," I blurt out.

Clark's eyes widen. He shakes his head, obviously struggling to keep the smile plastered on his face. "Charlotte, what are you talking about?"

"You're cheating on me," I repeat, with more confidence this time. "With…" I reach into the dark recesses of my damaged brain. "With Haley."

I can see Clark debating whether or not to deny it. Finally, he drops his head. "I'm sorry," he says.

I don't know what else to say. I have a feeling it's all been said already.

"The thing is," Clark says softly, "you and I didn't have a great marriage. I wish we did. I wanted things to work out so badly but…" He takes a breath. "Then I met Haley, and we just fell in love. I didn't mean for it to happen."

"Oh," I say.

I thought I'd feel satisfaction in making him admit it, but weirdly, I don't. All I feel is like I've been punched in the gut. He doesn't even seem like he feels all that bad about it. I thought Clark was my savior, but I was wrong. I have no savior.

"Look, I'm going to be straight with you, Charlotte," he says. "You need my help. And I could really use the money from your disability payments. To be blunt, I've gotten myself in a bit of financial trouble. So maybe we could have a mutually beneficial arrangement."

I feel a little bit confused. I didn't think my disability payments were that high. It wasn't enough for my mother to pay for help around the house. But I guess it's enough for Clark.

"Believe me," Clark goes on, "there are plenty of married couples out there who are only together for financial reasons. It's actually better this way, that we're both clear about our arrangement." He pats my right hand gently. "I felt bad lying to you about Haley."

My throat feels suddenly dry. "So you don't... feel anything for me?"

Clark gives me this pitying look that makes my stomach turn. "In public, I'll pretend. I know that's really important to you. I'll act like we're just a normal couple. Like I'm still really devoted to you since you got hurt."

"And you'd still keep seeing Haley?" I ask in a small voice.

Please say no.

"I'm in love with Haley," he says like I'm stupid for suggesting otherwise. "The arrangement between you and me would be strictly platonic."

"So if I wanted to be with another man...?"

Clark laughs. "Are you serious?"

My cheeks start to feel hot. "What does that mean?"

"Charlotte," he says, shaking his head. "I know you don't have a lot of insight into your situation. I mean, that's what the therapists say. But I think it's better for you to realize that you're not in any position to be in a relationship with a man. I mean, I'm not sure if you're aware of how you look right now. But... it's just not going to happen. Ever. I think it would be cruel for me to act like it's some sort of realistic possibility."

"Why not?" I ask, then instantly wish I hadn't said anything. I'm not sure I want to hear the answer to that question.

"Why not?" Clark repeats. "Charlotte, I don't even know where to begin. Half your skull is missing. You're wearing a diaper. You can't even sit up without practically falling over to the left side. I really don't foresee any man jumping on that, you know?"

"Yeah," I mumble. I wish Clark would leave. I wish we didn't have training right now.

"You're really lucky that you have me," he adds. "Because if you didn't, you would have no one for the rest of your life. No man, anyway. So you should be really grateful to me."

I look down at my sheets. I can't look at Clark right now. I'm worried he's going to make me tell him how grateful I am to him.

"So we have a deal?" Clark asks me.

I have this feeling that the old Charlotte never would've agreed to this. But then again, maybe she would have. After all, she was the one who married this guy.

"Okay," I hear myself saying.

Chapter 49
Five Months After

The next morning, Clark comes in early again to train with Valerie. He does more of the work in helping me get dressed. (Correction: dressing me.) It still feels weird that Clark is dressing me. I mean, this is the man that I *married*, that I used to make love to, and now he's basically my nurse. But I guess it's something I'll get used to.

After Valerie leaves, Clark stands over me. He never sits down to talk to me, the way my mother does.

"Listen," he says to me. "I was just thinking about the living arrangement after you get out of here…"

"Oh," I say.

I don't know what he's getting at. I'm going to be living in my old apartment, right? Isn't that the whole point?

"The thing is," Clark says, "Natalie says that you should have a hospital bed at home. So I was thinking maybe we could put the hospital bed in our spare bedroom and you would sleep in there."

"And where would *you* sleep?" I ask.

"Well, in the master bedroom," Clark says.

Excuse me? That apartment is *mine*. I owned it before Clark came along. If anyone should get the master bedroom, it should be *me*.

"I might need more room for my equipment," I say carefully. I don't want to let on how incredibly angry I am.

"There's plenty of room for that in the spare bedroom," Clark says. "And I'm going to need more room because both Haley and I will be staying there."

What?

I manage to say, "What?"

"Charlotte," Clark says, shaking his head. "You said you were okay with me continuing my relationship with Haley. That's part of our arrangement."

"I didn't know she was going to be living with us…"

Clark shrugs. "What's the difference to you? We'll tell people she's your nurse. Actually, she could really help out with things. Your care is a lot of work."

No. *No.* I don't want this. I don't want my husband's girlfriend having any part in my care. And I certainly don't want her sleeping in my bedroom.

"I don't think it's a good idea," I say.

"Be reasonable, Charlotte," Clark says with a frown. When he looks at me like that, his cheeks seem really hollow and his Pacific blue eyes seem almost evil. I can't believe I ever thought he was attractive. "Look how much I'm doing for you. Would you really be so bothered by Haley staying with us? You probably won't even notice."

I feel tears pricking at my eyes. I'm afraid to say anything else because I don't want him to see me cry.

Maybe Clark notices that I'm really upset, because he says, "We'll talk about it later."

We'll talk about it later. That's exactly what my mother used to tell me when I was a teenager and she knew that I wasn't going to get my way.

It's obvious that I don't have any choice about this woman living in my home. What can I do about it? Nothing. I'm just going to have to learn to deal with it. Like every other goddamn thing.

It's time for my Walking Group, so Clark takes me there. He doesn't speak to me as he pushes me down the hallway. When we get to the group, he positions me next to Angela, then after a moment of hesitation, he pats me on the shoulder and waves goodbye.

Naturally, Angela notices that our goodbye was less than passionate. "Well," she says. "He may be hot, but he's a real cold fish."

I turn away, not really wanting to get into a discussion about it.

"Doesn't he ever kiss you?" she asks with a wink.

I feel my face getting hot. I'm embarrassed to tell anyone what Clark said to me yesterday, but at the same time, I feel like I have to talk to *somebody*. I can't exactly tell my mother. And Angela is probably my best female friend here.

I lower my voice. "It's not like that between us. Not anymore."

Angela frowns. "Like what?"

"Like, he's not interested in having that kind of relationship with me anymore."

Angela's mouth falls open slightly to reveal her cigarettes-stained bottom teeth. "Did he say that?"

I nod.

Angela punches the armrest of her chair. "Are you serious? That asshole really *said* that to you?"

She's talking too loudly. I look around self-consciously. I see Jamie sitting about four feet away, but he's looking in a different direction. I don't think he's listening. Good.

"It's not that surprising, is it?" I mumble. "I mean, he's helping me with all this gross, personal stuff. And it's not like I look so great right now. It's not like any man would want to... you know..."

"Did he *say* that to you?" Angela is practically screaming now. Her brown eyes are huge.

"Keep your voice down," I hiss at her. "He didn't say it to be mean. He's *right*."

"He's *not* right," Angela retorts. "Charly, you're gorgeous. Any man in his right mind would think so."

"Please keep your voice down," I say again. "I know you're being nice, but it's *not true*. It's better to be realistic."

"I'll prove it to you," Angela says.

I watch as Angela starts studying the male occupants of the room. Oh God, what is she going to do? I really wish I hadn't said anything to her.

Finally, Angela's eyes rest on an elderly man sitting across from us. He is possibly the skinniest man I've ever seen in my life. His wrist and forearms are all bones. He looks like he hasn't eaten in years.

"Henry!" Angela barks at the man.

"Eh?" Henry replies. He's probably as deaf as he is skinny.

"Charly over here," she says loudly, jerking her thumb at me. I want to crawl behind my wheelchair and hide. "Do you think she's pretty?"

"Eh?" Henry says again. "Speak up, young lady!"

Angela is practically shouting now: "DO YOU THINK CHARLY IS PRETTY?"

Henry looks me over carefully. He's so old, I'm not convinced he isn't blind. Finally, he nods his approval.

"She's real nice looking," he says. "But she'd be prettier without wearing a helmet. I don't know what it is with you young people and your fashion statements."

"Thank you," Angela says to Henry. She smiles at me triumphantly. "See? Men still think you're pretty."

"I don't think that counts," I say, rolling my eyes. "He's about a hundred years old. He probably thinks anyone under the age of seventy is a catch."

Angela nods thoughtfully. "Oh, I see! So you're looking for the opinion of a man your age. Is that right?"

I have a bad feeling I know where this is going. "I'm not looking for an opinion. Really, Angela."

But Angela isn't about to let this go. She jerks her head to the right and her eyes rest on Jamie. He's staring straight ahead, but his ears are really red. I'm starting to suspect he's been listening to our conversation all along.

"Mr. Knox," Angela says. She's smiling really wide right now. "May I obtain your opinion on something?"

Jamie shakes his head. "What is it, Angie?"

Angela looks back at me, "Now here we have a man who appears to be… I'd say, mid-thirties. Jamie, how old are you?"

"Thirty-six," he mumbles. He looks like he wishes he were somewhere else as much as I do right now.

"There you go," Angela says.

"Angela, don't…" I try to say, but Angela holds up her hand.

"Now we have a *very* important question for you, Jamie," she says. "We were hoping you could help us out."

Jamie shakes his head again, staring down at his lap. "Do I have to?"

"You do," Angela confirms. "I just need you to tell us whether you think our friend Charly here is pretty or not?"

Jamie is quiet for a minute before he lifts his eyes to meet mine. The flush in his ears enters his cheeks. "She's beautiful," he says.

"Well, there you have it," Angela says, nodding in satisfaction. "Not only have we gotten a younger man to confirm that you are attractive, but we've managed to make both of you blush adorably."

I don't know why Angela went through that stupid exercise or what it proved. Obviously, Jamie only told me I was beautiful because what else could he say. He couldn't be honest. He's too nice for that.

CHAPTER 50
Five Months After

"Who is that handsome man I saw you with in the hallway this morning?" Helga asks me while we're waiting for our Thinking Skills Group to start.

"That's my husband," I tell her.

Dr. Vincent, who seems to have grown even older in the last few weeks, adjusts his Yankees cap and raises his bushy eyebrows. "I thought your husband was the one who tried to kill you."

"No, *dummkopf*," Helga says. "It was a burglar!"

I don't bother to correct either one of them.

Angela shakes her head in disgust. "I'm still not entirely sure that the husband is innocent."

Helga thankfully ignores Angela's comment. "He is the most handsome man I've ever seen," she gushes. "I think he is even more handsome than the one with the shaky hands." She smiles at me. "I'm sure you agree, Charly."

Do I? Actually, I've grown very fond of the one with the shaky hands, even if his hands aren't so shaky anymore. Jamie may not be as classically handsome as Clark, but he's boyish and sweet looking. Every time he smiles, I feel good. Clark doesn't make me feel good. Not anymore.

"And this must be the ring!" Helga says, snatching up what I vaguely recognize to be my left hand from across the table.

Helga gazes down at the diamond thoughtfully. Valerie recently had my mother bring in my engagement ring because she thought it might help bring attention to my left hand. So far, it hasn't worked.

"That's a big diamond," Dr. Vincent comments. "Eh, Helga?"

Helga drops my hand down on the table, a troubled look on her face. "Yes…"

"What's wrong?" I ask.

Helga sighs loudly. "You know I used to be a jeweler, and I am sorry to say this to you, Charly, but this is not a diamond at all. It is what they call cubic zirconium. Fake diamond."

Angela gives me a pointed look. "Charly, did you know it was a fake?"

I remember how impressed I was when Clark presented that diamond ring to me. It was before I knew he was out of a job. After I found out the truth, it never occurred to me that Clark shouldn't have been able to afford a big diamond. "It doesn't matter," I murmur.

Amy comes into the room, holding the box for Taboo again. I've gotten a little bit better at the game, but it's still hard for me. I've had a total of twelve years of higher education, but here I am, struggling to play a party game. It's sort of depressing.

"Why don't you go first, Charly?" Amy suggests.

Do I have a choice? I select a card from the bunch. I stare at the word at the top, which I have to get everyone else to guess:

AND

That doesn't sound right. How am I supposed to get everyone to guess a conjunction? I stare at the card, trying to figure out what clue I could give. This game is really hard.

"Are you ready?" Amy asked me.

"Not yet," I mumble.

What clue could I possibly give for the word "and"? And the taboo words that I'm not supposed to say don't make sense either.

"I don't think I can do this one," I tell Amy.

She frowns. "Why not?"

"It's not even a real word," I say. Technically, "and" is a real word. But most of the clues are nouns. This isn't fair.

Amy looks over at my card. "'Husband' isn't a real word?"

Oh. I guess I missed the left side of the word.

"She's too slow," Dr. Vincent complains. "Maybe I'll go first."

Dr. Vincent pulls off his Yankees cap. It's the first time I've ever seen him without the baseball hat on his head, and my eyes are immediately drawn to a lesion on his scalp. He has a firm, red-colored, crusty nodule protruding from his skin that is at least a centimeter in diameter.

"You have skin cancer," I hear myself say.

All four set of eyes in the room turn to stare at me. "What did you say?" Amy asks.

"Dr. Vincent," I say, my eyes still pinned on his scalp. "You have skin cancer on your scalp. You need to have somebody do a biopsy, but my guess is a squamous cell carcinoma from the appearance. It's a slow-growing cancer, but it does have potential to spread to lymph nodes and other organs. So the sooner you can get it removed, the safer you'll be."

Dr. Vincent reaches up with the shaky hand and gingerly touches the nodule. "Really?"

"You should listen to her," Angela speaks up. "She's a skin doctor."

"Thanks, Dr. McKenna," Dr. Vincent says, smiling at me.

And I remember how satisfying it used to be, making those diagnoses. I miss it sometimes. So much.

Amy squints at the lesion herself. "Dr. Vincent, we can make you an appointment with a local dermatologist if you'd like."

He nods. "Yes. Yes, of course."

There's a long, tense silence in the room. Finally, Amy shakes her head at me. "I don't get it, Charly. You can diagnose skin cancer, but you can't get through one stinking round of Taboo?" She cocks her head to the side. "I think you're holding back on me."

If only that were true.

———

I have that dream again.

I don't know why. Barry is in jail. He can't hurt me anymore.

The dream starts with my looking into Barry dark eyes. *Hi, Dr. McKenna. Remember me?* He raises the gun and points it at my face.

And that's when the left side of my world disappears. I lie on my back, listening to the footsteps on my left side. I keep straining to see if Barry is still there, if he's left me to die.

And then I hear his words whispered in my ear:

"You deserve this."

I wake up shaking for the first time since Kyle Barry went to jail.

CHAPTER 51
Five and a Half Months After

Ever since Clark entered the picture, Jamie has stopped having meals with me in the hallway. The truth is, he's nearly stopped talking to me entirely. When we sit together in Walking Group, he barely looks at me. I don't know what I did or said to upset him so much, but sadly, it feels like our friendship is over.

The next morning, in Walking Group, I end up sitting next to Jamie. It wasn't my choice. The nurse who brought me to the group put me there. And I felt like it would've been rude to ask her to put me somewhere else.

So now I have to endure the fact that Jamie basically isn't speaking to me.

Unlike me, Jamie is now sitting in a regular chair, because his balance has improved to the point where he walked to the group instead of being pushed here in a wheelchair. So he could theoretically relocate to another chair. But he doesn't. Maybe he's also afraid of being rude.

"I saw Sam yesterday," I say to him, recalling how I watched Karen bringing Sam into the hospital yesterday evening.

Jamie looks at me in surprise, as if he didn't expect me to talk to him. He nods a bit warily. "Yeah," he says. "He came to visit me."

"He recognized me," I say. I still feel pleased about that.

"Of course he did," Jamie says. "He really likes you."

That makes me smile. "He does? Really?"

"Yeah." Jamie grins and rolls his eyes. "He thinks you're cool. Cooler than me."

I laugh. "I saw that Karen was with him. So, um, I guess that's working out, huh?"

I watch Jamie's face, holding my breath slightly.

"Yeah," Jamie mutters. "More or less. It's not ideal, but it is what it is."

"So are you getting back together with her then?" I ask.

Jamie narrows his eyes. "What's the difference to you?"

I just look at him, unsure what to say. I'm not sure why he seems so irritated by my question. He seemed willing to talk about Karen in the past.

Finally, Jamie sighs. "We're not getting back together. Not in this lifetime."

Natalie comes over to us because it's Jamie's turn to walk. She helps him to his feet, but once he's upright, she barely has to touch him. He only loses his balance once while walking to the other side of the gym. It's a far cry from when he first got here, when it took her and Steve together just to keep him on his feet.

He's made so much progress. He's gotten so much better. Unlike me.

Jamie is at the other side of the room when I feel a hand on my shoulder. I look behind me, and see that Clark is standing there. I don't know what he's doing here though, because he's not supposed to come until after my group is over. He's half an hour early.

"You're early," I say. I feel pleased. Usually, Clark is half an hour late.

"I've got to take off early today," Clark explains. "Valerie said that we could start half an hour early."

"But I've got my Walking Group," I protest.

Clark shakes his head. "So what?"

"So I'm supposed to be walking."

"Charlotte," Clark says irritably, "we've already been through this. You're not going to be walking at all when we get home, so this is all completely pointless. Why don't we work on the important stuff?"

He's right, of course. There's really no point in having Natalie drag me across the room. But I like doing it.

"Can't I just walk once?" I ask.

Clark shakes his head again. "Charlotte…"

I see that Jamie is approaching us, still walking with his cane. I look up at Clark pleadingly. "I'm next."

For a moment, Jamie's eyes meet mine. I know what he's thinking. He's heard every word that Clark has said to me, and that's why he's so angry. But he must understand that I don't have a choice here. This is my only option.

"Fine," Clark says. "*One* walk. But you've got to make it quick."

What happens next happens so quickly that if I turned away for a minute, I would've missed it. Jamie is right next to his chair, but instead of sitting down, he lays the ball of his hand against Clark's chest and shoves him. Hard. Hard enough that Clark stumbles backwards, trips on a mat, and falls to the floor. Right on his butt.

For a moment, Clark just sits there on the floor, looking completely stunned. I look over at Jamie, who has a small, satisfied smile on his lips. And I have to admit, I feel a little bit pleased myself.

That lasts all of ten seconds. It takes that long for Clark to scramble to his feet, looking beyond furious. I see his hands ball into fists.

"What the hell?" he yells at Jamie. "Did you just *hit* me? What the hell is *wrong* with you?"

Jamie just blinks innocently. "Sorry about that. I lost my balance."

"Sorry?" Clark growls, his face turning purple. "You did that on *purpose!* That wasn't an accident."

Natalie steps between the two men, her arms outstretched to keep them separated before another punch could be thrown. "Please calm down, Mr. Douglas," she says. "I'm certain that was an accident. Wasn't it, Mr. Knox?"

"Of course," Jamie says, his eyes darkening. "Why? Do you think you did something to my friend Charly that would make me want to hit you?"

Clark's blue eyes widen and he finally gets it. "You need to mind your own business, asshole," he snaps. "Or do you want me to rip you apart?"

Jamie doesn't look worried, but maybe he should be. Before his accident, I'm certain that Jamie would've been a good match for Clark in a fight. Clark does work out, but Jamie is clearly in pretty good shape as well. But now that Jamie's balance is off, Clark would definitely have the edge. I wouldn't want to see them in a fight.

Luckily, Natalie intervenes. "Mr. Douglas," she says tightly. "I'm going to have to ask you to leave this group. And if you make any more threats against my patients, I'm going to have Steve here escort you from the building."

Clark looks like he has more to say, but he looks from Natalie to the hulking Steve, and wisely keeps his mouth shut. He looks down at me, and I'm certain he's going to order me to leave with him, but then Natalie says, "I'll bring Charly out to you as soon as she finishes her walk."

"Fine," Clark grumbles. He shoots Jamie one last dirty look before he storms out of the gym. Natalie rushes over to shut the door behind him.

With Clark gone, I figured Natalie was going to walk me. Instead, she comes back to where Jamie is sitting, and places her fists on her hips.

"Jamie," she says in a stern voice. She's a small woman but she's really tough when she needs to be. "We all know you hit him on purpose."

"He deserved it!" calls out a voice from my left. It sounds like Angela.

Jamie just shrugs. "He *did* deserve it."

Natalie hesitates. I want her to tell everyone that my husband is a nice guy, and they shouldn't give him a hard time. But she's not going to say that. Because she doesn't believe it.

"It doesn't matter," she says. "You don't hit people just because they make you angry."

"Sometimes you do," Jamie retorts.

Natalie raises her eyebrows at him. "Is that the sort of thing you would've done before?"

Jamie is quiet for a minute. "I'm not sure," he finally replies. "I guess not."

"I know you felt like you were standing up for Charly," Natalie says, more gently this time. "But I don't think she wanted you to do that. Did you, Charly?"

I shake my head. "No," I say. "I wish you hadn't done that, Jamie."

Jamie looks at me and his eyes are very sad. "Is that really true?"

"Yes," I say.

It's the truth, not just what Natalie wants me to say. I know Clark very well, and I know that Jamie has made him furious. Jamie doesn't have to deal with him being furious though. I do.

"I'm sorry, Charly," he says softly. "It's just hard to see…"

"I know," I say quickly, before he can complete his thought. "It's okay."

Jamie seems like he might have more to say, but Natalie cuts him off by getting me up for my walk. As she helps me across the small gym, I can't help but wonder if this might be the last time I walk for the rest of my life.

CHAPTER 52
Five and a Half Months After

As I predicted, Clark won't stop fuming about what happened in the gym today. Even as Valerie is teaching him how to bathe me, he is noticeably sulking. And he's definitely angry with me. He practically scrubs the skin off my shoulders until Valerie tells him to be a little bit more gentle.

Even though Clark said when he first came in that he had somewhere to go, he sticks around after Valerie is done with her session. I can tell he wants to hash out the whole thing one more time. I wish he would leave, even though it would mean I'd have to go in the hallway in my wheelchair.

"So who was that guy anyway?" Clark asks me. "Is he, like, some good buddy of yours?"

"No," I reply quickly. "I hardly know him."

Clark narrows his eyes at me. "Didn't he say that you were his friend?"

He's my best friend here. Or at least, he used to be.

"I don't know," I say. "He's got a brain injury. He doesn't know who his friends are."

"He didn't look that bad," Clark grumbles. He starts pacing across my room. "He hit me pretty hard. But I mean, I wouldn't have fallen over if he didn't catch me off-guard."

"Of course not," I say.

"Maybe I should pay him a visit," Clark says, pausing mid-stride. "What did they say his name was? Knox?"

"I don't remember," I mumble. "Really, I barely know him."

"I don't want you talking to that guy anymore," Clark says, folding his arms across his chest. "Okay, Charlotte?"

"Okay," I reply. My voice sounds tiny.

"What?" Clark cups his hand over his ear. "I didn't hear you."

My cheeks burn. "I said *okay*!"

Clark nods his head in satisfaction. "Also," he says, "there are some other things we need to talk about. This whole power of attorney thing is bullshit, Charlotte."

For some reason, that sick feeling returns to my stomach. "What do you mean?"

"Before this happened to you, you filled out all this paperwork to give your mother power of attorney," he says. He's started pacing again. "But *I'm* your husband. I'm taking care of you. I should be managing all our finances."

I don't say anything.

"Don't you think so?" he asks. He stops pacing and stares at me.

"I guess so," I say.

Clark nods. "I agree. I talked with Dr. Greenberg and he said that if a neuropsychologist can declare you at least competent to make a decision about this, we can get the paperwork switched over."

"Okay," I say.

That sick feeling stays in my stomach. I don't want Clark to be in charge of my finances. I don't want his girlfriend living in my house, sleeping in my bed. I don't want any of this.

But more than that, I don't want to be stuck in a nursing home for the rest of my life. So I guess I don't have much of a choice.

———

They never give me enough food. I just finished eating my dinner in the hallway, but I'm still hungry. I'm also really thirsty, because they forgot to give me a drink. How could they forget my drink? And there are no nurses around anywhere to help me. I see one nurse in the hallway, but she seems to be giving a patient his medications.

I guess I can wait. I'm not going to die of thirst or anything.

As I sit and stare down at my empty tray, I notice that a few patients are coming back from their last therapy of the day. Coming up at the rear of the group is Jamie, who is walking on his own with only his cane. Nobody is helping him or making sure he's not about to fall.

Apparently, they've decided that Jamie's balance is good enough for him to walk on his own. Which means he'll probably be going home soon. I'm happy for him.

Jamie is about to walk past me, but then I see him hesitate. He stops in front of me. "Can I talk to you, Charly?" he asks.

I nod.

There's a stool about a foot away from my wheelchair, and Jamie grabs it so that he can sit with me. It makes me think of how whenever Clark comes, he never sits down. He always just stands next to me, which makes me feel like I'm a child. Of course, Jamie probably needs to sit. His balance is better but still not perfect

"Charly," he says in a low voice. "I just want to say that I'm really sorry about what happened this morning. I didn't mean to make trouble for you. I just got angry because…"

"It's okay," I say quickly. "Don't worry about it."

"Here's the thing," he says. He pauses for a minute, then he reaches over and I feel him take my right hand in his. His hand is warm, and I can feel the calluses that have been developing from using the cane. Warm hands, warm heart. His brown eyes meet mine. "I understand why you want to be with your husband. He has a lot more to offer you than I can."

What?

"I mean," Jamie continues, "I can't help you much. I can barely help myself. So I get it. I get why you'd want to be with him instead of me."

I feel like it's almost hard to breathe. What is he saying to me? Is he saying that he wants to *be* with me? *Why*? Why would he? Why would *anyone*? Where is all this coming from?

"But you need to know," he says in a voice that's almost a whisper, "that I think you're the most beautiful woman I've ever met."

That is clearly not true. I'm not the most beautiful woman he's ever met. I wouldn't have been even before I got hurt. But actually, I don't mind hearing it, especially from him. Especially with the way he's looking at me.

I hear him take a deep breath. "And I don't think you should be with any man who doesn't realize that."

I can't stop staring into Jamie's eyes. I want to tell him how much I'd like to be with him. I'd like to lean forward and kiss him. But if I tried to do it, I'd probably fall or do something else embarrassing. If I were normal, I could be with Jamie.

But if I were normal, I never would've known a guy like Jamie.

Jamie lets out a sigh and releases my hand slowly. "Anyway, that's all I had to say."

I just nod, still unable to completely catch my breath.

Jamie looks at me thoughtfully for a minute then he leans forward. My heart starts to pound and I'm certain he's going to kiss me. But he doesn't kiss me. Instead, he puts his hand on my tray of food, and spins it around. Suddenly, I see a lump of mashed potatoes, a dessert of angel food cake, and most wonderfully, a glass of water.

"Water!" I gasp. I reach for the cup of cool liquid and start to gulp it down. I don't stop until the glass is nearly finished. "I was so thirsty! Thank you!"

Jamie smiles crookedly at me. "No problem."

I watch him as he struggles to his feet, then limps down the hallway back to his room. I'm sure he'll be going home soon, and then he'll forget all about me. And I'm sure he'll find some other girl who's more beautiful than I am, especially since I'm not actually beautiful at all.

CHAPTER 53
Five and a Half Months After

The next morning, I see the eye doctor.

His name is Dr. Singh and he's "the best," or so I've been told. I saw him a few weeks ago about the problems I'm having seeing on my left side, and he suggested that a prism for my left eye might help me see better on the left. The prism will bend the light that comes from the left side and put it in my right visual field.

Unfortunately, I've been blessed with perfect vision, so there were no lenses to attach the prism to. Dr. Singh told me he'd come back after making me glasses.

Dr. Singh is a short, stout, dark-skinned man with a wide smile. He comes into my room holding up a leopard-spotted glasses case. "I've got your prisms for you, Mrs. McKenna," he announces proudly.

"Wonderful," I say. I wish I shared his enthusiasm.

Dr. Singh opens the case. Inside is a pair of giant tortoiseshell rimmed lenses. The left lens is covered in some sort of striped clear material. The glasses are probably the ugliest things I've ever seen.

"Try them on," Dr. Singh urges me.

I bite back my distaste. So what if they're ugly? Who cares what I look like anymore? Vanity is the least of my problems.

I pull the glasses out of the case with my right hand and slide them up my nose. I feel like a schoolmarm. I look up at Dr. Singh's round face. I don't notice any difference whatsoever.

"Well?" he asks me.

I shrug. "I'm not sure if they're helping."

I'm being nice. They're not helping.

"Well, give them a try today," Dr. Singh says. "They might help you functionally, even if you don't notice a difference."

I shrug again.

I mostly forget about the glasses until later in the morning, when I'm having a physical therapy session with Natalie. I'm sitting in my wheelchair, and she whips them out of her pocket.

"Those don't help," I tell her.

"Just give them a chance, Charly," she says.

This time, she slides them onto my face herself. Nothing becomes any clearer with the lenses on. Just like everything else, the glasses are a big disappointment.

"Okay," Natalie says. "Let's work on wheeling down the hallway."

"What about walking?" I ask.

"We're not going to focus on that anymore," Natalie says firmly. "I talked to your husband about it, and he definitely makes some good points. You're mostly going to be using the wheelchair when you get home, so you need to be able to control it better. You don't want to have to depend on someone else to wheel you around, do you?"

"No," I say.

She's right, of course. It's bad enough that I can't walk, but the fact that I can't even push my own chair is even more of a liability. I don't want to have to rely on Clark just to be able to get from the bedroom to the living room without bashing into ten things along the way.

And forget about wheeling around in public. That would be dangerous. If I tried to push myself down the sidewalk, I'd probably wheel right into traffic.

"Alright," Natalie says. "Put your hands on the wheels and go down the hallway."

I have to admit, I was a little bit skeptical about the glasses, but for the first time in all the times I've been doing this, I make it down the entire hallway without slamming into the wall on the left side. I've never ever managed to do that before. I feel ridiculously proud of myself.

"I did it!" I say.

Natalie is looking at me with a strange expression on her face.

"What?" I say, feeling suddenly nervous. "I thought I did a good job. I didn't hit anything. Did I?"

Oh God, did I hit something and not even realize it? That would definitely be a step back.

"No," Natalie says, "you didn't hit anything."

I just look at her.

"Charly," she says. "Do you realize that you were using your left hand to help wheel the chair?"

I look down at the left wheel of my chair and I see a hand on it. My hand.

"I don't usually do that?"

"Sometimes you'll put it on the wheel for a second or two," Natalie recalls. "But this time you had it on the wheel for the entire time. I've never seen you do that before."

I bite my lip. "So that's good... right?"

Natalie nods. "Really good."

I touch the ugly glasses on my nose. "Do you think it's the prism lenses?"

"Maybe..." Natalie frowns. "I mean, the prisms definitely help some patients a lot. But I can't say that I've ever seen anything quite this marked."

"I didn't think they were making a difference at all," I admit.

Natalie nods again, looking thoughtful. "Let's keep trying."

We go down the hallway several more times, and I don't bump into the wall once. And each time I use my left hand to push the wheel. Natalie is over the moon happy for me, and I'm pretty pleased myself. I'm baffled that these glasses could be making such a big difference, but I can't argue with the results.

———

Clark is expected to come after lunch today, so I eat my lunch in the hallway alone. I see Jamie walking by, and I try not to stare. He's alone too, gripping his cane in his right hand as he walks confidently down the hallway.

"Hey, Charly," he says when he sees me. He manages a crooked smile. "New glasses?"

My hand flies to the lenses on my face. I know these glasses are incredibly ugly, and I hadn't really cared before. But suddenly, I feel self-conscious. "Yeah," is all I say.

"They're cute," he said, even though they absolutely are not cute in any way, shape or form.

"Thanks," I say anyway.

He hesitates, lingering in front of me. "Can I... would it be alright if I sat with you?"

I look down at the watch on my left hand. It's a quarter to one, and Clark will probably be here soon. God knows how he would react if he saw Jamie out here sitting with me. "You better not," I say.

Jamie nods. But he looks sort of sad.

"I'll see you tomorrow in Walking Group," I tell him. Although I'm not actually sure that I'll see him. I think Clark has spoken to Dr. Greenberg about my schedule and how he didn't think it was a good use of my time to be in Walking Group. He makes a good point, but more than that, I think he's trying to get me away from Jamie.

It's hard to blame him for that one.

"Hey," Jamie says suddenly. "Who turned your tray around?"

"Huh?" I say.

Jamie gestures down at my tray of food. "You usually only eat half. You know I always turn it around for you."

I stare down at the empty plate of food in front of me. I hadn't realized it, but my tray did seem especially easy to navigate today. My drink was there, my side dish was there, my utensils were easy to find, and my dessert was there too. Usually locating all the parts of my lunch is something of a scavenger hunt

"I think it's the glasses," I tell him.

Jamie raises his eyebrows. "The glasses? Really?"

I shrug. It's the best explanation I can come up with.

Jamie looks a little bit skeptical though, and I can't blame him. No matter how much of a miracle these glasses are, it doesn't really explain why I suddenly started using my left hand. And it suddenly occurs to me that when I checked the time, I looked at the red watch Amy had put on my left hand to get me to pay more attention to it. I hadn't even had to think about it.

CHAPTER 54
Five and a Half Months After

These glasses are literally the ugliest glasses I have ever seen.

Like I said before, I've always had perfect vision. Mostly, it was a blessing, but there were actually some days I was jealous of people who needed lenses to see. When it was stylish, I would've loved to put on a pair of Tina Fey glasses. But you don't do that if you have perfect vision. It would just be pathetic.

These glasses are definitely not Tina Fey glasses. They're the kind of glasses that you see on a spinster librarian. And then one day, she takes off her glasses and you realize that she was beautiful all along, but you never knew it because she's had these horrible, ugly glasses covering half her face. That's what's I've got on my face right now.

But they're helping me so much, I can't hate them as much as they deserve to be hated based on appearance alone.

"It's like a miracle," I gush to Clark, when he arrives soon after lunch.

Clark has his nose buried in his phone, which is per usual. I wonder if he's texting with Haley. No, I'm not going to let that bother me.

"That's great, Charlotte," he says. He sounds distracted, which I'm used to, but even more irritating, his voice has a patronizing edge to it.

"I just have to get a nicer set of frames," I say.

"Who cares?" Clark says. "It doesn't bother me."

That's not surprising, considering that he hasn't even glanced in my direction since he walked into the room.

"They look like granny glasses," I say.

Clark shrugs. "So what? You really want to waste a bunch of money on a pair of fancy-looking glasses? Do you really think that's a good use of your finances, Charlotte?"

"Sure," I say.

He rolls his eyes. "It's *not*. That's why I'm helping you with your money. Because you don't know better."

"I don't see what's wrong with getting a pair of glasses that look nice," I say, frowning at him.

"What's wrong is that glasses are expensive," he says. "We're on a tight budget to begin with. It's not like you need to look like some kind of model."

Lately, it seems like I haven't had one conversation with Clark where he hasn't reminded me of how physically undesirable I am. I bite my lip. "But, Clark…"

"Charlotte, I said *no*."

And that's it. That's the end of it.

When Valerie comes into the room, she lets Clark do everything. Despite his apathy and chronic tardiness, he's gotten pretty good at transferring me in and out of bed, and getting me dressed. He hardly even struggles to get my arms through the sleeves of my shirt anymore. Maybe this will all work out after all.

"Much better," she tells Clark.

Clark smiles at the compliment. "I told you I'm a fast learner."

I look at my shirt. Clark buttoned it, but missed one of the buttons. All of the buttons are now off by one. "You missed a button," I tell him.

He looks at my shirt and laughs. "Yeah, I guess I did."

"Can you fix it, please?"

Clark flashes me an irritated look. "Oh, for God's sake, Charlotte... you're acting like some sort of diva today."

Am I really a diva because I don't want my shirt buttoned wrong? It looks so sloppy. I don't want to go around the rest of the day looking like this.

But it's obvious that Clark isn't going to help me.

I sigh, and start fixing the buttons myself. They're completely wrong and all of them need to be undone. I start with the top button, and have gotten two of them fixed when I feel Valerie's hand on mine.

"What are you doing?" Valerie nearly screams at me.

I drop my head guiltily. "I'm sorry. I just wanted to fix the buttons."

"But you're using your left hand," Valerie says, shaking her head.

Wow. She's right.

"It's the glasses," I tell her.

Valerie is still shaking her head. "No pair of glasses would do that."

I'm not sure what to say to Valerie, because obviously the glasses did do it. Unless she thinks I was faking my entire brain injury. Maybe I chopped off my own skull just for fun.

"I don't know," I say. "I just know that they work."

Valerie nods. "Thank God," she says.

CHAPTER 55
Five and a Half Months After

I wake up to a ringing sound coming from my left side.

I blink my eyes, taking a moment to adjust to the darkness in the room. The clock on the wall says that it's a quarter to eight in the evening, but the sun is down and it's pitch black outside. Under the best circumstances, it would be hard to locate an object on my left, but it's much harder in the dark, when I'm waking up from a nap.

Then I spy my glasses on the end table to my right side.

I grab the glasses with my right hand. Taking care not to poke myself in the eye with the earpieces, I slide the glasses onto my nose. I close my eyes for a second, then reach out to pick up the ringing phone with my left hand.

"Dr. McKenna?" a breathless voice says on the other line.

I freeze. Nobody has called me "Dr. McKenna" in such a long time. It hardly even feels like me anymore. "Yes…" I say.

"Dr. McKenna," the voice says, "this is Regina Barry."

My skull throbs slightly. I grip the phone tighter, uncertain what to say except, "Oh. Hi."

"I'm so sorry to call you like this." Regina Barry's voice is just as I remember—a mix of shyness and uncertainty. She seemed like such a sweet woman, plagued by a horrible skin condition. I was so glad to have been able to help her.

Well, at least until her husband shot me.

"How did you get this number?" I ask weakly.

"It wasn't easy," she admits, "but I have my sources."

That sounded ominous.

"Why are you calling?" I ask, now gripping the phone so tightly that my knuckles are white.

"I just…" Regina Barry hesitates. "There's something I had to tell you. I couldn't live with myself if I didn't."

I shake my head. "Okay…"

"The thing about my ex-husband Kyle is," she begins, "he would *never* have shot you because he was angry about you breaking us up. That doesn't make any sense."

I frown at the phone. I can't believe Regina is defending her husband. After everything he'd done to her. And to me.

"Believe me," I say. "He's the one who shot me. I remember it."

"No, I don't doubt that," Regina says. "I believe he's capable of it. I just… I don't think he did it because he was angry that I left him." She pauses. "The truth is, Kyle couldn't care less that we got divorced. He was happy to be done with me, in fact. He only cared that he got half my money."

"Half your money?"

"My father owned a successful business," she explains. "He left me a fair amount of money in his will. I wouldn't have believed it at the time, but now I suspect that the only reason Kyle married me at all was for financial reasons. He... has a bit of a gambling problem."

"Oh," I say, because what else can I say?

She takes a deep breath. "Anyway, the thing is, Dr. McKenna, you were so kind to me, and you helped me so much. More than anyone else in my entire life. So that's why I had to talk to you."

I'm having trouble following what she's talking about. Maybe it's the brain injury. "I don't understand."

"I read this article about you online the other day," Regina says. "I just got curious about you, since... well, you know. And until I read that article, I never realized that Clark Douglas was your husband."

"Oh," I say. This conversation is making me tired. I wish I could go back to sleep. "Yes. He is."

"The thing is, Dr. McKenna," she says, "I *know* Clark."

"What do you mean?" I ask impatiently. My head is starting to throb. Maybe my nurse could bring me some Tylenol.

"Dr. McKenna," Regina Barry says, "Clark was my neighbor. He lived in the apartment down the hall from me and Kyle for several years."

The throbbing in my head intensifies sharply. "*What?*"

"Clark and I were neighbors," Regina repeats.

I shake my head at the phone. "You must be mistaken. Maybe it's a different Clark."

"I doubt that," Regina snorts. "Clark Douglas—crazy good-looking with those ridiculously blue eyes. Sort of hard to forget. Clark and Kyle were, like, best friends for a while…"

No. That's not possible.

"And he was dating this gorgeous brunette model," Regina goes on. "Or wannabe model… it seemed like she mostly did waitressing. I think her name was Heidi. No, Holly."

"Haley," I say.

"Yes!" Regina yelps. "That's it. Haley. God, I hated the two of them." She amends, "Well, all three of them, really."

The throbbing in my head is making it hard to focus. Clark couldn't have been neighbors with Kyle Barry. It doesn't make any sense. After all, the only reason I gave Clark a chance for a second date was that Kyle Barry was threatening me, and Clark heroically stepped in and…

Oh.

Oh God.

"Did you tell this to the police?" I ask Regina.

"I tried," she says. "I called several times, but I kept getting transferred to answering machines. I left my contact information, but nobody ever called me back. I don't know. It felt like they thought the case was pretty much wrapped up and they weren't interested in any new information." She pauses. "So I decided to call you instead."

"Yes," I say weakly. The throbbing pain in my temple has become so severe, I'm afraid my brain may explode. Especially since I don't have a skull anymore to hold everything in place.

"Dr. McKenna?" Regina Barry's voice suddenly sounds very far away. "Are you okay?"

"Yes," I manage. "But… I have to go."

"You sure you're okay?"

"Yes," I say. "I'm fine. Thank you for calling."

Before Regina can get out another word, I slam the phone back down on the receiver. I feel my breaths coming fast and hard. I need some Tylenol *now*. No, I need something stronger than Tylenol. Where's that nurse call button?

The door to my room cracks open, filtering in a tiny bit of light. I breathe a sigh of relief—the nurse is here to give me my goddamn pain medication. I'm going to have some nice oxycodone in a little cup of applesauce. Maybe my brain won't explode after all.

Except when I see the silhouette framed in the doorway, I realize it isn't my nurse at all.

It's Clark.

CHAPTER 56
Five and a Half Months After

For a moment, I feel a sense of fear so overwhelming, I can hardly breathe. All I can think about is Regina's words: *Clark was my neighbor. Kyle and Clark were best friends.* I watch Clark step into the room, shutting the door behind him. His blue eyes suddenly seem almost black.

"Clark," I manage, over my fear and the persistent throbbing in my temple. "What are you doing here? Visiting hours are almost over."

Clark comes closer to me. I feel like I barely recognize him. Those beautiful blue eyes, the chiseled features, the chestnut hair—they all seem like the features of a complete stranger. He walks right up to my bedside, close enough that I can smell the alcohol on his breath.

"No more screwing around, Charlotte," he says. He holds up a few papers in his hand. "I'm sick of the games. These are the power of attorney forms. I want you to sign them for me. Now."

"Now?" I squeak. "But it's the middle of the night…"

"Always with the excuses," Clark mutters. "Charlotte, without these forms, I can't even pay your mortgage and you'll lose your precious apartment."

"My mother has been paying the mortgage," I point out.

Clark doesn't seem to appreciate that answer. "Do you recognize the sacrifice I'm making for you?" he practically spits in my face. "I'm going to be dressing you, bathing you, wiping your ass. I'm the one keeping you out of a nursing home. You can't even sign a paper for me, you ungrateful bitch?"

Christ, where is that nurse call button?

"I thought it had to be notarized," I say in a small voice.

"I've got a friend who can do it," Clark mutters.

"Oh."

Clark places the paper on my lap then roughly shoves a pen into my right hand. I don't want to sign these papers. I really don't. But what else can I do? In a way, he's right. He's going to be doing everything for me. I *need* him.

Clark was my neighbor. Kyle and Clark were best friends.

The pain in my temple is almost blinding. I feel my hand holding the pen start to shake. I don't know if I could sign even if I wanted to.

"Sign the paper," Clark says through his teeth. "Sign it or I swear to God, I'll walk away right now. I'll leave you to figure out this mess all on your own."

I have to sign. I don't have a choice. I try to steady my hand enough to sign, but it's hard. I can't stop shaking.

"I'm doing you a favor, Charlotte," he goes on. "You realize that, right? Just like I did you a favor when I married you."

I stare up at him. "What?"

"Come on, Charlotte," he snorts. "You didn't really think that somebody like me would really be attracted to a fat, bitchy, ugly doctor? I did you a favor by marrying you. I *took pity* on you. But you were never grateful to me. You always just wanted more. You wanted me to work myself into the ground like you did. Or to have a *baby*, for Christ's sake. *God.*"

My throat feels almost too dry to get any words out. "That's not…"

"All you wanted was to be able to control me," he hisses at me. "Well, now you don't get to be the boss anymore. You're not the smart one who knows everything anymore. Who looks down on me because I'm not as good as you are. Because I don't have any money and my career is in the shithole."

Clark was my neighbor. Kyle and Clark were best friends.

"Clark," I manage. "I never…"

But Clark doesn't want to hear anything I have to say. He's on a roll.

"I've got news for you, Charlotte," he says. "You better learn to get a lot more humble or else your life is going to be really crappy. Nobody is going to put up with your shit anymore looking the way you do now. I sure won't."

I look into Clark's handsome face. I remember the first time I saw him, being so amazed that somebody like him could like somebody like me. And I was right. He never wanted me. He never liked me. Not really.

"Frankly," Clark goes on, "I feel like I've been putting up with it for far too long. It's sort of gratifying to finally see you get what you deserve."

Get what I deserve.

I deserve this.

You deserve this.

I stare at my husband, and suddenly the room starts to melt away. I'm in my apartment again. I open the door and there's Kyle Barry, holding Clark's gun. "Hi, Dr. McKenna," he says as he swings the gun in the direction of my face. I see his black eyes staring back at me. I hear the gunshot..

Next thing I remember, I am lying on the floor. I look up at the ceiling of my apartment, and I try to get up, but I can't. I feel too weak. I think I'm dying. Oh God, I'm dying.

I hear the keys in the lock. I hear the heavy footsteps, and Clark's voice calling out, "Charlotte?"

Clark. Thank God.

I hear his voice: "Charlotte?"

My vision is fuzzy but I can see Clark's face above mine. "Please," I croak. "Please. Call 911."

I expect him to pull out his phone and dial 911. But instead he just stands there.

"I can't believe it," Clark mutters. "I can't believe he shot you in the head and you're *still fucking alive*."

I watch as Clark sits down on the couch to my left. I don't understand it. Why isn't he calling?

"Clark," I gasp. It occurs to me that every word could be my last.

"I don't understand it," he says, shaking his head. "It's like there's no way to get rid of you."

I don't know what he's talking about. I want to beg him to please, please, *please* call an ambulance. But I don't have the strength to say it anymore. My vision is growing fuzzier every second.

"No," Clark says quietly. "I'm not going to call 911. Not until I'm ready." He stares down at me with his beautiful blue eyes. "Not until you're dead."

"Please, Clark," I whisper with my last ounce of strength. Pretty please with sugar on top. Don't let me die.

"Don't try to manipulate me, you bitch," he says. He leans in towards me. His lips part and he hisses the words in my left ear, "You deserve this."

With those words, my old apartment fades out and now I'm back in my hospital room again. I'm lying in bed and staring at my husband. I feel dizzy, like I might pass out. My heart is beating much too fast.

"You left me to die," I say softly.

Clark frowns. "What did you say?"

"You left me to die," I say again, this time enunciating each word clearly.

Clark's face changes. All of a sudden, he starts looking very nervous. He shakes his head at me. "What are you talking about?"

"I remember it," I say. My heart is beating so quickly now, it actually hurts. My temple is one big mass of pain. "You sat down on the couch and told me you were going to wait for me to die before you called for an ambulance. Except you didn't wait long enough."

"That's crazy," he says, his dark eyebrows knitting together. "You're hallucinating. You realize you have a brain injury, don't you?"

"I remember it," I say firmly. "I know what you did. And I know that you were friends with Kyle Barry."

The color drains out of Clark's face. "What are you talking about? Who told you that?"

"Regina Barry."

Clark just stares at me for a minute, as if weighing his options. I glance over at the door to the room. It's closed. I can't even see the light of the hallway through the space under the door. I know based on the screams I sometimes hear at night that the rooms are not soundproof, but considering I'm a brain injury patient, would anyone come running if I started to yell?

Where is that goddamn call button?

"What did Gina tell you?" he asks in an oddly calm voice.

"Enough," I say.

Clark takes a step back. He stares at the wall over my bed, his breathing disturbingly even.

"I'm not a bad person, Charlotte," he says softly. "I'm really not. I didn't mean for things to happen this way. Honestly."

I shake my head. "Did you ever even like me?"

"It's not like that, Charlotte." For a moment, he squeezes his eyes shut and he looks like he might cry. "My career was totally screwed… everything I ever worked for. I had all these debts. Then Kyle starts telling me about this doctor who treated Gina. 'Single, fat, rich, and desperate'—that's what he said."

Is that how Clark saw me the day he came in for that first appointment? It's painful to think about, maybe even more painful than my throbbing temple.

"It wasn't like I was repulsed by you or anything," Clark continues. He's still just staring at the wall. "It wasn't a sham, not exactly. I broke things off with Haley, and I was willing to give it a real try. I really was. I wanted to make it work, but…"

But I was too disgusting for him to ever actually be attracted to.

"When did you start up again with Haley?" I ask.

Clark is quiet.

I take a breath. "Was it before or after we got married?"

Clark doesn't answer me for a long time. Finally, he says, "Before."

That extra week in the Bahamas. I don't even have to ask him. I know that she must have been with him. I'm such an idiot.

"The whole thing was Kyle's idea," Clark says. "I swear. I'm not a murderer, Charlotte. He didn't get as much money as he expected from Gina, so he figured..." Clark shakes his head. "He told me to get the gun, to keep it unsecured..."

I don't know if it's the pain in my head, but I suddenly have the urge to throw up.

"I wasn't going to do it though," Clark insists. "I swear. I was going to ditch the gun and just... I don't know. Try to make it work. But then when you were going to end it..." His voice breaks slightly. "It's your fault, Charlotte. You were never honest with me. I wouldn't have had to go after your life insurance if I knew what you had in the bank."

I don't get it. I don't know what great quantity of money he's talking about. If I had that kind of money, I wouldn't be worried about a nursing home right now. Is he delusional?

"It was supposed to be done by the time I got home," Clark says. "Kyle was supposed to make it look like a burglary, and I was going to call the police when I found you. Except... you were still alive."

A tiny thread of hope surges in my chest. He said he was going to wait until I was dead, but he didn't. He didn't wait. He called for an ambulance while I was still alive. That's the only reason I'm still here now.

"So why did you call?" I ask. "I mean, before... you know..."

Clark shakes his head. "Your cat."

FREIDA MCFADDEN

"My cat?" I have no idea what he's talking about. "What cat?"

"Christ, you don't remember your cat?" Clark rolls his eyes. "That black stray that strutted around like she owned the place?"

A black cat...

Oh my God, Kitty! How could I have forgotten her?

But why is Clark talking about her in the past tense? How come my mother hasn't mentioned her or brought her to me in all the time I've been here?

Oh Jesus, did he do something to Kitty? Oh God...

"She slipped out when Kyle left the apartment," Clark says with a sneer. "Your neighbor came by to return her, and she saw everything. I had to call an ambulance. So that was that."

My stomach sinks. Clark didn't have a change of heart, after all. He only called because he was cornered.

"But why didn't Kyle tell the police you were involved?" I ask. "I mean, after they caught him."

"Because he isn't dumb." Clark focuses his attention squarely on me. "He's better off claiming he shot you in a fit of angry passion than admitting that it was planned for months. That's why he used my gun that he "found," and that's why we sent you that divorce paper. For second-degree attempted murder, he could get paroled in a few years. For first-degree attempted murder, it's a minimum of ten years, maybe life in prison. I explained it to him very carefully, and I know he'll keep his mouth shut."

Clark and I look at each other. The room suddenly seems very quiet and very dark. The pen has fallen out of my hand, forgotten. Until Clark picks it up and holds it out to me.

"So are you going to sign or not?" he asks.

I stare at him. "Are you kidding me? You just admitted to me that you planned my murder."

"So what?" Clark shrugs. "Nobody will believe you, Charlotte," he says. "I didn't shoot you. They caught the guy who did it and now this is all just your word against mine. There's no evidence that I had anything to do with it. Kyle will back me up."

"I don't care if they believe me," I say, the pain in my head fueling my anger. "But you're not going to get one cent of my money. Not one fucking *cent*, you asshole."

Clark's blue eyes darken again. I feel around with my left hand for the call button, searching desperately between folds of sheets and blankets. I want this man out of my room. The pounding in my head is so bad that I feel like my brain must be bleeding. What if my brain is actually bleeding? What if I'm going to die, right here, right now?

But no, I'm not going to die. It's just a headache.

Where is that goddamn nurse call button?

"Can you open the door to the room, please?" I croak. "I need the nurse. I… I have a headache."

"Charlotte, be sensible," Clark says in that oddly calm voice. "You don't want to end up in a nursing home. We have an arrangement."

I shake my head. "Clark, I think you should leave."

"No," he says. He starts moving in the direction of my bed. "No, I'm *not* going to leave. Not until we reach an agreement. One way or another."

What does this man want from me? I have no money. I can't work anymore. I don't get it.

All I know is that he wants *something*. And he wants it very badly.

Before she left, Valerie placed a pillow under my left arm to prop it up to prevent swelling. Even though it's hard to see on my left side, I can feel the pillow sliding out from under my arm. And then the pillow is in Clark's hands.

No. Oh my God, *no*. He can't. He *wouldn't*.

"Clark…" I whisper.

He doesn't say anything. He holds the pillow against his chest, one hand gripping either side. If I died right here, right now, would anyone wonder why? After all, I have a severe brain injury. I'm sick. My death is not out of the realm of reasonable possibility. For all I know, this headache is a sign that death is imminent.

In all honesty, it would be a bit of a relief in some ways—after all I've been through, to just be able to just let go. I can almost feel the softness of the pillow smothering my face. My life has become so difficult in so many ways. And sometimes it feels like things will never get better.

But I don't want to go. Not this way.

I look up at Clark's face. There's something really scary and unfamiliar in his eyes. He's gripping the pillow so hard that his knuckles are white. Again, he gets close enough that I can smell alcohol on his breath. He's definitely had at least a few drinks before he came here. And it's fueling his anger.

I can't stop him.

"Charly?"

It's Jamie's voice from outside the room. Relief washes over me. Before Clark can yell at him to go away, I scream out, "Come in!"

Jamie steps inside, holding his metal cane, and shuts the door behind him like he always does. When he realizes that Clark is in the room, he blinks in surprise. "Oh, I'm so sorry," he coughs. "I... I didn't realize. I'll come back later."

"Yeah, good idea," Clark says in a low growl.

No, Jamie! Don't leave!

"No," I say quickly. "Stay."

Clark glares at me and I can see his fist tighten around the pillow.

"I want a moment alone with my wife," he says through his teeth.

Jamie looks between the two of us and frowns. He finally notices the pillow in Clark's hands and his eyes widen. He won't leave me like this. I know it.

"Charly wants me to stay," Jamie says finally.

Clark folds his muscular arms across his chest and glares at Jamie. I can see the recognition dawning on his face. "I *know* you," he says. "You're the asshole who pushed me in the gym."

Jamie grins crookedly. "Yup, that was me."

Clark steps away from my bed and moves towards Jamie. "I've been wanting to talk to you again," he says. "About what happened. It wasn't really an accident, was it?"

Jamie stares at Clark, the smile fading from his face. "No, it wasn't."

"Clark," I say sharply. "You need to leave. Right now."

"Shut up, Charlotte," he says, whipping his face back to look at me. He says it with such anger. He hates me. My *husband* hates me.

I can see Jamie's eyes filling with anger as well. His left hand balls up into a fist. As much as I'd like to see him punch Clark, I don't want him to. Clark is in top physical condition right now. He can *destroy* Jamie. There isn't much I can do to help him, stuck here in my bed. Where is that call button? Is it even in my bed?

"Charly says she wants you to leave," Jamie says slowly. "So I think you'd better go."

Clark snorts. "Are you threatening me?"

"I'm just telling you to leave," Jamie replies in an even voice.

Clark keeps moving towards Jamie. If I were Jamie, I'd be terrified, but he doesn't even flinch. That's probably the brain injury.

"Back in the gym, you caught me by surprise," Clark says. "You won't do that again. I hope you know that I could break every bone in your face."

Jamie nods thoughtfully. "Maybe," he says. He looks at Clark for a minute. Then he takes the cane in his hand

and lifts it into the air. He grips it with both hands like a baseball bat. "This cane is made out of metal," he says, studying the long thin rod as he speaks. "I used to be pretty good at baseball. I'm pretty sure if I swing this at your face, I could break your jaw."

Clark's eyes widen.

"The difference between you and me," Jamie goes on, a pleasant smile spreading across his lips, "is if I break your face, *I* won't get in trouble."

For a moment, I'm sure that Jamie is going to swing his cane square into Clark's handsome face. And you know what? I really want him to do it. I want him to shatter that perfect jaw. I want his jaw to be wired shut so that he can never smirk at me again.

But Jamie holds the cane steady in the air.

"Fine," Clark growls. He turns around to give me one last look. "You're making a big mistake, Charlotte."

Jamie drops the cane, letting it fall to the ground. I watch Clark's hand on the door to my room, and I wonder if he'll run. I wonder where he'll go to escape the punishment for what he did to me. For what he tried to do to me. I don't even care anymore. I just want him gone.

But before Clark can get the door open, Jamie grabs him by the arm. With his bare hands, Jamie shoves Clark hard against the wall, and presses his forearm against my husband's windpipe. Clark gasps for air and Jamie stares him straight in the eyes.

"What were you trying to do to Charly with that pillow?" Jamie snaps at him.

"Let me go, you asshole," Clark gasps.

Jamie releases him for a split second, pulls back his right arm, and punches Clark square in his perfect Aquiline nose. Clark screams as blood pours from his nostrils, and Jamie replaces his forearm against his neck.

"I repeat," Jamie says, "what were you doing to Charly?"

The door to my room cracks open, then swings open entirely. I recognize Grace, my evening nurse. Her eyes fly wide open when she sees Jamie pinning a bloody Clark to the wall.

"Mr. Knox!" she yells. "Get off him *right now!*"

Jamie glances over at Grace, then glares into my husband's eyes. "You'll have to make me."

He just earned himself a lot more time here.

It takes two big orderlies and a vial of sedative injected into Jamie's ass before he can be pried off Clark. I honestly had no idea he had it in him. The whole while, he keeps yelling, "He was trying to suffocate her with a pillow! I saw it! I saw it!"

And by the end I'm crying too. I can't stop sobbing until I get my own vial of sedative, mine injected into my arm. And when Grace asks me why I'm crying, I tell her, "He tried to kill me. My husband tried to kill me."

CHAPTER 57
Six Months After

Clark is in jail.

As it turned out, while Clark was trying to suffocate me with a pillow, Kyle Barry was singing like a bird in prison. I guess he finally got pissed off about the fact that he was the only one getting punished for planning to shoot me. When Clark was finished getting his nose set in the ER, the police were waiting to arrest him.

Jamie is the local hero. Officially, nobody will say it's a good thing that he broke Clark's nose, but everyone is shaking his hand and clapping him on the back. As for me... well, he saved my life. What else can I say?

"I was worried," I confided in Jamie as we sat together eating dinner the next night. "I didn't think you'd be able to take on Clark."

Jamie made a face at me. "Gee, thanks a lot, Charly."

"Well, your balance isn't perfect," I pointed out.

"True," he admitted. "But I took him by surprise. Also, remember: I did bartending. Taking down drunk idiots is part of the job description. As soon as I smelled the gin on his breath, I knew I could take him."

We haven't discussed the fact that my husband tried to kill me or why. I'm not sure it says anything good about me that the person I married wanted me dead.

As for my rehab, I've gotten markedly better since I got those glasses. But the weird part is that even when I'm not wearing the glasses, I'm better at using my left side. I can get my left hand on the wheel of my chair without prompting, and I can dress my upper body almost entirely by myself. I do sometimes bump into things on the left side when I'm wheeling my chair, but much less than I used to.

"You're doing amazing, Charly," Dr. Greenberg said to me after watching me do a transfer with Valerie. "I always knew you had it in you."

I bit my lip. "Can I ask you a question, Dr. Greenberg?"

"Of course."

I asked the question that had been swirling around my head ever since I remembered what Clark did to me: "Is it possible that the reason I was having so much trouble seeing things on my left side was because I saw something so terrible on my left side that I needed to block it out?"

To his credit, Dr. Greenberg considered my question thoughtfully. "You're talking about conversion disorder," he said. "That's a psychiatric condition where you have a neurologic response like numbness or paralysis in response to a stressful situation."

"I know what conversion disorder is," I said. "I *am* a doctor, after all."

"Well, *sorry*, Dr. McKenna," Dr. Greenberg said, grinning at me. "Anyway, it's possible, I suppose. But in your case, I'd say it was unlikely. Your brain injury was on the right side, so the weakness and numbness and neglect of the left side is perfectly explained by your injury."

"But how come it just got better all of a sudden?" I asked.

"Well, the prism lenses helped," Dr. Greenberg said. "But that can happen with a brain injury. As the blood gets reabsorbed, there can be a sudden, marked recovery. I would guess that's what happened to you."

I guessed that made sense.

"Although the question remains," Dr. Greenberg added with raised eyebrows, "what is it exactly that you think you saw on your left side that was so horrible?"

I'm not sure exactly how I stammered my way out of that one.

The one piece of bad news is that I still can't go home from here, most likely. I can't make it to the bathroom on my own, and that's requisite before my mother can take me home. But I've been trying not to think about that.

So yeah. That's that. On to more good news:

At long last, I am allowed to be alone in my room. That means no more meals in the hallway. I worried it would mean no more meals with Jamie, but instead, he's taken to bringing his food tray into my room to eat with me. At least for dinner. Every night.

I know what you're thinking. Jamie and I are supposed to be walking (wheeling?) off into the sunset by now. Once again, real life is a bitch.

I don't know exactly what happened or what went wrong. Maybe Jamie has just been thinking differently about me since he's recovered so much faster than I have, which would be completely understandable. After all, Clark thought I was unattractive at my very best, and I'm definitely not at my best now—miles from it. Or maybe he asked me too many times and he got sick of being rejected. Or maybe, despite his protests to the contrary, he and Karen are trying to make things work. In any case, it's become clear that Jamie and I are just friends, and likely will stay that way.

Really, it's a good thing. A relationship would be far too complicated now anyway.

No, that's a lie. This completely sucks.

A couple of days after Clark's arrest, I'm eating dinner in my room with Jamie next to me. We're watching television like we usually do, an old episode of *Friends*. Joey is explaining about "the friend zone." I think that may be what happened between Jamie and me. We've been friends too long, and now he can only think of me as a friend. He's lost any sort of romantic interest in me.

"It's true, I guess," I say suddenly. "I mean, about the friend zone."

Jamie turned away from the television to look at me. "You think so?"

I shrug, sorry I said anything. "I never had a relationship with a guy I've been friends with first," I say thoughtfully. "So I'm not entirely sure."

"Well, maybe that's been your problem," Jamie says.

I shrug again. "Maybe."

Jamie is looking at me in a way that makes me feel really self-conscious. I wonder if he feels embarrassed about all the things he said to me before. I mean, I do know what I look like. Half my skull is missing, half my body doesn't work right, and to make matters worse, now I've got the ugliest glasses in the world perched on my nose.

"Charly," Jamie starts to say, but he gets interrupted by a knock at the partially open door.

The door swings open the rest of the way, and Dr. Greenberg enters the room. His tie has little brown teddy bears on it. When he sees me, his face crinkles up in a smile.

"Here's our new superstar!" Dr. Greenberg says.

I feel my cheeks get hot, but actually, I'm really pleased about all the progress I've made lately.

"And I've got some more good news for you," he says. "The neurosurgeon has scheduled your surgery for two weeks from now."

I stare at him. "My *surgery*? Why do I have to have surgery?"

Dr. Greenberg laughs. "You want your skull back, don't you?"

I reach out and touch my helmet. It's been so long that I'd almost forgotten that getting my skull put back together was even a possibility. I was starting to think I'd be stuck with the helmet for the rest of my life. "But… how?"

"They made you a new skull," he says. "It's all ready for you."

"That's awesome," Jamie exclaims, his brown eyes wide. "Charly, I'll get to see what your hair looks like!"

I roll my eyes at him.

"I'm just going to take off your helmet for a moment," Dr. Greenberg says. "I just want to take a quick look at your incision. So try not to fall, okay?"

I bite my lip. "Can't we do it later?" I ask.

I don't want to admit it, but I'm reluctant for Jamie to see me with my helmet off. Yes, he's seen me with it off once before and didn't seem particularly disturbed. But that was a long time ago, before he was recovered. I'm pretty sure if he sees me now with half my skull missing, he'll react the way Clark did. Anyone would.

"It will just take a minute," Dr. Greenberg promises.

Before I can protest again, I feel him loosening the straps under my chin. Jamie is watching us with fascination. I feel the weight of the helmet lifting off my head and the cool breeze against my sweaty scalp.

"Yes," Dr. Greenberg says. "That looks very well healed. And the craniectomy site is quite sunken."

"Wonderful," I say as I reach for the helmet.

I can't even manage to look at Jamie. If he had even the slightest bit of sexual desire for me, I'm sure it's now completely evaporated.

"So like I said," Dr. Greenberg continues, he helps me strap the helmet back in place. "Your surgery will be in two weeks, and you'll leave straight from here to go to the hospital."

"And will I come back here after the surgery?" I ask.

The smile fades slightly from Dr. Greenberg's face. "No, we discussed it and we think the best thing is for you to go straight to a nursing facility after your surgery."

"But Charly is doing so great now," Jamie speaks up.

"We think it's for the best," Dr. Greenberg says. "But don't worry. You'll get home soon. I'm sure of it."

I'm not so sure. I'm getting better faster now because I'm getting so much therapy. But I won't get nearly as much in a nursing home. Maybe I will get home eventually, but I can imagine being stuck there for months, maybe even years.

"Okay," I finally say.

It's obvious that no matter what, I don't have a choice in the matter. But it's okay. I'll make it home eventually. I'm determined.

Dr. Greenberg rests his hand briefly on my shoulder then bids me good night, leaving Jamie and me alone to finish our meals. I look over at Jamie, who is calmly eating his chicken a la king like nothing even happened. He isn't screaming in terror or running to the bathroom to retch.

In fact, he doesn't seem at all rattled by having seen me without my helmet.

"Sorry you had to see that," I tell him.

Jamie is chewing a bite of his sandwich. "See what?"

"Me without my helmet," I say, feeling my cheeks grow hot again.

He shrugs. "I saw it before."

"You remember that?"

"Of course." He grins. "Remember I told you it looked like somebody took a bite out of it? And then you let me touch your brain."

"I remember," I say.

He shrugs again. "I don't know. What's the big deal? It's no worse than the huge scar I've got on *my* head."

It's not anything like that. You can't even *see* the scar on Jamie's head anymore. It's completely concealed by his hair. He looks entirely normal. He looks like a nice, normal, good-looking guy. I look anything but normal. And the truth is, no surgery is going to fix that.

CHAPTER 58
Six Months After

One thing that hasn't improved magically since I got my glasses is my ability to make it to the bathroom on time. I'm better than I used to be, meaning I've got maybe a twenty-minute window rather than a five-minute window. But twenty minutes goes fast, especially since it takes me at least five minutes to get to the toilet once the nurse comes.

I'm sitting with Jamie in my room, watching television, when the urge comes. I hit my call button, but I see from the time that it's the afternoon change of shift. That means the nurses are signing out to each other, and they won't have time to run to my room unless I am actively dying. And the last thing I want is to pee in my pants in front of Jamie.

"What's wrong?" Jamie asks me, noticing the look on my face. I swear, sometimes I think he can read my mind. Sometimes I even think he can read the part of my mind that's damaged beyond repair.

"I need to use the bathroom," I mumble, not really wanting to get into details.

Jamie raises his eyebrows. "Is it urgent?"

He gets it, of course. This is a guy who also needed to hit the call button to use the bathroom not that long ago. I wonder if he ever didn't make it in time. Not that I'd ever ask.

"Kind of," I admit.

He glances up at the clock on my wall. "Change of shift," he notes. He really does get it. He looks at me thoughtfully. "I could help you to the bathroom."

Oh God, no.

"That's okay," I say quickly.

"I can do it," Jamie insists. His brown eyes are wide and earnest. "I've seen like a million transfers. Anyway, you can walk now mostly on your own, right?"

"Not entirely."

"I'll just help you stand up and then hang on to you while you walk," he says. "It'll be fine."

On the outside, he appears to be mostly recovered from his head injury, but the fact that I recognize that this is a bad idea and he doesn't makes me wonder.

"My balance is great," he insists. "I took a balance test this morning and I got a perfect score. A *perfect score*, Charly."

"What about when I'm on the toilet," I say. I'm not really going to let him do this, but I play along for the moment.

Jamie thinks about it for a minute. "I won't leave, of course. But I'll look away. I won't see anything, I swear."

Jamie stands up and positions himself in front of me. I have to admit, he *does* seem like he might be able to do it. He's sturdy and strong, and he *has* seen me walk with the therapists a million times, like he said.

Taking my silence as tacit approval, Jamie leans forward to help me stand up. I can't help but notice that he smells nice. Clark always smelled like his cologne, but Jamie isn't wearing any. Who would wear cologne on a rehab unit? Anyway, he just smells clean, like fresh soap and shampoo. The pleasant scent and the heat of his body makes it a little bit hard to concentrate on not peeing in my pants.

I grab onto Jamie's neck and feel the muscles in his shoulders. I know this is a bad idea, but it's really hard to focus on that right now. I'm just going to let this happen. Deal with the consequences later.

Of course, the consequences come sooner than I thought. The second my butt rises up off the chair, an alarm goes off. If either of us were thinking clearly, we would've realized that this was going to happen. But instead, we both freeze. Jamie clearly has no idea how to shut off the alarm.

Fortunately, the alarm does its job. Seconds later, Kim, my nurse for the day, is rushing into the room. Her eyes widen when she sees us. "Charly!" she exclaims. The bags under her eyes deepen as she glares at Jamie. "Jamie Knox, what do you think you're doing?"

"Charly needed the bathroom," he says sheepishly. He adds, "It was urgent."

"And *you* were going to help her to the bathroom?" Kim asks, shaking her head in disbelief.

"I was going to cover my eyes," he says, his ears turning bright red.

Kim shakes her head again, but it's hard to tell if she's angry or amused. Maybe both. "Jamie, go back to your room. I'll help Charly."

Kim helps me to the bathroom, and thank God, I make it on time. It's been at least fifteen minutes. When she gets me back in my wheelchair, she turns the alarm back on.

"I had been thinking you might not need the alarms for much longer," she says, clucking her tongue. "But I guess you do."

No, no, no. I don't want to be making backwards progress at this point. Anyway, this isn't my fault. "It was all Jamie's idea. He really wanted to help me. I told him not to."

Kim laughs. "I believe it. Your boyfriend is certainly very dedicated to you."

My face feels suddenly hot, and it's not entirely due to my giant helmet. Although it's *partially* due to my giant helmet. "He's not my boyfriend. He just wants to be friends."

Kim raises an eyebrow at me. "Oh *really*? Is that what he said to you? Because I'm fairly sure that's not the case."

Maybe it used to be the case. Before Jamie's brain was entirely healed. But right now, it's very clear he's not interested in me. "You're mistaken."

Kim gives me a knowing look. I remember that look, from back when I was an intern. It's the look of a nurse who knows much better than I do.

"Let me tell you something, Charly," she says. "Every time that boy isn't here or in therapy, he is out at the nursing station talking about you. 'Where is Charly? When is her therapy going to be over? Could I take her down to the cafeteria? Could I take her out on the porch?' Or he's telling some story about something you did or said that he thinks we ought to know." She smiles. "Granted, some of it is probably his head injury. But I think the head injury is just messing with his self-restraint so that he can't keep his mouth shut about how crazy he is about you."

I shake my head. "It's not what you think."

"What's wrong?" she asks in a teasing voice. "Don't you think he's cute? *I* think he is."

She has no idea. I'm embarrassed to admit how much I think about Jamie.

"It's not what you think," I mumble again.

Kim shrugs her shoulders. "Believe what you'd like to, Charly. But I can bet you a million bucks that Jamie is out at the nursing station, just waiting for me to be done so he can come back in here."

I still don't believe what Kim is saying. I don't believe that Jamie could possibly be so happy to see me when he walks back into the room a minute later. His face does light up, but that's because I'm his friend. I mean, why would he be so excited just to hang out with me?

CHAPTER 59

Six Months After

The next evening, Jamie kisses Karen.

I see them while my chair is parked in the hallway, waiting for somebody to bring me into my room. I see Karen arrive alone, without Sam. Jamie meets her in the hallway and then he kisses her.

The best I can say is that it isn't a passionate kiss. They're not full on making out or anything like that. But that said, they're in the hallway of the hospital. You can't make out in the hallway of a hospital.

And then Jamie doesn't come by my room for dinner. That part hurts most of all. I understand that he'd rather be with her than with me, especially if he's trying to make it work. But he'll only be here a little bit longer. I wish we could keep pretending.

It's close to eight o'clock when I hear the knock at my door. I'm sitting in my wheelchair, watching television by myself. I figure it's my nurse, bringing me medications. But it's not. It's Jamie.

I notice right away that he isn't holding a cane. Apparently, his balance is good enough that he doesn't need it anymore.

"Hey, Charly," he says. "Can I talk to you?"

"Sure," I say, nodding at the chair next to me.

I already know what he's going to say: *Charly, I've decided to get back with Karen.* And you know what? I'm okay with it. I'm going to be completely supportive. I'm going to tell him he's doing the right thing. I'm going to pretend to be really happy for him.

Except he doesn't tell me he's getting back together with Karen. What he ends up saying is much worse.

"I'm going home tomorrow," he says.

I stare at him for a second then I burst into tears. It's not my finest moment.

"Don't cry," he pleads with me, taking my hand in his. "Please don't cry, Charly. I'm really sorry."

I feel ridiculous for crying, in all honestly. It was obvious that he was going home soon. He's practically all better. But I can't seem to stop sobbing. "Why didn't you tell me sooner?" I sniffle.

"I just found out today," he says. "I wanted to tell you right after therapy ended, but then…"

But then Karen came by. And that took priority. I get it.

"Charly?" he says, giving my hand a squeeze.

I pull my hand away from his to grab the box of tissues on the table in front of me, and I start wiping at my eyes. I'm not hysterical anymore, but I don't trust myself to say anything without sobbing like an idiot.

"Please say something," he says. He looks so cute, with his eyebrows scrunched together in concern. I hate

Karen. *I* want to be with Jamie. This is so unfair. I'm going to miss him so goddamn much. "Please?"

I just shake my head.

Jamie squeezes his eyes shut then opens them again. "I only live in Brooklyn… not very far. I can't drive yet, but I'll take the subway over to visit. I promise."

"You don't have to do that," I say, swallowing hard.

"I want to," he insists.

Bullshit. He only just recently had brain surgery and he's trying to put his life back together again. He's got a kid to take care of. He isn't going to hop on the subway to come see me just because I'm crying. Even though I wish he would.

"You can visit Angela too," I say.

Jamie rolls his eyes. "Charly, I like Angela a lot, but if I'm sitting on the subway an hour, it's to see *you*, not her."

I'm not sure what to say to that. The truth is, I doubt he's getting on the subway to see either of us. Anyway, I'd rather change the subject than listen to his empty promises.

"Are you going back to work?" I ask him.

He shakes his head. "Not right away. I wanted to but… I saw the neuropsychologist a few weeks ago and he felt like I couldn't… I mean, that I wasn't ready yet."

"Ready for what?"

Jamie sighs. "I don't know. He was giving me all these problems with money and I used to be so good at that stuff. I was always so quick at math, but somehow I was having trouble, even though I knew the problems were easy. Anyway, he felt like it might be a little while before I could balance the books like I used to."

"You've gotten so much better," I point out. "I'm sure you'll be able to do it again."

"Yeah, maybe." He shrugs like it's no big deal, although I can tell it's something he's really upset about. "If not, I can always just tend the bar like my brother does."

"You'll be able to balance the books again," I say, more firmly.

Jamie lifts his eyes and forces a smile. "Yeah, well, you might be the only one who thinks that."

He looks so sad for a moment that I really want to reach out and give him a hug. Could I hug him? That wouldn't be weird, would it? I wouldn't want him to think I was hitting on him or anything like that. I'm sure he's completely mortified by the things he said to me about how he wished he could be with me. I wouldn't want him to know just how attracted I feel to him right now.

I just wish that Jamie and I could have been more than friends. I wonder when the next time I'll be more than friends with a man will be. I have a feeling it's going to be a long time.

Maybe forever.

No, I shouldn't think that way. I should try to be positive.

At that moment, a nurse peeks her head into the room and seems surprised to find Jamie in here. "Visiting hours are over," she says.

In his NYU T-shirt and worn jeans, Jamie looks far more like a visitor than a patient. Unlike me. He holds up his left wrist with his white wristband. "I'm a patient," he says. "James Knox. Room 325."

"Oh." She blinks at him. "Well, in that case, you still need to get back to your room. Wrap up the conversation and leave."

Jamie rolls his eyes as the nurse stalks off. "Well," he says. "I guess I better go."

No. Please don't. Please don't leave me alone here.

"I'm leaving pretty early in the morning," he says hesitantly, as he gets up from the chair. "So I'm not certain I'll see you. So I guess… this is goodbye for now."

"Right," I say.

He holds out his hand to me and I shake it. I try to remember the feel of his warm hand in mine for later. I have a feeling that this will be the very last time that I ever see Jamie Knox.

"Bye, Charly," he says.

Somehow I manage to say "goodbye" without bursting into tears again.

Goodbye, Jamie. Thank you for being my friend when I didn't even know who I was. Thank you for turning my tray around during meals. Thank you for making me feel attractive again, even if it was just for a short time. Thank you for saving my goddamn life, whatever it's worth.

Thank you and goodbye forever.

"No," I hear Jamie say.

I look up, trying to figure out to whom he's talking. Then I realize that he's talking to himself. Either that, or he's talking to my door. I watch him as he turns around.

"I can't leave," he says, shaking his head. "There's something I need to do first."

He strides determinedly back across the room to sit down next to me. His eyes lock with mine, and before I can really process what's happening, he's leaning toward me. His lips are on mine. He's kissing me. *Jamie* is kissing me.

Lord, it's a nice kiss. It's just the right amount of soft and passionate. Just the right amount of lip and tongue. Somehow, I feel like I've been waiting for this kiss my entire life. And the way that Jamie is kissing me, like he can't stop himself, it makes me feel like he's been waiting for this his entire life too.

When he pulls away, we're both shaking.

Jamie stares at me, blinking quickly. "I'm sorry," he says softly. "But... I couldn't leave here without doing that."

If I could catch my breath, I'd tell him that I'm glad he didn't.

"I was in a haze after I hurt myself," he says, shaking his head. "Everything was so disjointed, I couldn't focus on anything. And then one day, I looked up and I saw the most beautiful violet eyes I'd ever seen in my life. And it was like everything got clear all of a sudden." He coughed and cleared his throat. "You cured me, Charly."

Okay, now he's being melodramatic. "I don't think I cured you."

"You did," he insists, picking up my right hand and holding it in his. "The whole reason I wanted to get better was so that I could get to know you. That's all I could think of."

"What about your son?" I remind him. "You wanted to get better for him too."

"I love my son more than anything," he says with a sad smile. "But I couldn't even remember his name back then. All I could think about was you. Charly, Charly, Charly. And even though I'm better... I still think about you. All the time, actually. Like, the first thing I think about when I wake up is what you might be doing and how I want to see you. And when I go to sleep at night, I'm excited about seeing you the next day."

"Jamie," I murmur. "I know you think I have pretty eyes, but... that's not really the basis of a relationship."

"That might be the first thing I noticed about you," he admits, "but it's not why I'm in love with you."

He didn't just tell me he's in love with me. This is just too unbelievable. This is a dream that I'm having where I'm going to wake up any minute.

"You have such a good heart," he says. "I could see it that day when we were playing with Sam. When you get hurt like we did, it's harder to conceal who you really are anymore. I *know* you, Charly. I know you really well, and I don't want to be away from you."

It might be the sweetest thing that a man has ever said to me.

Still, I can't help but ask: "What about Karen?"

He frowns. "What about her?"

"She's Sam's mother," I point out. Plus, she can walk, she can talk normally, and half her skull isn't missing. And PS, she's gorgeous. "And… I saw the two of you kissing in the hallway today."

"Kissing?" He blinks at me. "Karen and I were not kissing. I promise you that. I mean, maybe I kissed her on the cheek or something. I'm attempting to be civil to her, you know?"

"You were with her for two hours…"

"We had to sort through a new custody agreement." He rolled his eyes. "It took *forever*. I was so pissed off, because I knew it was my last night here and I just wanted to get to your room—it was all I could think about. Believe me, we weren't in there necking or anything. I have zero interest in Karen."

I think he means it. Or at least, he thinks he does.

Jamie takes a deep breath. "Okay, I said what I had to say. Now it's your turn to say something."

Except I don't. I just sit there, staring at him. There's something in my throat that's making it hard for me to talk.

Jamie runs a shaky hand through his short hair. "Please say something, Charly."

I swallow down the lump in my throat. "What do you want me to say?"

"I don't know." He smiles crookedly. "Something along the lines of, 'Please kiss me again, Jamie.'"

I want him to kiss me again, don't make any mistake about it. I can still feel his lips on mine, and my cheeks are still tingling from where he touched me as he drew me close. But here's the deal: it occurs to me that, like me, Jamie has an entire life to put back together. He needs to focus on his career and his child. As much as I want him, it would be selfish to keep him from what he needs to do. I would be a distraction.

This will be the hardest thing I've ever had to do. Well, after recovering from a brain injury.

Maybe Jamie's right. Maybe I do have a good heart. Maybe I'm not just a selfish bitch, like Clark made me think I was.

"I'm sorry," I whisper. And I shake my head.

It's all that I have to say. I watch Jamie's face fall, and I just feel so incredibly guilty. Really, I feel like the worst person in the world, even though I'm doing this for him. And I suspect that on some level, he probably knows that I'm doing it for him. I mean, how could I not like Jamie? He's so cute.

He doesn't try to dissuade me, which is a good thing, because I'm pretty sure I wouldn't have the willpower to resist him again. If he kissed me one more time, that would be it. Instead, he just stands up.

"I guess I'm not surprised," he says.

I'm not entirely sure what he means by that, but he doesn't say it in a mean way. I can't imagine Jamie being mean to me the way that Clark was. He's just not that kind of person.

Once again, I watch Jamie head for the door. Except this time, he doesn't turn around. "Goodbye, Helmet Girl," he whispers as he leaves.

CHAPTER 60
Six and a Half Months After

When I see my friend Bridget walk into my room, I almost start to cry.

Bridget has been my best friend since we met our first semester of college, when we were randomly assigned to be roommates by the Great Roommate God. To be honest, for the first month, I found Bridget incredibly annoying. She talked way too much, she had *way* too much clothing and make-up and hair products, and she mostly just seemed like a complete ditz. Plus she left her curling iron on my desk and it scalded my hand.

Then one night, the two of us went to a party together. We got rudely snubbed by a couple of frat boys who didn't think we were attractive enough to hook up with that night, which made me feel like I was too ugly to live. The whole thing made me feel awful about myself, but amazingly, Bridget didn't even care. "Screw them," Bridget said to me. And the two of us proceeded to get very drunk on Jell-O shots, and spent the entire night giggling and talking together.

I can't even remember how long it's been since I've last seen Bridget. I'm not entirely sure whether I'm happy, sad, relieved, or angry that it's been so long since she's visited. These days, my emotions are sort of a mystery to me.

She looks so familiar to me, with her red hair and slight double chin and the gold chain from her grandmother that she's worn around her neck every single day I've known her. It reminds me of the fact that I'm still the same person I was before. I'm still Charly. I'm not just some brain-damaged cripple.

"Charly!" she cries out when she sees me sitting there.

Honestly, I would've thought that it would be awkward, considering the fact that I'm sitting in a wheelchair and wearing a giant helmet on my head. But it isn't. Bridget comes over to me and hugs me for like ten straight minutes. And sometime during those ten minutes, I really do start to cry.

When Bridget pulls away finally, her eyes are red and moist too, which makes me feel slightly less embarrassed about the whole thing. "I missed you so much," she says softly.

Um, so why didn't you visit me?

"You look great," Bridget says.

I roll my eyes at her. "I look terrible. Be honest."

"You don't look terrible," she insists. "You just look like… you're going to go out and play in a game of football."

I roll my eyes again, but this time I laugh.

Bridget pulls out a bag of presents. It's mostly food. Cookies and brownies and chocolate. Maybe it's a good thing Bridget hasn't been here to visit me sooner. I'd probably weigh two tons by now. I've got enough problems without having to use a bariatric wheelchair.

While Bridget is unpacking my goodies, she tells me about how Chelsea is doing, and updates me on Kitty, who is alive and well, and has been boarding at her place until I'm ready to take her back. While Bridget is babbling on, my mother comes into the room with a glass of apple juice and graham crackers that she got from the kitchen. Recently, I've been suspecting that my mother is abusing the free kitchen on our unit. She literally visits that kitchen every thirty minutes when she comes here. But I'm not going to say anything about it.

"Bridget," my mother says with a smile. "I'm so glad you were able to come."

"Yes," I say. And I can't help but add, "Finally."

Bridget and my mother exchange a look. Maybe I shouldn't have said that. Even though I'm angry, I don't want Bridget to get upset and not visit again. But you know what? I *am* angry. Why hasn't she been here before? She's my best friend. What sort of best friend doesn't visit me after I got shot in the freaking head?

"Charly," my mother says quietly. "Bridget has been wanting to visit you for a long time. Clark has been calling her and telling her that you were refusing to see anyone."

Bridget nods. "I told him that I was sure you'd want to see *me*. But he said that if I came, you'd never speak to me again. I didn't want to upset you, so I stayed away."

I sit there silently, absorbing this new information. I didn't think it was possible to hate Clark any more than I already did, but here we are.

"When I heard about Clark's arrest…" She shakes her head. "God, I couldn't believe it. I called your mother and asked when the earliest I could come see you would be. And… here I am."

I feel tears spring up in my eyes once more. I had genuinely thought she didn't want to see me, that she didn't care about me.

"Oh, please don't cry again, Charly!" Bridget says. I can see her own eyes are getting misty again too. "I'm going to have the puffiest eyes ever tomorrow!"

I almost laugh. That's the Bridget I remember.

She sniffles. "Anyway, I feel awful about what Clark did. I mean, I feel like it's partially my fault."

"Your fault?" I say.

Bridget nods. "Well, sort of. I mean, I was the one who told you to find the private investigator and get hard evidence that he was cheating. And I was the one who convinced you to hide your assets in those overseas accounts so that Clark wouldn't be able to get to them in a divorce. But seriously, who knew he was such a sociopath?"

Something that Bridget just said tugs at my memory. It's that nagging feeling something is there, right on the periphery, but I can't quite grasp it. I look over at my mother, who is staring at Bridget with wide eyes.

"What bank accounts?" she asks Bridget.

Bridget's pale skin turns red. "Oh, I'm sorry. Maybe it wasn't my place to say…"

"Bridget," my mother says slowly, "do you know something about Charly's finances?"

Bridget looks at me, as if for permission. I nod, as much for her sake as for mine. I'm still struggling to recapture that memory. I remember walking into a lawyer's office, something about overseas accounts…

"Charly was concerned that Clark would get all her money if they got divorced," Bridget says. "So I referred her to our lawyer. I think he was helping her set up some ways to hide or shelter her money."

My mother's eyes are still wide. "How much money are we talking about?"

"Oh gosh, I'm not sure," Bridget says quickly. "But it was a lot. I mean, *a lot* a lot. Charly used to do all these expensive procedures, like the hair transplants. But aside from that, when I was still at the company, I gave her all those tips about new drugs that were about to explode." Bridget smiles at me fondly. "Charly and I *cleaned up*. I used to joke that I paid for my entire wardrobe with drug money."

"But how much," my mother presses her. "Like… ballpark?"

"Two and a half million dollars," I say.

Mom starts choking on her apple juice. That's what she gets for abusing the kitchen. "Charly, you remember this?" she manages between coughs.

I shrug. "Sort of."

Suddenly, everything seems to make sense. Clark wasn't after my meager disability payments or my apartment. He must have found out about the money I had tucked away, and that's why he suddenly started visiting me again. He needed me to sign over power of attorney so that he could access it. And then he would've disappeared with his girlfriend. And I would have had nothing. Really nothing.

She shakes her head. "Charly, if you have that kind of money, you realize that you don't have to... I mean, we'll have enough to hire help and you wouldn't have to..."

I won't have to go to a nursing home. I can live with my mother. This money changes everything. Everything.

Bridget is so shaken by all this that she rips open the box of chocolates that she brought then stuffs one of them in her mouth. Then a second. "I can't believe you didn't *know*," she says, as she chews through caramel and nuts. "I wish I could've told you."

I do too. It would've saved me a lot of grief. Actually, if I had never met Clark in the first place, it would've saved me a lot of grief. But that's life.

At least now I can finally go home.

CHAPTER 61
Six and a Half Months After

Today is my last day in rehab and I'm absolutely terrified.

Tomorrow morning, before the sun even comes up, I'm being transferred to an acute hospital. They're going to open up the scar on my scalp, and close up the defect in my skull. My new skull is going to be made out of plastic… a material called polymethyl methacrylate. Dr. Greenberg told me the name of the material yesterday, and somehow, miraculously, I've been able to retain it. I think that's pretty amazing, considering a few months ago I couldn't retain my first name.

Granted, the only way I could remember it is that I've been repeating those words to myself over and over again: *polymethyl methacrylate, polymethyl methacrylate.* But still.

There was sort of a party for me today on the rehab unit. My mother brought in a bunch of mini cupcakes, and all the nurses and therapists told me how much they were going to miss me. Valerie, who I always thought hated me, actually gave me a hug and told me she thought I was going to do great. Then she told me I was her favorite patient, which was clearly a lie, but that's okay.

After my surgery, I'm going to spend a few days in the hospital, provided everything goes well. And after that? After that, I'm going home.

My mother contacted the lawyer that Bridget had recommended to me. We located close to three million dollars in offshore bank accounts. It may not be the kind of money that will provide for me the rest of my life, but it's enough to hire help for me to come home. It's enough money that I can take my time recovering and figuring out what I do want to do with the rest of my life.

And I thank God every day that Clark didn't get his hands on it.

Anyway, it's a nice last day overall, but it's bittersweet. Partially because of how terrified I am about tomorrow. And partially because of the absence of one person.

Jamie.

Jamie wasn't here today, obviously. I didn't expect him to be. He knew today was my last day, at least he did the last time he was here. But aside from the memory problems he has (for obvious reasons), he's got a lot on his mind right now. He's got a business to resurrect, a son to raise, and his own recovery to think about. In reality, it would've been a miracle if he showed up today.

But that didn't keep me from hoping.

I keep going over that last conversation with Jamie in my head. You know, the one where he told me that he loved me and I shot him down for his own good because I'm just such a wonderful person. I keep imagining some other outcome, maybe one where I told him that I loved him back. And I could have kissed him again.

I really enjoyed kissing him. I still think about it. A lot.

But what's done is done. Jamie is back home with his family, and I'm about to have brain surgery. I'm sure in a few months, he'll forget me completely if he hasn't already. He'll move on to someone else. Maybe Karen, despite his protests. Or maybe somebody totally new.

As for me, it's going to be a long time before I can move on to someone else. Maybe never. There are some things that Clark was right about.

Dr. Greenberg makes it to my room at the end of the day to say his final goodbye. I'm lying in bed at this point, watching television and trying to forget about tomorrow. As if an episode of *Family Guy* is going to help me forget I'm about to have brain surgery.

"Nervous?" Dr. Greenberg asks me.

I can't manage to look him in the eyes, so I focus on his tie. This one has multicolored balloons on it. "A little."

"Don't be," Dr. Greenberg says. "This procedure is usually very successful. It may even help you in your recovery."

I frown up at him. "How?"

"Well," Dr. Greenberg says. "Usually your skull protects you from the pressure of the atmosphere on your brain, but now you don't have that protection. So you've got this steady pressure on your brain all the time. Putting your skull back on will get rid of that."

"Great," I mutter.

Dr. Greenberg smiles. "Take it from me, Charly, in another few years, you're going to walk into this place to say hello and none of us are going to recognize you." He adds, "And you'll probably make us all call you Dr. McKenna."

I don't think that's likely. But it's a nice thought.

"Maybe you can give us all free hair transplants," Dr. Greenberg, patting his balding scalp.

"Deal," I say with a laugh.

Dr. Greenberg wags his finger at me. "I'm gonna hold you to that, Charly."

I'm not worried. I don't think I'm ever going to be doing hair transplants again. And even if I do, most of the staff is female here. So I'm pretty safe.

"By the way," Dr. Greenberg says, "there's a package that came for you. It's over at the nursing station. Do you want me to go get it?"

"Sure," I say.

Dr. Greenberg trots off, while I sit and wonder what the package could be. Maybe something from Bridget. Probably more chocolate.

Then he returns, holding a simple but beautiful basket of flowers, which he deposits on my right side. He winks at me then leaves me alone to search for the card.

It takes me a couple of minutes, but I finally find the white card nestled between a tulip and a lilac. It's handwritten, using shaky lettering:

Dear Charly,
Good luck! I can't wait to see your hair!

Love,
Jamie

I close my eyes as I hold the card in my hand. I hope he does get to see my hair. I really do.

Epilogue
One Year Later

I don't know why, but before I go out to lunch with Bridget, I put on a layer of lipstick.

I'm not a lipstick kind of girl. I wasn't before, and I'm not now. Bridget is the one who's into layering her face with paint. I mean, if it's a date, sure, I could put on a layer of lipstick and maybe even spring for some mascara. But it seems silly to put on lipstick just to go out to lunch with my best friend, even if it's just a shade of rose that doesn't stand out much. Especially since the last thing people are going to be looking at is my face.

But what the hell. Sometimes it's fun to look nice. And I don't see myself going on any dates in the near future.

As I'm painting my face, I notice that Kitty has been watching me the whole time. I show Kitty my make-up and she meows in approval. I took her back from Bridget a few months after I came home, and I've been spoiling her even more rotten than before. That's what she gets for helping to save my life.

I grab my cane before I head downstairs. After a year, that's what I'm left with. A sturdy metal cane with four prongs at the end that keeps me from losing my balance when I walk. For short distances, I could probably go without it. But the alternative of winding up flat on my face on the sidewalk is so unappealing that I prefer to use the cane.

Let me tell you something about walking with a cane: people stare. You don't even realize how rude people can be until you've given them something to stare at. Back when I first left the hospital, and I was still using the wheelchair a lot outdoors, you'd think my hair was on fire based on how much people stared at me. The hemi-walker attracted fewer stares, but it was still pretty bad.

The cane attracts the least number of stares, but people still look twice, probably wondering why a young(ish) person like myself is hobbling around with a cane. If I were eighty years old, I'm sure I wouldn't be quite as much of a spectacle. But after a year, I've gotten used to it. Well, sort of.

Other than the cane, I do look pretty similar to how I looked before. My hair is still growing back. It's short and practical, but then again, it was short and practical before. The only difference is that this time it's not my choice. My face is slightly asymmetric if you look carefully. If I don't concentrate, sometimes I drag my left foot when I walk. I also still wear glasses with the prism on the left lens, although I've gotten a much cuter pair than the ones I had in rehab.

Anyway, all told, considering I was shot in the head, I think I look pretty damn good. Especially compared with Clark.

The last time I saw Clark was when he pleaded guilty to first-degree attempted murder. I was very ready to testify against him, and I heard that Jamie was too, as well as Kyle and Regina Barry. It seems like his lawyer convinced him that taking the plea bargain of twelve years in prison was smarter than going through a trial and getting a life sentence.

I watched Clark at the sentencing, dressed in a suit that fit him poorly given all the weight he had recently lost. I guess prison food is even worse than hospital food. His hair was disheveled and he looked every day of his forty-two years. The brightness was gone from his blue eyes.

Whenever I'm having a bad day, whenever my muscles are feeling tight or my balance is off, or I'm just generally feeling sorry for myself, I think about Clark's sentencing. And I feel a little bit better. Like maybe there's some justice in the world.

When I get downstairs, Bridget is waiting for me in the lobby with her daughter Chelsea. I'm glad now that Bridget opted to take a few years off to be a stay-at-home mom, because now she's around to keep me company. And I get to see my goddaughter a lot too.

"Where should we eat?" Bridget asks me.

"Old McDonald's!" Chelsea cries out.

"Veto," I say. As much as McDonald's excited me back in rehab, there's no way I'm going there today.

We end up going to a diner a couple of blocks away—although not the diner that Clark and I used to go to, which is forever tarnished. We almost always go somewhere in a five-block radius around my apartment. I still feel unsteady enough on my feet that I don't want to take a long walk. But the weather is nice, at least. As I walk down the block, I feel the breeze lifting the strands of my short hair from my face.

On days like this, it doesn't seem so bad that I'm taking an extended hiatus from work. Other days, I feel like I'm losing my mind. The truth is, I miss my job desperately. I miss the challenge of medicine and seeing patients and having a purpose and... well, all of it.

Cognitively, there are still some issues. I'm not back to where I was before. But I spoke to my old advisor from residency, and he told me he thought there was a path for me to get back to working again. It might be a long, hard road, but I'm determined to do it. Even if it takes me ten years, I'm going to be Dr. McKenna again. I'm determined.

Although unfortunately, it will mean that I'll have to give everyone who works at rehab hair transplants.

Weirdly enough, I end up ordering a cheeseburger and french fries at the diner, which is pretty much what I would've gotten if we were at McDonald's. I'm sad to say I've grown too old for McDonald's. Their fries just sit in my stomach like a big ball of lead.

As I watch Bridget picking at her turkey sandwich, I can't help but notice she looks a little bit green. I've known Bridget for a long time and I recognize that green face.

"You're pregnant," I say. It's not a question.

Bridget glances at Chelsea then grins sheepishly. "Shh, we don't want her to know quite yet."

"Bridget, that's wonderful!" I exclaim. "Congratulations! How far along are you?"

"Three months," she says.

Three months. Bridget used to tell me everything, but somehow she kept this from me.

"I just…" Bridget murmurs. "I know you have a lot on your plate, and I didn't want to…"

No, I get it. She doesn't want me to feel bad about her joyous news when I'm recovering from my husband trying to have me killed. She knows that I used to want a child. Before.

Do I still want a child? When I look at Chelsea building a snowman out of her mashed potatoes, I think to myself that yes, yes I do. But at the same time, I'm nearly forty. I don't even have a potential boyfriend on the horizon, much less a guy offering to father my offspring. So I'm thinking it's not going to happen.

I feel bad about it, but I know I'll get over it. If I can get over being shot in the head, I can get over anything.

I've eaten about half a cheeseburger when I feel something hit my shoulder. Whatever it was didn't hit me very hard. More like a light tap. And then I feel it again on my thigh.

I look up at the ceiling. Is there some sort of leak right above me? I put my hand on my shoulder but it doesn't feel wet to me. I must be going crazy. Could this be related to my head injury? Some late sequela?

And then I feel something hit me on the back of my hand. And I see it too. A tiny green ball. I stare at it in confusion for a minute, then I pick it up to examine it further.

It's a pea.

"Charly," Bridget whispers to me. "There's this totally cute guy two tables over who keeps staring at you."

Before Bridget can tell me not to, I pivot in my seat. And just as I suspected, there he is.

Jamie.

Oh my God, it's Jamie.

He waves to me as his ears turn slightly red. He's sitting across the table from Sam, who seems oblivious to our interaction.

"You know him?" Bridget asks me.

"Yes," I say. "From rehab."

Her eyes widened. "So he's... messed up?"

I shoot her a look, and she has the good grace to seem embarrassed. "Well, why don't you invite him to sit with us?"

Before I can tell her not to, Bridget has leapt out of her seat and marched over to Jamie's table. I just sit there, feeling really self-conscious. The truth is, I've thought about Jamie a lot in the last year. Mostly, I've beaten myself up for heroically rejecting him. Sometimes I think it was the dumbest thing I've ever done. And that includes marrying Clark.

It's possible that if there were some other man in my life, I would have been able to attempt to forget him. But there hasn't been. Considering I've spent the year recovering, I haven't really been up to the task of dating. And considering what I look like right now, I don't feel quite ready to put myself out there. Maybe someday. I don't know.

As I watch Bridget speaking softly to Jamie, I wonder if he's started dating again. I'm sure he has. Of course he has. Especially now that he isn't a full-time single father. Anyway, what woman wouldn't want to date a great guy like him?

I don't even realize I'm holding my breath until I see Jamie stand up from his chair. Sam scurries over to our table ahead of him, but pauses for a second when he sees me. He studies my face for a minute, then his eyes turn into saucers.

"Charly!" Sam screams. He looks back at his father. "Daddy, it's Charly! From the hospital."

"I know," Jamie says, his eyes never leaving my face.

I manage a weak smile. "It's you."

He nods. "You have beautiful hair, Charly," he says, then adds softly, "I knew that you would."

And then my mouth goes completely dry.

———

The five of us actually have a nice lunch together. It's a little awkward, but the quiet moments in the conversation are filled by sweet Sam's adorable attempts to befriend little Chelsea. And Bridget manages to refrain from asking Jamie about his head injury, which is a miracle in itself.

"It's so great that we ran into you," Bridget says, as the check arrives.

"It really is," Jamie says, scooping up the check before Bridget or I can even reach for it. "We should do it again sometime."

"Absolutely," Bridget says enthusiastically.

They both look at me. I shrug. "Sure."

I can tell Jamie is hurt by my lukewarm reaction. I want to smack myself in the head. Why am I so scared of letting him know how I feel?

Maybe because I'm scared that he's moved on.

Jamie takes care of our bill, just as both kids start complaining that they need to use the bathroom.

"I'll tell you what," Bridget says, "Why don't you let me take the kids to the bathroom and you two go ahead and wait outside?"

I know what Bridget is trying to do and I sort of hate her for it. What does she think is going to happen exactly? And anyway, I don't want to be alone with Jamie.

"Sure," Jamie says. "Thanks, Bridget."

I grab for my cane. For a moment, I feel self-conscious about my walking, but then I remember that Jamie was around when I was much worse than I am now. Still, I have to pay extra attention to everything I'm doing, so as not to walk into a wall. Not that I usually walk into walls, but it seems like something I could definitely do right now.

When we get outside, it seems like the temperature has dropped several degrees. I feel myself shiver. Jamie keeps looking at me, wringing his hands together. Finally, I hear him take a deep breath.

"Look, I have to be honest," he says. Uh oh. No great sentence ever started that way. "This isn't a coincidence or anything. Running into you here, I mean. I came here to find you."

"Oh," I manage. I guess I'm not all that surprised. We're at least an hour subway ride away from where Jamie lives.

"We were standing in front of your building for like an hour, waiting for you to come out," he says. He grins sheepishly. "I had to bribe Sam with candy in order to make him wait."

"You could've been waiting a long time," I point out.

He nods in acknowledgment. "I know. I probably shouldn't have brought Sam, but I figured if I was with him, you wouldn't refuse to talk to me."

"Why would I refuse to talk to you?"

He raises his eyebrows at me. "You don't remember our last conversation? Where I told you that I loved you and you told me to get lost?"

I roll my eyes. "I don't think I was that mean."

"No," he admits. "You were actually really nice about it. But that was the basic idea."

He's looking at me really intently. It's making me feel breathless. "It was for your own good, you know."

"Was it?" he says, raking his hand nervously through his hair, making it stick up a bit. I wonder if he can feel the scar when he does that. I wonder if it still itches the way mine does. "The thing is, maybe you think it was for my own good, but the reality is, I haven't been able to stop thinking about you all year. There isn't a day that goes by where I don't wonder what you're doing and wish I could see you. It's really distracting, actually."

A long silence passes between us. I don't know what to say. I want to tell him that I've been thinking about him too, all the freaking time, but I'm still not sure if that's the right thing to do. We both have so many of our own issues. The two of us together would be a disaster.

At least, I *think* it would be. It could be. Or it could be great.

I can see that Jamie is getting more and more anxious the longer that I'm silent. Finally, he blurts out, "Have you thought about me at all?"

God, how could he ask me that? He was my best friend in rehab. He stood up to Clark and maybe saved my life. Does he think I'm some sort of unfeeling bitch?

"Of course I have!" I retort. "I think about you all the time! Every day, I…"

And then I catch myself, blushing. I've said too much.

"Charly," he says, taking my hand in his so that I have to release the cane. I don't pull away, even though I probably should. "I know you're thinking this is a stupid idea, but it isn't. I promise you."

I just shake my head at him.

"You wanted me to get my life back together again," he goes on. "Well, I have. The business is doing fine. Great, even. Sam and I are great. My life is back together, as much as it ever was." He pauses to take another deep breath. "The only thing missing is *you*."

He's very convincing, I have to admit.

"Charly," he says, scratching his chin nervously. He has adorable stubble on his face, which reminds me of the way he looked in rehab, when they didn't have time to shave him for a day or two. "Please say something."

The last time he said that, I told him he needed to leave and never see me again. I guess I had more willpower back then. I can't make myself tell him to go away this time. I'm pretty sure I'm going to just have to let this thing happen between Jamie and me.

So anyway, I kiss him.

In retrospect, it may have been a little bit stupid to kiss a guy without great balance when mine isn't so good as well. We could've very easily ended up on the ground. I could tell he was struggling to catch himself for the first ten seconds. Luckily, he was standing with his back to the restaurant, so the glass of the window caught us.

And once the fear of falling has been safely dealt with, he gets pretty into it. We both do. Actually, we kiss for like five straight minutes. Or as long as it takes two small kids to use the bathroom.

It's a lovely kiss. No, "lovely" isn't the right word. "Lovely" would be a pretty bouquet of flowers. This kiss is everything: soft, passionate, sexy, life-changing. As he pulls me closer to him, lacing his fingers into my hair, all I know is that this can't be the only kiss.

When we separate for air, Jamie is looking at me in a way that no other man has ever looked at me before in my entire life. And I know this is different. *He's* different. He's the one I've been waiting for.

"I really missed you, Helmet Girl," he whispers.

Except I'm not Helmet Girl. Not anymore.

But maybe it was all worth it if it got me here.

ACKNOWLEDGEMENTS

When I first told my husband that I was going to write a novel about a woman who was shot in the head and must identify a killer whose identity is locked in the left side of her visual field, he said to me, "You know who the killer should be? It should be her evil Siamese twin who is attached to her on the left side."

I rolled my eyes. "Great idea," I said.

"Really!" he said. "In the climax, she can look in the mirror and see that the twin has been there all along."

"I don't think that will work."

"It definitely won't work if you won't even *try*."

When I finished writing and editing *Brain Damage*, I asked my husband if he had any interest in reading my book.

"Is that the book where I thought you should have the evil twin be the killer?" he asked.

"Yes."

"Did you end up doing that?"

"*No*."

"I don't think I should read it then," he said thoughtfully. "I mean, if I read it, I'm just going to spend the whole time thinking how much better it would be if only it had the twist with the Siamese twin. I think that would just ruin it for me, because I'd be thinking—"

"*Never mind!*"

It's hard to get people to read your unpublished writing, even family and friends.

On that note, I'd like to thank all the people who put in their time and effort to make this book what it is. My mother read *three* separate drafts of *Brain Damage*. My father even read the book, and offered the advice that I should publish this one "for real" (instead of publishing it in Imagination Land, like my other books). Special thanks to Jessica Schuster, whose pointed critiques I must read with a shot of whiskey, but my books wouldn't be half as good without her. I also want to thank the always wonderful Dr. Orthochick, Katie, Jenica Schultz, Dr. Eve Shvidler, and Dane Miller.

But most of all, I want to give a huge shout-out to the patients I work with, and the therapists and other staff members who form our team to help them to recover. You guys are all an inspiration to me. And if any of you have evil twins attached to your left side, I will totally let you know about it.